SUICIDE THURSDAY

ABOUT THE AUTHOR

Will Carver is the international bestselling author of the January David series and the critically acclaimed, mind-blowingly original Detective Pace series that includes *Good Samaritans* (2018), *Nothing Important Happened Today* (2019) and *Hinton Hollow Death Trip* (2020), all of which were ebook bestsellers and selected as books of the year in the mainstream international press. *Nothing Important Happened Today* was longlisted for both the Goldsboro Books Glass Bell Award 2020 and the Theakston's Old Peculier Crime Novel of the Year Award. *Hinton Hollow Death Trip* was longlisted for the *Guardian*'s Not the Booker Prize, and was followed by two standalone literary thrillers, *The Beresford* and *Psychopaths Anonymous*.

Will spent his early years in Germany, but returned to the UK at age eleven, when his sporting career took off. He turned down a professional rugby contract to study theatre and television at King Alfred's, Winchester, where he set up a successful theatre company. He currently runs his own fitness and nutrition company, and lives in Reading with his children.

Follow Will on Twitter @will_carver.

Also by Will Carver and available from Orenda Books:
Good Samaritans
Nothing Important Happened Today
Hinton Hollow Death Trip
The Beresford
Psychopaths Anonymous
The Daves Next Door

SUICIDE THURSDAY

WILL CARVER

ORENDA BOOKS

Orenda Books
16 Carson Road
West Dulwich
London SE21 8HU
www.orendabooks.co.uk

First published by Orenda Books, 2022
Copyright © Will Carver, 2022

A catalogue record for this book is available from the British Library.

ISBN 978-1-914585-38-8
eISBN 978-1-914585-39-5

Typeset in Garamond by typesetter.org.uk

Printed and bound by CPI Group (UK) Ltd, Croydon CR0 4YY

For sales and distribution, please contact info@orendabooks.co.uk

This one's for me.

'Fiction reveals truths that reality obscures.'
—Jessamyn West

'The only cure for grief is action.'
—George Henry Lewes

PROLOGUE

I type:

> Mike is dead. From behind, it looks as though he is
> sitting on his living-room floor with his hands in
> his lap, staring into the mirror.
>
> And maybe that is true.
>
> His eyes are open. But Mike is definitely dead.
>
> Two cuts. One across the top of each thigh.
> There's more blood on the floor than left inside his
> body. And some of that blood has been mixed with
> Jackie's tears. She found him like this.
>
> And the look on his face is one of relief, and the
> look on hers is mourning and sorrow and all her
> Catholic guilt. He is gone. She is lost. I'm
> somewhere in between.
>
> Suicide is a beginning for those left behind.
>
> This was not a cry for help. This was serious and
> thought out and deliberate. Mike wanted to die. But
> a look at the scene from the front – a different
> angle – and his hands are not resting on his lap.
> They're in his legs.
>
> He tried to stop it.
>
> They're both sitting on the floor. Broken. My best
> friend and my girlfriend. Blood on their hands.

Too dark, maybe. Gruesome. In this situation, you don't know
what is going on, how events transpired, the reasons behind the
decision to end a life. It's easy to focus on the wrong thing, miss
what's important, what's right in front of you.

Again:

Apparently, the triangle is the strongest shape. The three sides push against each other perfectly so that a great force is required to misshape or break the bond between them.

That's how we work. Mike. Jackie. And Me.

How we worked.

Mike cut his legs open and bled out on his newly polished floor. Whatever he was secretly feeling, it warped our triangle and made us weak. Our compassion must not have been equal to his self-loathing. Our love was not enough to cancel out his despair. Understanding is often outweighed by self-interest, benevolence by guilt.

Now all that is left is a line. A faint line between myself and my girlfriend, Jackie. A continuum, where one end is her and one end is me.

One side is fact and the other is fiction.

And somewhere in the middle is the truth.

Too bleak. Nobody wants to read about decaying social values and humankind's growing disconnection with one another. It's abstract. Obscuring what the story is really about.

In my mind, it plays out like a film.

Once more:

INT. MIKE'S FLAT - NIGHT
(Mike is sitting on the floor, opposite a mirror, in a puddle of his own blood. Jackie cries opposite him.)

          ELI (V.O.)
Someone once said, 'Things turn out best for people who make the best of the way that things turn out.'

I got a phone call a moment ago telling me that my best friend has just killed himself and, in a way, it has filled me with hope.

Maybe one day I will be able to put an end to something.

CUT TO BLACK.

WEEK ONE

MONDAY
(THREE DAYS BEFORE SUICIDE THURSDAY)

118, 117, 116...

It's far too quiet in the office on Monday, which gives me more time with my own thoughts than is healthy.

I need a distraction: the radio perhaps, or kids screaming in the streets, or maybe even some actual work to do – anything, just to prevent my own nauseating voice from whizzing around inside my head, splitting and overlapping and altering into a maddening crescendo in the key of G, which resonates through my very being like the antithesis of orgasm. But I'm thankful: it's nearly the end of the day now.

94, 93, 92...

With my hands poised, middle finger of my left hand on *Ctrl*, index finger on *Alt*, I count down the seconds of my last two to three minutes at work, the index finger of my right hand hovering trigger-happily over the *Delete* button, ready to log off.

It's been yet another gut-wrenching, soul-destroying, waste-of-time day in which I feel as though I have offered the world nothing and achieved even less.

Don't get me wrong, I'm not depressed. It's not depression, it's not frustration either; it's not even annoyance. It's an amalgamation of all these sentiments playing off each other like some kind of sick, satanic, symbiotic mess of emotion. I get annoyed because I don't believe in depression; thus, I get frustrated with myself. The fact that I am constantly frustrated, well, that is just depressing.

Fruproyance. That's my word for it, the neologism that best expresses my combination of frustration, depression and annoyance. As you can see, I have kept depression's involvement to a minimum but that is probably a result of something my therapist would call 'fruproyance anxiety'. Of course I'm anxious; it's a relatively unknown condition.

It's not that I want to bring down the mood of those around me, but how can I help it? It's come to the point where stagnation is seen as a compliment. At least my mind is still active, even if my enthusiasm is on life support. I'm constantly thinking of new ideas, of sex with Jackie, of Mum's cooking, of Nick Drake lyrics, of money, of getting out of work, getting out of work to go and meet Mike.

I should be thinking more about Mike but I'm not, I'm too self-involved for that. I should be spending as much time with him as possible because in three days' time it will be Thursday; in three days, none of this will matter to me because in one, two, three days, Mike will be dead.

47, 46, 45...

So where does that put me?

Here, I suppose. 17:29 on a Monday afternoon, drowning in the monotony of another laborious day in the marketing department of DoTrue. That's right, DoTrue, capital D, capital T. A little-known computer manufacturer that opened an office in the UK two years ago. It's my job to publicise their presence. Can you think of a more pointless occupation?

I have a degree in English language and phonetics from King's College. Three years slogging it out with future leaders and Nobel Prize winners to end up here trying to think of interesting ways to market a new RoHS-compliant chassis, which conforms to the latest BTX design parameters, promoting smoother air flow over the mainboard and processor. It's not the kind of creative writing that I am pursuing.

22, 21, 20...

I can see my boss pacing.

That's never a good sign at this time. It means that he is mulling over an inspirational end-of-day speech.

He is insipid. An infant straight out of university who landed a highly paid position of power after earning a first-class degree in 'How to Convert People into Numbers' combined with a course in 'Advanced Fear and Misery in the Third Reich'.

His look reduces me to a barcode in an ever-growing population of corporate whores. But the thing that really annoys me, the thing that I hate most, is the way he tries to instil a semblance of confidence and encouragement by punctuating his lectures with the phrase, 'Okay, now let's do some good.'

'...So, in conclusion, our forecasting has to be spot on as we move into Q3, when we can certainly expect a ramp in the notebook market. Okay ... now let's do some good.' As if anything we do makes the slightest difference to the world.

9, 8, 7...

Oh shit, he's coming out.

5, 4, 3...

'Ring, ring, ring,' a woman's voice sings.

And I'm saved.

'Ring, ring, ring.' There it is again. Pick up the phone. Please, just pick up your bloody phone. My fingers are still poised over the keyboard but in my mind they are pressed together in prayer.

'Riiiiiii-iiii-ii-ii-iii-iii-iiing.' The trilling vibrato that I usually hate to hear has just prevented a further twenty to thirty minutes of a Danny Elwes harangue about teamwork and targets and forecasts and e-shots and sell-out and sell-in and price lists and percentages and on and on and 'let's do some good' and on and on again and, finally, he answers his phone.

I remember the day he got the ring tone for his mobile of that fucking woman singing ring, ring fucking ring. He was so proud. He let everyone know how much it cost him. Loser. I laughed to myself thinking it probably wasn't the first woman he had ever paid money for. But that doesn't matter now, he is back in his office and I resume the countdown.

2, 1...

Delete.

I'm logged out, standing up, jacket on, bag in hand, walking, walking, past the boss, walking, out the door and onto the bus. The number eighteen bus which takes me sixteen minutes and drops me right outside The Scam – my local pub – which is sixty-four steps from where I live.

TEXTS

Are you there?
I haven't heard from you all weekend.
Did you do it?
Oh, my God. You did it.
Did you do it?
Please answer me.
I'm messaging a dead man.
Fuck. You did it.

I didn't do it.

Jesus Christ. You're alive.

Unfortunately.
Sorry to make you worry.
I was going to do it.

What happened?

I needed to see my family.
Before I leave them.

That's still your plan?

I have to. I know that.
I've seen them. They have no idea about how I feel.
I don't even know what I'm waiting for.

You have to stop putting off and putting off.
There's never a right time. You could do it right now.
Do it.

MONDAY
(THREE DAYS BEFORE SUICIDE THURSDAY)

The sixteen-minute bus ride isn't the toughest commute, and the sixty-four-step journey to my front door isn't particularly arduous, either. I suppose this minuscule portion, this fraction of my everyday life, could be considered easy; I have an easy life in this respect. I start to enjoy myself; I even gain pleasure from the routine of it.

This is where my day really begins.

Almost everyone on here can be pigeonholed as a 'young professional'. They all look relieved to be out of the office, they all look uncomfortable in a suit or sensible blouse, and they all have a mobile phone in their hands, even though they've been glued to some kind of screen all day.

We just want to block out the din of the world around, separate ourselves from reality for a moment.

Nothing online is real.

Yes, it's surprisingly peaceful on the bus.

It has always interested me why people do not talk on public transport but this bus journey is a particularly anomalous phenomenon: it is silent except for the tinny treble sound coming from the cheaper earphones, but that eventually fades into white noise. The few elderly ladies aren't even talking. It's too late for school kids to be on here but there is one girl in school uniform who I assume has been in a detention until now, maybe for being disruptive in class, but even she is quiet, in contemplation.

I use the tranquillity of my environment to relax, read the paper or a book; but usually I spend the time scribbling ideas into my pocket notebook; ideas that I can work on when I get home; ideas for my latest masterpiece.

I hang at the back of the bus and jump off while it is still moving, slowing down before it pulls into the stop. The world seems so loud outside. I lift my headphones from around my neck, place them over my ears and select a song. Kirsty McColl, 'Days'. It's the soundtrack to my life for the next sixty-four steps or so. At this moment of every weekday, I am always thankful.

I stand still for eight seconds until the first time she sings the word 'days'. It feels like the right moment to start walking to the beat, to begin my journey.

My first smile of the week.

I walk.

Sixty-four steps doesn't necessarily constitute a journey. Sixty-four steps. Twelve after I turn left again, which is the back of The Scam, then I hit a shop called Furry's, which only sells vinyl records and eight-tracks, my next eight steps. A butcher's, sixteen steps. He always waves even though we have never exchanged a word. An alley that leads to the back of the butcher's, two steps; a newsagents, ten steps; an off-licence, twelve; and a quaint coffee shop run by two war veterans who always waffle on about conflicts that nobody has ever even heard about, but they are harmless, eight steps. Then you arrive at my house.

I noticed the place about four years ago during a time I was spending most mornings at Gaucho's, drinking coffee and etching musings into my slowly biodegrading notebook. I was unemployed and scrounging £43 per week off the state, which barely covered my coffee bill, but I was more determined than ever to finish a novel that particular year.

The truth is, I have never managed to write anything beyond a first chapter; 733 first chapters, in actual fact. Mum had read and kept them all, every last one, boxed and stored in her attic chronologically according to time written.

Why would I ever need 733 first chapters?

It acts as a constant reminder of a key issue in my life, I suppose.

I can't finish anything.

By the summer of that year I was no nearer to completing my novel than I was at the start. Slowly running out of options, fate intervened and took my mother, leaving me with a pile of cash, three months of sequestered living, elevated *fruproyance* and a level of suspended animation that would rival even the most indolent of catatonic ticks.

But the money gave me something that I didn't have before.

Choice.

So I bought up the lease on the old place next to Gaucho's that has been closed since the mid-seventies; a place called Pretzel Logic. It was brown and damp, and the windows had been boarded up and covered in graffiti. It was mainly the obvious 'Ben 4 Charlie 4 Eva' kind of graffiti, with a few call-girl flyers and cards pinned to it, plus an old poster for a band named Turquoise Indigo, who looked like a Latino Supremes tribute group; also part of an unfinished poem or song that I copied down in the hope that maybe I could complete it for the person who started it. 'So, What Now?' A simple title and I'm not sure why I seem to love it so much. Maybe it's because I relate to the fragmentation of the piece. I keep it with me all the time; I even kept the wooden panel it was written on.

So this place used to be a pretzel joint thirty years ago but failed because the salty bread that makes you crave liquid for a week never really caught on over here like it did in the States. When I tore down the wood to clean the place out, it smelled like pretzels. Not old pretzels either, fresh ones. Fresh, never-before-touched, brackish loaves, delicately prepared for an ignorant British public afraid of change.

Three years I have lived here now, and it still smells like fucking pretzels.

I've always liked the smell of paper. You know? New books, old books. Oh, old books. That damp-page aroma. That stagnant essence of wildebeest; the pungent, animal-like stench that disperses from the sleeves as the unappreciated novel gasps for air and unleashes its dankness, causing a one-foot orb of moisture around the unknowing reader's head. I love that. But you don't get that here. You get pretzels, and that's one thing that will never change.

I spend the majority of my time on the ground floor of the three-level apartment building that I almost own thanks to Mum's untimely departure from this mortal coil. No bigger than a twelve-year-old girl's bedroom, the space on the bottom floor acts as my office, my therapist's office, and the 'first chapter' library.

All the first chapters that I have ever written are now here. On shelves, currently arranged according to their genre but that can change by the day depending on mood or my need to distract myself from actually writing a second chapter.

I had an idea. To make money doing something that I actually enjoy. Isn't that the dream?

I would open a shop of first chapters – more of a cubby hole, in truth. By using my ability/curse as a prolific starter, I would provide an invaluable service to those who suffer from writer's block. They could come to my shop, my business, and buy a first chapter that I had written – to get them on the right road; to motivate and inspire them.

Fundamentally, I was going to sell my ideas, my hours of factual research, my own experiences and peccadilloes; I was going to sell them, like my soul, to the Devil Herself. All I would ask is that I would be credited with the first chapter of the novel which was to remain as unchanged as possible if the author were ever to be published.

It was novel. Quirky. Maybe even innovative. There's a possibility that I could get bogged down in the legalities if anyone ever did make something out of my ideas, and maybe that would take the fun out of it. So, for now, they act as a library. A reference. A memento of my life's work. Until the weekends, when those eight shelves of paper are open for aspiring creatives to peruse.

A clear indication of my worthless existence to date.

I lied. It's not really my therapist's office. This is something else that I made up.

Fiction.

Another thing that I started.

Initially I just said that I had begun seeing a therapist to get out of something that I didn't really want to do; but now I see my 'therapist' every Thursday, sometimes on a Tuesday, if I need the space. It gives me an excuse to be alone, to write without interruption. For two hours every Thursday night, nobody calls, nobody bothers me, because writing is supposed to be a solitary occupation. Writers need to be alone in order to fully immerse themselves into the world they are creating.

Sometimes I just lie on the therapist's couch that I bought especially for the library, place a Dictaphone on my chest and let go. I get out any thoughts I have about Jackie or Mike, situations from work, stories that others have told me, I release them and use this as a stimulus to start another chapter. It's cathartic.

It's time alone. Just the two of us. Myself and my conscience, my counsel.

My fake therapist.

The only person I can trust.

Me.

But Mondays aren't about therapy. So I should have time to sort something I have been putting off.

SUICIDE **THURSDAY**

He is sitting there.

When they find Mike, he is just ... sitting there.

It doesn't really look right.

Is there actually a *right* way to kill yourself?

He is sitting there, on his floor, his wooden living-room floor. Recently, he decided to take a home-study French-polishing course, and this was his first conquest, his own lounge. He was so proud. And I am glad. Glad it has had a recent spruce because it makes the job of mopping up the blood much easier: it hasn't soaked into the wood – although it did fall between some of the cracks. It shouldn't really do that but it was only his first attempt.

He is sitting there. Dead. But actually sitting up.

Sitting, on his newly self-polished wooden floor, leaning against his used-to-be-pea-green two-seater sofa. It used to be that colour but, over time, and through lack of care and more attention paid to the wooden floor, it has turned brown.

It isn't a dirty brown, although it is dirty. It is the kind of brown you get when you try to make purple by mixing red and blue poster paint. Of course, this never works so you end up adding yellow ochre to brighten it, then a green to darken it again. Then you think, perhaps white will lighten it up so the brown is more detectable, but this turns it grey. So you add red and blue again, maybe cadmium yellow this time.

That is the colour of Mike's sofa.

I don't know how it got like that, probably some self-taught, home-study, dye-your-own-sofa-to-match-your-new-room course. Gone wrong. It was only his first attempt, though.

So, he is sitting there. Sitting up. Sitting, on his newly polished floor, leaning against his badly dyed and eroding sofa. One of those sofas your aunt had in the eighties. With the gold tassling that frames and segments each rectangular section of this monstrous furnishing.

Mike is sitting there with his hands in his legs.

Not on.

In.

In his legs.

Slitting the wrists can take far too long. I can remember him saying that he could never slit his wrists; of course, I took that to mean that he would never kill himself. Not that he would do this. Some people slit their wrists in the bath. I always thought that maybe it dulls the pain or something, but actually it still hurts. A lot. It just looks like you are in a bath full of blood. Perhaps people do it just for the imagery or drama. That would be too clichéd for Mike.

Obviously.

If you slit your legs, you enter a whole other league.

It can no longer be misconstrued as a cry for help.

You mean business.

You want to die. And you want to die quickly.

In your thigh, just above the sartorius muscle, where the skin on your leg creases before your hip, there is a pretty major artery with a sign on it saying: 'Please do not cut here.' Mike chose to ignore this sign.

Cutting this area will cause you to die very quickly, without the aching agony that a wrist slashing incurs. Ten seconds and you're gone. Left leaning against your sofa, bleeding on your cowboyish attempt at French polishing a floor, your blood oozing out of you and seeping down the cracks that would not have been there if you had just paid the £250 for a professional. You are left as a dry, pathetic husk. But maybe that is the way you want to be remembered.

But wait. There is a solution. You can stop the pints of blood from dropping out of your leg. There are, in fact, two options. Putting pressure on the wound will buy you some time, but your own hands are not powerful enough. The only way to stop it, to generate the necessary amount of pressure, is for someone else to stand on the gaping gash with their full weight. You could probably get up and walk to a hospital one mile away if you had only slit your wrists.

However, if you are on your own and therefore do not have this luxury, there is something else you can do. Calling for Miss Fagan across in flat fourteen will not help: she only weighs about four stone, soaking wet. Take your hands, extend your fingers and dig them inside, deep inside the slash. This should block the bleeding. Then you can phone an ambulance with the other hand.

That is, unless you have cut both legs.

Mike had opted for this extreme method of suicide and obviously had second thoughts because his hands were lodged into his thighs up to the second knuckle of each finger.

I stare at him. Sitting there. French-polished floor; eighties sofa; hands in legs; piece of glass on each side, which he's used to jab into the artery; hands in legs; a mirror directly in front of him so that he could watch himself die, hands in legs, hands in legs, hands in legs.

That's all that there is in the entire room.

Well done, Mike.

Not bad, considering it was only his first attempt.

After what seems like a twelve-minute gaze, I start to smile.

Maybe he did it for me.

MONDAY
(THREE DAYS BEFORE SUICIDE THURSDAY)

I turn my key and am immediately greeted by a backdraft of pretzel aroma.

And I know that I am home.

Kirsty McColl hasn't quite finished her serenade so I lie down on the couch listening to her; I let her finish. Because she can.

I'm jealous.

I want to start writing because I had a great idea on the bus for a comedy set in a hospice for the terminally ill, but there is something that I have to do that I have been putting off.

This Friday, it is our six-year anniversary, and I want to do something special with Jackie.

Jackie. My long-term girlfriend.

Something else I can't finish.

At first it was fine. Not great. Just, well, fine. When I first saw her, she didn't bowl me over with good looks: she is not *good*-looking. She is average. Not girl-next-door, either. More like the younger, underdeveloped sister of the girl next to the girl next door.

The girl who lives a couple of doors down.

I make the call to À la Gare. A fairly exclusive restaurant in Islington built inside three train cars. Jackie loves these kinds of quirky places that sell expensive French cuisine. Anything with *à la* in the name is good enough for Jackie. But then again, apparently I am good enough for Jackie, so that doesn't say much about her taste.

The maitre d' tells me that I am lucky, that they have just had a last-minute cancellation.

I ponder my apparent luckiness for a second.

'Okay, well, thanks for your help.'

'*Bon. Merci.* See you both on Friday.' He sounds genuinely pleased.

'Eight o'clock,' I confirm.

'*Oui.* Yes, eight o'clock.'

And I hang up.

This year it will be different. Last year I was so nervous that I drank a bottle of Pinot Noir and nearly asked her to move in with me. This year, I am going to do it properly.

Two beers, the starter and main course, and that's it.

That is when I will finally do it.

Friday, the day after Suicide Thursday, I am definitely, one hundred per cent, surely and without doubt going to finally do it.

This Friday, I am going to break up with Jackie.

I am going to finish something.

Thanks, Mike. I'll get the message.

JACKIE

It's Monday evening, work is over and, of course, Jackie heads straight to church.

Sitting in what is essentially a partitioned-by-chicken-wire shed, opposite the horrific image of a pale, skinny, bearded Jewish man nailed to a couple of pieces of wood, Jackie waits, perspiring inside the dark oak casement of the confessional. Her priest, a man she has known since birth, perches himself behind the divide in semi-darkness, like a rape victim on an American talk show: concealing his true identity; hiding behind his veil of secrecy, of morality, of faith.

She runs through the Bible in her mind until she hits Romans 14:14:

'Nothing is unclean in itself, only to him who thinks anything to be impure, to him it is impure.'

And so begins her torture: the guilt that can only come with a faith in something that decrees a person's every action can be interpreted as a sin.

She's Jackie McConnell.

It's been twenty-eight hours since her last confession.

'I have had impure thoughts,' she self-deprecates.

'Continue, Jacqueline.' Father Farrelly says this as if he is going to understand Jackie's problem, which isn't even a *real* problem, but he is just there to judge her. That's his job.

Judge.

Jury.

And executioner.

She continues to explain her issue, the fact that she had a dream about another man. She lies and says it is a man she has never seen before, but it was Mike she dreamed about – she will confess to this on Wednesday.

Why is she apologising for something that happened in her subconscious? How does she have control over that? If you believe in the gospels, God created us all from thin air, which begs the question, who created air, thin or thick? Allegedly, humans were created by a God who decided to also give them free will. So how is it Jackie's fault that she had a dream? But what is the point of religion if not to make one feel perpetually guilty.

Jackie's experience should not be seen as impure. Eli purposely brought on a thought just yesterday regarding Jackie meeting a terrifyingly brutal and untimely end. This was a conscious thought that he invoked, not God or Allah or LSD or anything else. He made it happen and, in return, it made him happy. Delighted, even. Delighted because, on most days now, he sees Jackie's death as the only way out of their relationship.

Father Farrelly listens intently to what Jackie has to say. Tutting in his head and fondling his rosary beads, he passes the sentence because this is a tribunal at which Jackie is at once the accuser, the accused and the witness; Father Farrelly merely acts as judge. He decrees that five decades of Hail Mary's should suffice – that's fifty *times* not fifty years – each one starting with an Our Father and ending with a Gloria Patri.

Because that will make all the difference.

Jackie lights a candle before leaving the church. She starts her six-minute walk back to Holloway Road and begins her own personal Monday night regime.

TEXTS

Okay, I'm gonna do it.

What? Now?

You were right. I can't keep overthinking it .

I can't spend every day like this.

I don't want to feel this way, you know?

So, tonight?

Not tonight.

You're not making any sense.

I don't have everything in place.

Tomorrow.

Definitely?

Definitely.

JACKIE

Arriving at her flat, she is greeted by Descartes, her cat. There used to be two of them – cats, that is – but, unfortunately, Camus lost all nine lives in one go to an elderly gentleman in a Fiat Punto. The good news for Descartes, however, is that with one solitary remaining dependent, Jackie can now afford to provide the very best in feline cuisine.

Pros and cons.

Jackie squeezes the contents of the gourmet sachet into a pink plastic bowl – it looks remarkably like the duck terrine Eli made the mistake of ordering on their five-year anniversary meal at the restaurant of some TV chef that Jackie has a crush on.

He thinks she spoils the cat and, as a result, it has become quite snobby.

That's right. Jackie's cat is a snob.

I think, therefore, he is.

Pouring herself a large glass of Sauvignon Blanc from an open bottle in the fridge, Jackie kicks off her shoes and heads for the Bluetooth speaker Eli bought for her when his mum died. Luckily for her, but not necessarily her neighbours, the soundtrack to *The Bodyguard* is still cued up on the speaker's app. She dances around the living room with her eyes closed, sipping her wine and occasionally spilling droplets onto the laminate floor, which Descartes then samples.

He laps them up but secretly he is looking down at her because he feels that a 2004 Pinot Noir would go better with his meal, he knows it's a perfect accompaniment to any game dish.

By the second chorus of 'I'm Every Woman', the first glass of wine is finished. Jackie sashays into the bathroom, puts the plug in the bath, hits the hot tap on and then pours in a muscle-relaxing bubble bath that smells of elderflower, all in time with the music and all the while singing along with Ms Houston, who is now being muffled by the splashing of water.

Jackie unbuttons her blouse two notches and sashays back to the fridge for more wine. Descartes has finished his duck terrine with a mêlée of seasonal vegetables washed down with a few drops of after-dinner wine, and feels he now deserves a nap and some valuable alone time.

After another short stint on the dance floor, shimmying in time to 'Queen of the Night', Jackie is marginally out of breath and sweating enough to justify her bath. She drops out of her work outfit and leaves it on the floor to get wet. Standing in front of the mirror now, in her underwear, she gives herself a miniature scrutiny. Firstly, from the front, where she examines her breasts, then a side shot, where she sucks in her stomach but not by much, and then a view from behind; she tugs a little at her waistband.

Slowly lowering into the tub, trying not to scald herself, Jackie lies back with the glass of wine still clutched in her hand, her head just peeping above the bubbles, listening to Whitney trilling on with 'Don't make me close one more door', waiting to hear the faux-powerful key change so popular in modern pop music, and she thinks of Eli and what he might be doing. It's not too dissimilar from what she is doing, except Eli's bath is a therapist's couch, his wine is a black coffee with two sugars, his Whitney is the jazzy muzak from the coffee shop next door, and his thoughts are not about Jackie: they are consumed with the need to get this idea down on the page without distraction. He has a title: *A Home to Die In*.

Of course, that doesn't happen, Jackie has taken her mobile phone to the bathroom.

She dials Eli's number, and a picture of some smiling numbskull who looks remarkably similar to someone he used to be flashes on her screen until he picks up.

'Can I come over?'

He really doesn't want her to because he has to get the idea down before he forgets it.

But still, for some unfathomable reason that can only be deciphered by his therapist, who is not even real, Eli says yes.

A HOME TO DIE IN
(WORKING TITLE)

BY ELI HAGIN

F I R S T **C H A P T E R**

His home was perfect. And not in that sterile, Scandinavian minimalist, dentist-waiting-room aesthetic that seems to be perpetually en vogue. There was character. Exposed brick. Shelves of books. Things. Tangible things that have been collected because they are one-of-a-kind or interesting or quirky. And it could be too much but it's just right.

The place is living.

It's lived in.

The *DONT WALK/WALK* sign outside the bathroom is genuine – complete with its lack of apostrophe. It once graced the streets of Manhattan in the 1950s and was ignored by New Yorkers every day.

The *On Air* light in the study was once a daily feature of a BBC radio studio.

The Godfather cinema one-sheet poster in the hallway – back when they were folded, not rolled – has some light damage from its display at the Cinematograph Theatre in Shepherd's Bush in 1972. Some would think it would devalue the piece, but, for Anders Stirling, it was added patina that made it unique.

It was real, it had lived, and it was old.

Much like the man himself.

All of these pieces of character and history had found the perfect home. A home that Anders Stirling had crafted to reflect his passion and personality.

And now they are collecting dust.

They're dying.

Just like Anders.

And he can't live among his things anymore because he needs care. And his family have put him in a place where he can be cared for by strangers because they can't take the burden themselves. And they're hopeful. Hopeful that his time will be easy passing. That he will go quietly into the night. And they will sift through the paintings and the artefacts and statues and furniture. And they will not keep any of it because it would add too much colour to their monochrome homes and clean lines and no clutter, and nothing that sparks an ounce of joy.

The vultures are circling.

As is Mrs Silverman. Every day, she walks a circuit of the freak show that is Anders' new home, Star Acres, his home to die in. A hundred and thirteen times, Mrs Silverman paces the carpets up and down and around. The equivalent of six miles per day. She is 103 years old. A vegetarian. And doesn't look like she's going anywhere soon. She is, at once, an irritation and an inspiration.

Most days, Anders thinks that it would be easier if he would just die. He's not inspiring anybody in there, he's too pissed off with the hand he's been dealt. He curses God and his family and rotten luck. But he can't let go. He won't let this disease take him.

He wants to fight.

For his Murano glass hanging lamp in the upstairs hallway. For his nineteenth-century Winfield Portable Campaign rocking chair. For his gilt overmantel mirror. His chinoiserie planters.

Regency writing desk. And the oil painting of the piano player in Bemelmans Bar at The Carlysle Hotel, New York.

Carrie saunters in to Anders and says, 'I don't know how women find this comfortable.'

She's a decade older than Anders but looks younger. Her hair is full and thick, you can tell she was a beauty in her day. There seems to be a hue that covers her. Some kind of blurring. A real-life photo filter that gives an analogue warmth. Like she has stepped off the set of some seventies porn film. And that wouldn't be a shock because she is overly sexual.

Carrie lifts her skirt as she speaks and shows Anders what she is talking about. She's too old to be wearing a thong and she seems to have put it on the wrong way around. Anders can see how it splits her right up the middle and he knows that's what she wanted him to see.

'No thanks, Carrie. I already ate, this morning.'

'Next time.' She smiles and kicks her heel up as she exits.

He can't be here any longer otherwise he's going to give in.

Mrs Silverman walks past and Anders calls out to her. He's drawn to her. He likes old things. And she's a walking antique.

'You mind if I join you.'

'Only if you can keep up.'

He knows it's a joke but Anders is worried he will be too slow. But he has to try. He has to succeed with this first step. Otherwise he will never escape in time.

It's only a few pages but I think it sets up Anders Stirling. There's some intrigue there. What is his plan for escape? Will he die? What is his illness? And there's the opportunity for an eccentric ensemble cast of characters. It could be the idea that gets a second chapter.

My phone buzzes. It's a text from Mike. There's a back and forth for a few minutes but it's enough to throw me off my rhythm. So, I pour myself a glass of red wine. Perhaps it will act as a creative lubricant.

I should push on with a second chapter for *A Home To Die In*, but something else has been floating around in my mind, and I want to get something down before I forget

I write, *Bud Ellis loved the movies.* And Jackie calls.

I ignore it, this time. She'll probably call back. She never quits.

SUICIDE **THURSDAY**

Arriving in Mike's block on the night of his suicide, I am petrified at what I might find when, really, I should probably feel privileged.

In flat forty-one, a Puerto Rican immigrant has fallen asleep in front of the TV, which is showing a repeat of a BBC documentary about narcolepsy. He's warm underneath his multi-coloured blanket; it took his grandmother two years to crochet it. He's dreaming about the brunette in flat eighteen.

The grocery assistant who lives in flat twelve has lied to two student actresses about working in casting. Now one of them is riding his dick while the other muffles his hearing with her thighs and smothers his face with her firm, shaven, not-so-delicate area. He can barely breathe but he doesn't really care.

This man will eventually understand the irritation of constantly itching and burning genitals as a result of one night's unprotected pleasure during which he contracted herpes. The girls know that they have it, but they don't really care either. There's a moral there somewhere.

Number twenty-three let their cat out for the night. It pisses against the door of flat twenty-five where a drunken Mr Thompson, who hates to be called Mr T, is dying in his sleep. His wife lies virtually comatose with a smile on her face and her eyes open. He's still warm and no fluids have been excreted just yet. They've been married forever but it will be a relief for her that he's gone.

The cat moves on, passing a seventeen-year-old girl arriving home two hours and twelve minutes late from a party at which her best friend fucked three different guys and left her on her own. She had an awful night, couldn't get a lift home, and her dad is waiting up for her with a belt in one hand and a cigar in the other. She is about to take a beating and a burning. Her mum knows it happens but lets it continue.

Flats four and six are empty and smell like wheat. The guy in flat seven works in an office and has an early start. Mrs Fagan is having difficulty getting out of the bath in flat fourteen because she relaxed with too many glasses of Port.

And here, in number fifteen, I think I've got it bad because my best friend has just killed himself and a police officer is refusing to acknowledge the blatant Catholic symbolism of Jackie's bloody hands.

I go quietly. I have nothing to hide. It was suicide.

It's one of the best things that has ever happened to me; to my creative life. Already, I have so many new ideas.

As I'm led down the corridor, hands cuffed behind my lumbar region, I hear the screams of cigarette burns, the echo of multiple, faked, diseased orgasms; I'm hit by the smell of the recently deceased, the taste of Jackie's perfume, and that odd sense you get when a television has been left on standby. These senses build into a swelling crescendo until I am taken outside the building into an unprecedented silence.

What a beautiful, perfect evening.

TUESDAY
(TWO DAYS BEFORE SUICIDE THURSDAY)

What the hell was I doing last night letting Jackie come over?

I feel an overwhelming need to vent but I can't, not for at least another eight hours and forty-nine minutes. I have to wait to get out of this fucking office before I can get back home and sweat it out with my fake therapist. Still, on the bright side, I have managed to get through eleven minutes of my working day before thinking about getting out of here.

I need to talk about this. I can't keep internalising everything, I learned that in my last session. I can't discuss this with Mike because, although his loyalties should lie with me, recently, when it comes to Jackie, he looks at me like I'm president of the Bill Cosby appreciation society.

There's nobody here to talk to. It's just me. Me and Sam. Sam Jordane.

He sits opposite me. I probably see his face more than I see Jackie's or Mike's, although after Thursday, I'll see Mike's face everywhere I go.

Sam isn't my superior, but he's not my equal either. He's the kind of employee who may have had a dream to do something great once but life just got in the way. Now he is stuck in a job with no prospect of progression but, because he has been here so long, he has convinced himself that what he does is actually important. And, honestly, I'm not actually sure what he does.

He does do a lot of things which make it very difficult to form a connection with him about anything that is not either strictly work-related or a topic *he* wants to discuss.

If I wanted to know what time our meeting will be on Wednesday, he won't tell me it will be at nine o'clock. Oh, no. He will say: 'O nine hundred hours.' This, in his warped little mind, is a subtle reminder to me that he was once a soldier and actually fought in a war. He was probably a chef in the Gulf or sheep-counter in the Falklands or a road sweeper in Kosovo. He never talks about it. Apparently he's not allowed to. So now, if I want him to stop talking to me, I just ask him how many confirmed kills he has.

We start each day the same way.

'Sooooo.' He elongates this until he has finished typing the last few words of his email, so I know he is busy and working. He clicks send. 'Get up to anything good last night, then?'

Oh yes, Sam, I really wanted to knuckle down to work and get some writing done. You see, I have this great new idea for a story about crumbling social values and the blur between fantasy and reality, but instead I agreed to have my girlfriend over to distract me with sex, which I'm fairly sure we both use as a tool to forget the meaninglessness of our existence even if only for a short while.

But this isn't what I say.

'Oh, you know, sat in, watched a film.' I don't even finish before he starts telling me about his own idiosyncratic routine.

'Well, I got home late from work again.' Of course you did, Sam, you value your job more than your own family. 'Alice wasn't pleased, obviously.'

Yes, Sam, that's right, it *is* obvious. Obvious to everyone but you that you deliberately use DoTrue to your advantage, leaving your poor exhausted wife, who you don't want to be with anymore, to take care of the children that you don't want to be around anymore. And you emotionally starve them of any love that you are incapable of providing anyway. That's two points for predictability and a bonus point for stating the obvious.

When did I get so bitter? Something to talk to my therapist about later.

Surely he won't continue this torture by telling me something his kids did recently, which is just annoyance with their indiscipline dressed up as a cute nostalgic yarn. A tale of woe disguised as cheery anecdote. A horror story impersonating a bedtime fable.

'And then, to cap things off, Harry got into bed with us last night and woke us up this morning at O four hundred by pissing all over the bed.'

For God's sake, Sam, sort your kids out, you're a military man, for crying out loud.

I don't really know what to say to this, so I stare vacantly at my screen, but I can't get what I did last night out of my head. Jackie just seemed so cleansed when she arrived, and she was in such a frivolous mood it made everything so easy. I think she must have finished her Hail Marys on the Tube before she got to my place.

I have to shake off these thoughts.

I only have until close of business today – Sam would say C.O.B. – to finalise a marketing plan for a new back-to-school campaign for laptops – Sam would say B.T.S. I bore myself thinking about it and, only sixteen minutes into my working day, my fingers gravitate toward the position known as log-off.

Sam never logs off. If he did any work, he'd probably burn himself out.

My computer makes a noise that jolts me back into reality, notifying me that I have mail.

It's from Jackie:

Hey you, thanks for last night. It was great ;-)
Miles of smiles,
Jackie xxx

THINGS I HATE ABOUT THIS

ONE: The way she calls me 'You'. She thinks it's cute; I think it's patronising and fake.

TWO: When people use punctuation to make smiley faces or other equally pathetic cartoon hieroglyphics to denote the emotion of the preceding sentence. It's a butchering of our beautiful language.

THREE: Those stupid little sayings like 'miles of smiles' and, oh, I don't know, 'pixie-dust kiss droplets' or whatever she says. I'm thirty years old this year. Just write *from Jackie*, or, if you truly believe it, *love Jackie*.

FOUR: Jackie. The part that reminds me I am still with Jackie. Why can't I just finish with Jackie? I really can't understand why I do this. It's not fair on her and, more importantly, it's not helping me.

'I need the BTS campaign by C.O.B., Eli. Don't forget.'

Oh shut up, Sam.

'I'll have it done by two o'clock,' I tell him. He looks at me like there's more information to give. 'Fourteen-hundred hours,' I add, as though he has no comprehension of the way almost everyone expresses time. Stupid rest of the world, getting their times wrong.

I pretend to concentrate on my screen but I'm staring through it, daydreaming, recollecting what I did last night.

The first chapter to *A Home To Die In* had written itself, as it often does. But something else was bubbling.

So I wrote that, too.

I had set up the fundamental characteristics of my lovable anti-hero, Bud Ellis, a man so obsessed with the movies that he tries to live his own life according to Todorovian principles. A theory that states that original order must be disrupted by a complication, only to be resolved and order regained in the end. Inevitably, this would involve Bud sabotaging his own relationship in the hope of rekindling the love affair and restoring the 'order' he'd had before.

Unfortunately for Bud, I was not planning on giving him the happy ending he was so confident of attaining because, well, the world just isn't that perfect – that just wouldn't be realistic. Bud had to learn the hard way that life cannot imitate the bubble-gum, silicon-injected, neon-lit fantasy celluloid world he had come to believe was the ideal.

I couldn't wait to get this all down on the page.

I'd just typed the word 'Chapter'. Every word preceding this had just flown effortlessly from my brain through my fingers and onto the screen of my laptop, but as soon as I wanted to start the second chapter, every single letter felt like it took a lifetime.

C – Felt like I could have watched the entire *Godfather* trilogy in the time it took for this solitary letter to materialise, maybe even throwing in *Apocalypse Now* for good measure.

H – I could have translated the *Encyclopaedia Britannica* into ancient Mayan.

A – A still-life oil painting of my newly replenished fruit bowl.

P – Run a bath.

T – Get a degree in biochemical engineering – whatever that is.

E – Invented my own language made up of only vowels and numbers.

R – Collected a thousand ants and arranged them into order of height.

2 – Delayed finishing another second chapter because Jackie decided to just turn up after I ignored her first call.

So now I am sabotaging my own relationship with my writing. Putting myself off the task at hand. I am mirroring my new creation, which means that my writing can be misconstrued as semi-autobiographical and I don't want that. I hate being asked that question. 'Oh, is Bud Ellis based on you?'

No, you fucking idiot. I'm not that two-dimensional. His persona is probably linked to the smallest part of me. I mean, has Stephen King ever had his ankles broken by a crazed fan? Does J.K. Rowling know of an extra platform at King's Cross and are the trains still late there?

This question infuriates me almost as much as Sam's pointless pontificating.

'Did you see my email?'

Sam has emailed me even though he sits less than four feet away from me; and he has cc'd Danny because he thinks that will definitely make me do whatever he has asked if the *real* boss is involved.

Hi Eli, please insure the B.T.S. campaign is complete by C.O.B. today.
Regards,
Sam.

I already told him this would be done by two p.m. So not only has he spelled 'ensure' wrongly but he brought me out of the dream before I got to the part where I had sex with Jackie, she made love to me, and we both fell asleep completely unfulfilled, uncomfortable and apathetic.

I can't get back into the reverie of last night so I grunt acknowledgement towards Sam and buckle down to my futile promotion and, well, no one wants to hear about that.

JACKIE

She types:

Hi Eli,

You seemed distracted last night. We had a good time, right? I just felt like there was something on your mind. You can talk to me, you know?

She deletes.

Hey Babe,

Last night was great. I'm so pleased I came over. I love waking up next to you in the morning. Did you have something on your mind? I felt like you might have been thinking about a new book or something. Are we meeting up later? Let me know.

Too soft. Pandering. She's a strong, independent woman. She doesn't need to cower to a man.

Again:

You were off this morning. I swallowed your come but I'm not swallowing this bullshit. What the fuck is going on with you?

Jackie smiles and deletes slowly, one letter at a time. The natural catharsis of honesty, of being true to who you really are.

She breathes. And smiles again.

Miles of smiles.

Eli can't finish anything. Jackie knows this. She knows how he feels about DoTrue, she has read many of his first chapters – maybe all of them – but something niggles at her. If Eli was no longer interested in her, if he wanted to break up, he couldn't do it. He couldn't finish their relationship. Maybe she couldn't do anything. Maybe she couldn't push him hard enough to make him do it.

But she doesn't want to do that. She doesn't want him to break up with her. She loves Eli. She wants him to succeed.

To write a second chapter.

And a third.

So, she writes:

Hey you, thanks for last night. It was great ;-)
Miles of smiles,
Jackie xxx

He's not finishing anything over that.

TEXTS

You know how you're going to do it?

> I've been looking into it.

You don't want to get it wrong again. You want it to work.

> Yeah. I guess.

You guess?

Second thoughts?

> ....

What does that mean?

All of this talk and now you're backing out?

Is that it?

Is that it?

> No. Nothing like that. I know what to do this time.
>
> Once I do it, there's no turning back.
>
> It only ends one way.

You just drink some fucking bleach.

Or you dive off the tallest building you can find.

> Who's doing this, me or you?

You. I hope.

> I've got a better way.
>
> You'll see.

Don't want to tell me?

You'll see.

FAKE **THERAPY**

This is how it goes:

```
INT. ELI'S OFFICE/FAKE THERAPIST'S OFFICE

     FAKE THERAPIST
And how are we today?
     ELI
'We' are fine.
     FAKE THERAPIST
Take a seat, Eli.
```

(Eli walks over to the couch and lies down, staring at
the ceiling.)

```
     FAKE THERAPIST
So, we're getting straight into it today. Last time,
we spoke for a while about your relationship with
Jackie. How have things been there since?
     ELI
We had sex. The sex was good. There's no issues in
that department. We know what works, by now. But …
I'm not sure I really wanted to have sex?
     FAKE THERAPIST
Are you saying she forced you against your will?
     ELI
Ha! No. Nothing like that. She didn't tie me to a
chair and gag me or anything. Just that … well…
     FAKE THERAPIST
Go on.
     ELI
```

I was busy, you know? I was doing something.
Writing. Something new. Something that could go past
a first chapter.
    FAKE THERAPIST
But you chose sex over your work?
    ELI
No. It wasn't that. I ignored her call the first
time.
    FAKE THERAPIST
But you picked up the next time.
    ELI
Yes. I was struggling. The words weren't flowing as
well as they were at the start of the evening.

(The fake therapist nods but says nothing.)

    ELI (CONT'D)
I just … I just can't seem to say no to her.
    FAKE THERAPIST
You think that perhaps it was you who used Jackie,
rather than the other way around?
    ELI
What do you mean?
    FAKE THERAPIST
She could be the reason that you didn't write a
second chapter. She becomes your excuse. Someone to
blame instead of taking responsibility yourself.
You said that you were struggling at that point…

A back-and-forth ensues. I tell her that I am listening, that I am
hearing what she is saying, I appreciate her words and I will give it
some thought. Textbook stuff. Then, after a string of platitudes and
silences designed to make me talk more than I want to, and a few
minor breakthroughs, I tell her about the chapter I wrote.

ELI

I wrote a new chapter.

FAKE THERAPIST

How do you feel about it?

ELI

I hate it.

FAKE THERAPIST

You hate it?

ELI

I've already moved on to something new.

FAKE THERAPIST

What's this one about? The one you hate.

ELI

It's about this old guy. Anders Stirling. A collector, maybe a bit of an eccentric, but he's put together this wonderful house filled with curiosities and one-offs. To him, it's perfect. But he's unwell and is forced away to die in a home that is not his own.

FAKE THERAPIST

Where did this idea come from?

ELI

You're a book blogger now, too?

FAKE THERAPIST

Hostility, Eli. It's just that it reminds me of something you said about your best friend, Mike. Isn't he currently working on his own home? He's doing something to his living-room floor that he believes will make the space 'perfect'.

This time I *am* hearing what is being said and I'm giving it some thought. And, for a fake therapist, there's a great deal of insight. Mike's floor is almost finished and in two days he'll be dead. He wants to die in his own home. That's his choice.

If subconsciously – or otherwise – I know this, why am I not trying to help him? Why am I writing about it, trying to obscure it in some way?

I agree with my therapist. That real life is seeping into my creative life, into my fiction. Fuelling it, perhaps.

I look up at the clock on the wall and realise our session has come to an end. And not a moment too soon. I don't have the energy to talk about my other book idea. I don't want to focus on what it could mean or where it may have come from. And I certainly don't want to delve too much into Mike or some of the strange messages I have been receiving.

THE PRINCIPLE
(WORKING TITLE)

BY ELI HAGIN

F I R S T **C H A P T E R**

Bud Ellis loved the movies. They were his life. They were more than that. Because they were better than life. That silver screen was magical to him. At the cinema, he would sit on the front row just so the image hit his eyes before the people behind him.

In films the hero prevails.

The court case is won.

Santa is real.

The guy gets the girl.

Off screen, bad people win the lottery and it doesn't change them. It doesn't make them more philanthropic. The safety net of wealth isn't enough to make them care about others. In many instances, it makes them worse. They rarely lose all the money, see the error of their ways and earn it all back. They never screw up, rekindle broken friendships or learn a valuable lesson about honesty and integrity. It is just an awful person doing awful things, getting lucky, and continuing to be a piece of shit.

It would make a terrible movie.

Much like Bud's own life. Continually taken for granted as a consequence of his idealism and naïveté. Crapped on at work, with women, by his mother. But it's all one note.

Crap on crap on crap.

That's not how movies work. Even the bleak Scandinavian ones.

It's a simple principle. Establish your story, how things are. This is *order*. At some point, introduce a complication, something that changes the path for the characters the audience is invested in. This creates *disorder*. By the end, have this complication resolved. Better still, get your protagonist to learn something valuable about themselves. *Order* is regained.

Order. Disorder. Order regained.

There's your movie.

Life isn't like that. It's filled with injustice and suffering and it all ends too quickly.

But Bud Ellis, with his rose-tinted glasses and optimism and celluloid dreams, disagrees. Movies are better than life. So, if you could make your life more like a film, doesn't that mean life would be better?

Ashleigh is perfect. She's a teacher. Idealistic. She won't let the bureaucracy of the school system knock that out of her. She's intelligent, thoughtful, determined, a great cook, and the crazy thing is that she is head over heels for Bud Ellis. And he feels the same way. Bud isn't perfect by any means, but he is perfect for Ashleigh, and she is easily the greatest thing that ever happened to him in his thirty-five years on this planet.

Bud wants to spend the rest of his life with Ashleigh.

And that, he tells himself, is the reason he has to cheat on her.

It's all too 'one note'.

Love on joy on happiness.

Sure, he could go through the rest of his life feeling content, happy even. They could raise a family. Get married. Finally make his mother proud. But it wouldn't be movie love. They wouldn't be Bonnie and Clyde, or Rose and Jack. They're not running from the law or fighting the class system or cancer or prejudice.

They haven't triumphed over adversity yet.

If anything, it's a lottery win.

And that doesn't always change people for the better.

So Bud will cheat, even though it is eating him up inside.

Because he can't get the girl back if he doesn't lose her first.

MIKE
(TWO DAYS BEFORE SUICIDE THURSDAY)

Phase 1: Mike wakes up at 8:55, just as he does every morning. Not weekends, though. Mike doesn't set his alarm on the weekend. It's his treat; a gift to himself. But every weekday he is startled to consciousness by the sound of the 'snooze tune' on the radio. Or the 'snooze *choon*', as it is often referred to. This spelling denotes something more than just a song. A sound that exceeds the limits of human experience and can therefore only be known hypothetically. An instrumental arrangement so poignant that it can only exist outside a material universe so as not to be limited by it.

In reality, there is nothing transcendent about the choice of morning mantra. It is a gimmick marketed as a design to keep listeners in bed that little bit longer before they actually have to make the decision to get up and be late for work or grab the phone and call in sick, ultimately grinding the wheels of industry to a halt with their endeavours.

This is Mike's routine.

It's not an action that makes him late, though, or even early, for that matter. No. Mike doesn't work at the moment. He's not even *between jobs*. This is just something he likes to do. It gives him a moment of happiness.

This morning's mind-numbingly soothing but nonetheless emotionally powerful serenade was 'You've Got a Friend' performed by James Taylor. A beautiful rendition of a Carole King classic, and Taylor's voice is so silky sweet that you actually feel as though you can taste it.

But the three and a half minutes of dreamy pleasure is just another daily reminder, to Mike, that fun is fleeting; it is pain that endures and gives life its meaning.

Mike goes back to sleep until 11:00.

Phase 2: With his eyes still closed he then ascends from his bed of self-pity and takes a laborious trek down the hallway in his underwear to the bathroom. Jackie thought it would be a great idea to put a large mirror in there behind the toilet. This is fine for her, but for Mike it means watching himself urinate every single day. It might make the room look a little bigger but it isn't necessarily inflating Mike's confidence to the same extent.

Daytime TV is **Phase 3**. A talk show hosted by a former obituaries editor of a small local paper in the south of England who now refers to his or herself as a journalist-come-therapist, and reinvents their persona by opting to lose their family name and go under the guise of single-name stardom. It's usually not anything cool like Pele, Prince or Aristotle either: it's something ridiculous like Godfrey or Jaunita or Derek.

Not only do they feel qualified to call themselves a journalist because they worked on the most unchallenging section of a local newspaper, but they believe they can offer advice to a public with problems because they were once called fat at school or the tabloids have uncovered an addiction to Lemsip.

Mike opens a new pack of wheat-based cereal that he only bought because it came with a free scratch card. He scratches the card with the handle of a spoon while he waits for the milk to warm in the microwave. Eli told him that this would give him cancer but that's the least of Mike's problems.

No three amounts were the same; he got four pairs.

While most people would accept this as mathematically probable, for Mike it is another confirmation that he is, in fact, a loser.

Will the world be a better place without him, though? No.

But will it be any worse off?

Mike takes his bowl and sits down to yet another paternity test or makeover while Boris or Daisy or Enrique offer trivially prosaic and shallow sentiments, followed seamlessly by a floor manager raising a placard instructing the audience to dish out a rhapsody of cheering and adulation designed to confirm that what they are hearing is correct and the applause subsequently explodes the ego of Daphne or Norman or Nikki spelled with two Ks and an I.

The show concludes with an overwhelmingly obvious final thought that explicitly states 'beauty is on the inside', or 'in the eye of the beholder', or something equally inane. Obviously this theory isn't based on the forty minutes of 'making over' an overweight, unattractive gaggle of unemployed reprobates who are being paid to air their deepest insecurities on national television, but the audience laps it up anyway.

It's sad for Eli (and Jackie), but their friend Mike falls contentedly into this demographic.

Phase 4: Comfortably numb, Mike heads for a twelve-minute shower to wash off the smell of Monday, and sets to work varnishing his new living-room floor so it is fully prepared in time for Suicide Thursday.

It's a shame because the episode on Friday of Sigfried or Belinda or Tarquin is scheduled to deal with depression and self-harming. Mike would think this was ironic except he didn't really understand what the word meant; his understanding was based on a song by Alanis Morrisette which Eli had tried to explain should actually have been called 'Unfortunate'.

With the floor stripped and sanded, Mike takes a rest on his sofa and reads the first chapter that Eli wrote a few days back. He scribbles a few notes down on a scrap of paper, just a few words that he thinks best illustrate the themes and motifs of the prose he has digested.

Mike is Eli's blurbist, or, as he likes to call it, 'blurb artist'. Every week Eli writes two or more new (first) chapters and every week Mike collects the latest could-be-masterpiece. He reads it on a Monday and/or Friday, writes a blurb as if it were a finished novel, then returns it.

Eli likes to keep Mike involved. This small act keeps him going because he's not working full-time and truly believes that at least he is doing something worthwhile.

He shares this delusion with his best friend.

Nevertheless, the fact that there is no chapter for him to work on this week gets him worried that there may be something wrong with Eli. In what seems to be an act of true altruism, he texts Eli asking to meet at The Scam later for a few pints and a chat.

Eli accepts, not knowing that Mike has secretly sent the same text to Jackie.

It's so common, now. The dopamine release that comes with online recognition or endorsement is similar to the effects of drugs. Instead of entering into a meaningful conversation with one person, we ask the same question to five or ten different people. Then wait. Wait for a response. The more responses, the more we are liked.

Popularity is an addiction and it kills.

Mike does this. He sends the same text to everybody. The only difference is that Eli and Jackie are Mike's everybody.

This will be the last night they will all be together to see Mike with a full ten pints of blood coursing through his body.

TEXTS

You're a real piece of shit.

What?

Where did that come from?

Just joking. :-)

Getting your attention.

Feeling better today?

Yes. I wish I wasn't like this.

What do you mean? Like what?

Such a fucking waste of space.

Nobody will even miss me when I'm gone.

That's how I genuinely feel.

I will.

I'm not talking about you.

But you'll forget about me, too.

What do I even offer?

I don't know what you want me to say.

You want me to tell you how brilliant you are?

You want me to tell you that you are loved?

You know that.

You know the people that care.

But you still have to do this.

I know.

It's the only way, now.

I know.

TUESDAY
(TWO DAYS BEFORE SUICIDE THURSDAY)

I manage to hit the 2:00 deadline that I set myself, which gives me three hours of nothing-to-do.

Sam thinks I am still battling with the final version of the back-to-school campaign, but the passion he sees in me is in fact the excitement arising from my triumph over the online, fiendishly difficult sudoku puzzle that has taken me almost twenty-one minutes to complete.

'It's 4:25, Eli. Can you fire the campaign over to Danny in five minutes? Don't forget to cc me in.'

He doesn't even look at me when giving this instruction. He's not the sales manager, and Ash is the top salesman, so I'm guessing he just wants to feel like he is in control of something because he probably can't even handle the organisation of his own sock drawer.

I decide to send it straight away as it was actually finished over two hours ago. But instead of putting Sam on the cc line of the email, I put his name alongside Danny Elwes on the 'to' line. In Sam's small feeble mind, he sees this as him being on equal terms with the managing director, and I can leave him to reflect on that for the rest of the day while I kill time by either sitting on the toilet playing solitaire on my phone or drinking coffee and walking around.

I can really smell that extra cup of espresso on my breath when I leave work, so before I get the bus I decide to dive into a newsagent to get something minty to chew on. As I go to pay for my sugar-free spearmint gum, I hear someone call my name.

'Eli Hagin.' He has a very low, booming voice, perfect diction. Received Pronunciation with an occasional whistle when saying words starting with an S – the way Brian Blessed might sound if he had a throat lozenge stuck to the roof of his mouth. 'How the devil are you?'

I can't remember his name.

'Hey ... man. I'm good. How is it going?' I stutter through my insincerity.

I remember selling a first chapter to this guy when I had the idea for the shop and I didn't like him then, either.

His voice really does not fit his appearance. You expect him to be rotund with a beard full of breakfast remains and browning at the ends of the hair around his mouth where he smokes a pipe. He's not. He's very slight of frame. Probably vegetarian, that's very trendy at the moment. He does have a beard, though; it's grey. But his hair is black. Looking at him, it's obvious that his hair could not be naturally black. So he obviously dyes it. He does not look young; he looks like an idiot. It's not even a full head of hair. It's bald on top with short hair around the sides.

Like Max from Guess Who?

This sorry excuse for a human being wants to *look* like a writer.

He looks like a geography teacher.

'I am doing very well, thanks to you.' Here it comes. My worst nightmare realised. 'I finally finished my novel. I've been in to s(whistle)ee S(whistle)cott Edgar agency today for representation and they are very interested. S(whistle)o, er, thanks again and, erm, I won't forget to credit you for the first chapter if they let me. Got to get publis(whistle)hed first, obviously. Okay. Nice to s(whistle)ee you again, anyway. And thanks(whistle) again.'

He started to get nervous towards the end of his clearly rehearsed speech. I was dreaming of pulling his heart out through his chest. Perhaps it was clear from my expression. And what an appallingly dire and unimaginative vernacular; how is he going to get published? He needs to play with the English language a little more; experiment with words and turn of phrase.

I am totally bummed out now, as if the tinkle of the bell as he edged out the door was some Pavlovian stimulus for the instant ignition of self-loathing and denigration.

I want to ask him which idea he has butchered. Which epic is now a collection of short fables for children, or which comedy is now a deconstruction of the psyche of women in Middle America during the 1850s. I know he's done it. I can see it in his corduroys with sandals and socks. He's fucked up something that I could never finish.

Who's to blame for that?

I pay for my gum and leave. The bus is late. I lean against a poster for a new mindless blockbuster movie. Everything sounds so loud and I feel the envy swelling inside me, upsetting me.

A tortured or tormented soul is supposed to be beneficial to any artist. So the way I feel most of the time should be helpful to my writing, but it's not.

I'm self-destructive. I know that.

My obsessive need to create means that if I exist for a moment without the satisfaction that comes with that act, I retract within myself. I feel it happening now, my writing is getting worse. I wonder whether this is really what I am supposed to be doing.

I need to talk to someone. To vent. Who do I have? Mike is probably busy plotting his own intricate death; Jackie will just agree with everything I say because she thinks it will make me feel better; my boss is useless at almost every simple daily task; my therapist is imaginary; my mum has been dead for four years; and the only recent contact I have had with the real world is with a wannabe writer who has mistaken a mild case of autism for literary talent. I can't turn to religion either. That would make me as hypocritical as Jackie.

All I have left are the two partially senile war veterans who own the coffee shop next to my house. A coffee shop spelled with a double P and an E. Gaucho's Coffee Shoppe. How contemporary.

So that's where I go.

To see the Teds.

Those two war veterans who share a name, share a contemporary Coffee Shoppe and, if it wasn't for the fact that they also share old-fashioned military views on life, you would swear that they were sharing bodily fluids after they turn out the last light on the Gaucho's sign every night at 8:30. They're not, but you would be excused if you thought it.

Usually, they speak utter nonsense. But every now and then, they strike a resonant chord within someone. Maybe that's the reason the Teds are so popular: a society of people waiting for an answer, too lazy to find it for themselves. They look for it in books and film and art and religion and social media and travel and fraudulent psychics and aliens and science, and when that runs dry, when that stops being *easy* and they are still no closer to the answer, when they are at the point of realising that the solution lies within themselves, within us all, as the possible moment of epiphany approaches, they seek the wisdom of a pensioner with life *experience* and a mochaccino to die for.

The Teds couldn't be anymore similar yet anymore different from each other. One Ted is the beverage maker but he is a man of few spoken words who is most comfortable sitting on a high stool next to the espresso machine, writing on scrap pieces of paper and napkins.

Sketching.

Scribbling.

I have had the privilege of reading some of his poetry, and it is both insightful and funny; I think he feels he can share it with me because he believes we are *both* writers. Although the majority of his work is poetry or short stories, he has a look in his eyes sometimes when 'the youth of today' stroll past him; a look that only a war veteran can give. It says 'I'm putting you on my list' as he scribbles on a tea-stained serviette. I would love to read that piece of original literature.

The other Ted is the real worker. Taking orders from pimple-faced art students who want to pay for one cup of low-fat-double-shot-half-caf-no-foam-extra-hot-vanilla-latte with coins. Taking abuse from the elderly who consistently complain about the inflated prices compared with those in 1943 – yet still come in every day and make one cup last for three hours. This Ted doesn't write, but he's one heck of a story-teller.

I'm so deluded that I think his stories hold the answers, when, really, I should be looking at my own.

It's fairly busy when I walk in. The crowd of businessmen and teachers who need an after-work caffeine infusion has dissipated from the city centre, where they sell products to people that don't really need them and can't afford them, or give extra attention and tuition to kids who don't really need it while others who do are left behind.

I give the Teds a welcoming wave.

'Afternoon Eli,' Ted says, already halfway towards the espresso machine to make my usual: a black coffee; blacker than night on a moonless night.

'Hagin,' interjects Ted, saluting me with his pencil before dropping his gaze once more towards his napkin and continuing with his musings.

I choose a seat with my back deliberately towards a brunette fiddling with her glasses as she works away on her laptop. If I look at her I'll end up taking a seat on my therapist's couch later and abusing the only image I have of her. I don't want to see that she might be working on a spreadsheet or something else totally uncreative and worthless to humankind. I don't want to sully the daydream that after finishing work for the day, leaving behind the office job that she hates, she has become so engrossed in writing her novel that time has ceased to exist for her. That's why I can't bear to look at her. I need to know that there are others out there. That we are not all in a world full of sell-outs.

A world full of Jackies, on the long road to the middle.

Ted brings my coffee over to the table and pulls up a chair for himself.

'I know how you feel.' He looks me directly in the face, his stare so intent it burns through my pupils and scorches my retina. 'Let me tell you a story.'

And then it comes. The story, the seemingly unrelated yarn that slots into my brain, occupying the gaps in my imagination and altering my life. The anecdote that will delay my epiphany, my recognition of where I am going wrong, by three or four days. But right now, it seems to be exactly what I need. The realisation I have is valid. But it's not going to help.

'1943, Operation Husky. Italy.' Of course, the battle of Penne Carbonara. I'm being cynical but he always starts his stories with this punctuating exposition, expecting the listener to have an encyclopaedic knowledge of battles. 'I'm in No Man's Land, on lookout. We are sat there. Just sat there, and Cox decides to booby-trap a toilet. He realises that if he puts a grenade into a tin snuff box, it is exactly the right size to pull out the pin and hold the trigger down, preventing explosion until the tin is disrupted in some way that the trigger is released and then' – he smashes his hand on the table – 'BANG.'

I nearly soil myself.

Now, everybody knows not to go into the toilet, and nobody does. Italians who do not speak or read English, however, do not understand the no-entry slogans. An elderly man wanders into the toilet, despite a shout from Cox telling him to stay away.

But it's too late.

He goes in, leaving his grandson outside to watch.

He watches his tanned-with-sixty-years-of-olive-oil-soaked-skin-cancer grandfather enter the toilet, only to be expelled into the atmosphere moments later in the form of a centillion particles that once shaped the complex compound that was Anastagio Calvino. An innocent man; a man who left a permanent scar on his grandson's life, a man whose name roughly translates as *divinely bald*. Nevertheless, a man he was.

'The kid, Ilario, he never wept,' Ted continues. 'He watched his grandfather blown apart in front of his very eyes and shed not one tear. He stayed with us for a while, singing songs and dancing for us. Keeping us entertained on those long shifts. I can't remember what happened to him. The boy. The boy, Ilario. The boy who did not cry. The strongest man I've ever known.' He trails off with nostalgic reminiscence.

While this story seems to have no particular significance, I share it for three reasons that are stronger than misanthropy, cynicism or cathartics. Reasons more compelling even than its overtly romantic overtones laced with disturbing peculiarities.

I share it for these three reasons.

One, it is a great story, and I want that too.

Two, the kid never cried.

Three, it's true. True in Ted's mind, anyway. Ilario, Cox, Anastagio, the bomb, the snuff box, the mission, it's all true.

If you can convince yourself that your story is true, then you can convince others. Or maybe it's the other way round.

Either way, I find myself leaving Ted abruptly because I'm late for drinks with Mike. Cursing my unpunctuality, I decide to jog the remaining sixty-two steps to The Scam to feign effort and gain some reprieve.

When I arrive, I doubt that Mike has even realised I'm late. He's sitting there laughing heartily at a comment Jackie has made, which is very strange if you know anything about Jackie. Mike nods at me in recognition and holds an empty glass up to signify that it is my round.

I go to the bar and order three drinks – two lagers and a white-wine spritzer for Jackie. In my mind I curse Mike for inviting her, but what I don't realise is that this is not just a random Tuesday-night drinking session with his two closest friends.

No. This is his leaving party.

This is goodbye and, because I don't know that, I'm bound to fuck it up.

SUICIDE **THURSDAY**

The night that it happened, I remember the beginning. But that's about it. The beginning. The rest just didn't seem genuine. It happened, it was real, but in recollection, aspects now start to appear strange and, well, not whole.

I remember getting on at Finchley Road Tube station. I remember passing a busker wailing out a very credible reggae version of the Rolling Stones' 'Wild Horses'. I remember not giving money to a woman I classed as an 'alleged' homeless person using her baby to guilt people into giving away money that she would ultimately squander on drugs that would later be injected under her toe-nails or into her anus or something. I remember thinking that I was being narrow-minded and should turn back and give her some money after all. Real money. Paper money. A note that would afford her and her child the opportunity for actual nourishment. I remember deconstructing her within seconds to a cultural stereotype and not doing any of this, instead thinking that my own problems were harsher than she would ever have to face. So cynical.

On the train, I remember the toadstools that possibly held the secret to eradicating AIDS, like the ones I read about in the *Sunday Times* that grew out of a combination of faeces, vomit, urine and semen. I remember passing Swiss Cottage, St Johns Wood and Baker Street. I remember humming the Gerry Rafferty classic, as I always do, when I passed the latter.

I remember thinking about the Tube attacks.

Then I remember nothing. I know I must have changed trains twice but I just can't recall that. I didn't drop back into controlled consciousness until I arrived at Mike's and Jackie shouted at me – the point at which fact and fiction intersect.

'Why are you smiling?' She is shouting so loud that her voice gargles with a natural vibrato. 'Eli?'

'Maybe he did it for me,' I mouth, possibly even muttering the words under my breath.

'What? What are you saying?' She is starting to get hysterical.

All I can think to do is hold her.

I pace over to her gently so as not to alarm her even further, force the mop out of her hands and squeeze the remaining tears from her delicately withering and emotionally exhausted body. She seems to weigh nothing. In the space of a day she has transformed from a fairly young, fairly healthy woman into a frail, greying, lifeless pensioner. It's as if she has managed to catch, or at least develop, some seriously convincing signs of progeria.

At least I've managed to stop her from mopping up the blood or displacing it around the corpse, pushing it into the cracks and combining it with her tears. Now she's just in my arms, in shock.

I just hold her.

I don't think about me, or Mike, sitting there, hands in legs, in a mere of blood, diluted by the saline solution waterfalling from Jackie's tear ducts.

I'm thinking about Jackie. How she feels. How I just want her to know that she is protected and how everything is going to be okay.

Of course, it won't be okay, far from it, but that's the way I want her to feel.

So I hold her.

And I keep holding her until I manage to start convincing myself that I actually do love her. I must. I'm not even thinking about myself.

Mike watches on.

He did it.

He actually did it.

Two paramedics arrive with some bright-orange first-aid kits that clash with the used-to-be-pea-green two-seater sofa. I think it's the claret that has siphoned from my best friend's *profunda femoris* that causes the main colour collision, though. I keep a tight hold of Jackie while the paramedics submit to Death's intentions.

She's weary and motionless.

And I start to recall how I truly might feel about her.

Nothing like tragedy to bring people together.

A policeman enters shortly after to disturb the romantic moment I am attempting to share with Jackie. The woman I may well love.

The only person I have left, apart from myself.

The woman who loves me.

The still, lifeless, breathless, exhausted Jackie.

In shock.

In love.

Again.

The policeman stares at us. I am attempting to protect Jackie from the situation as she leans on me, drained of any last remnants of energy. The man hides his shock well; Mum would have assumed he'd been 'desensitised by the media'.

At this point, Jackie manages to summon up a modicum of strength, a spurt of energy, like those women you hear about that can lift a car on their own in order to save their trapped child. She pushes her hand against my chest, forcing herself backwards. Leaving her arm perpendicular to her body, she points a finger at me, turns her head slowly – Exorcist-scary slowly – and she starts to talk to the stalwart officer.

'It was him. He did it. It's all his fault.'

Thanks, Jackie. I love you too.

TUESDAY
(TWO DAYS BEFORE SUICIDE THURSDAY)

I'm unaware that tonight, in The Scam, sixty-four steps from where I live, I am spending my final evening with my best friend, Mike. I have no idea that I am going to skip work tomorrow just because I feel I deserve a day off – a 'duvet day' they call it.

And I don't even know whether Jackie wants a Sauvignon Blanc or a Chardonnay. Or whether she could even tell the difference.

Instead the thought that seems to be dominating the majority of my cognitive processes as I stand at the bar waiting patiently for a small Pinot Grigio is: why has Jackie been invited to what has to be – although I may not know it yet – the single most significant moment in Mike's life to date?

His pre-suicide drinks.

His last supper.

Not that I have a clue that's what this is, but why is Jackie here at all?

I carry our three drinks back to the table, a pint in each hand and the stem of the wine glass wrapped in my little finger. I sit down and attempt to get involved.

'I didn't realise you were coming tonight.' Not your textbook greeting, I know, and it's just the start of how I nearly ruin the whole evening.

They answer in stereo.

Mike invited me/I invited her.

I feel like they are ganging up on me. Conspiring.

Strength in numbers.

It's only a short pause, but we all know it's slightly awkward. I decide to take the high road. 'So what are we talking about?'

All seems to be forgiven. As if I'm always this rude.

'Well, my friend, Jackie was waxing lyrical about The Leap of Faith,' Mike says with a knowing smile towards his accomplice.

'Crikey, how late am I?' I look at my wrist even though I don't wear a watch. 'We're already discussing Kierkegaard? How bleak.'

My therapist would say that I was mocking the subject to belittle Jackie and turn the attention to me but, honestly, I just think it's too early to procrastinate over whether doubting the existence of a God actually makes you a better Christian. Even though I did not mean for it to happen, the conversation turns towards me.

'So how are you anyway, Eli? How comes I don't have a new chapter for today?' He swigs at his beer.

'Oh wow, have you started a second chapter?' Jackie interrupts with excitement. Hopeful.

'No, nothing like that. I've just been a little busy with work and stuff.' This is a lie. I have two new first chapters and I don't know which direction I'm going to go. I'm attacking it differently.

'Come on, Eli. You hate your job. If you start to care more about your "career"' – he makes the speech-marks sign with his fingers as he says career – 'than your real work ... well ... we're all fucked. That's not what it's supposed to be about.' (As if I'm their ticket out.)

He speaks so much sense for a guy that is ready to top himself. His mind seems so lucid for a person on the brink of extinction. And I feel a little uncomfortable discussing my own inadequacies.

'So ... the father of existentialism, eh? I think he is the reason I find Ibsen so unreadable.' My deliberately crude ploy achieves what I intended. Jackie feels uncomfortable and stands up.

'I just need to go to the ladies. Do you need another drink?' We both opt for a beer even though we're not even halfway through the one I just bought.

As she flounces towards the restroom I don't notice but both Mike and I are staring at the form of Jackie's buttocks in her deliberately figure-hugging skirt.

'I do have a chapter for you, Mike. I just reckon I'm close on this one. I think I would have started the next chapter if Jackie hadn't turned up when she did last night. I'll get something to you this week.' I half whisper, like I don't want anybody to know in case I jinx things. Subtly passing the blame to Jackie.

'That's brilliant, mate. I look forward to it.'

Is he lying? Does he know at this point that he'll never read it or is he still ambivalent about Suicide Thursday?

We chat superficially until Jackie returns with more drinks. Mike tells me about stripping his floor and something funny he saw on television, while I complain about Sam and the campaign they have me working on in the office.

Jackie returns.

'So ... what are *we* talking about?' Touché. We all laugh at what an idiot I am, and the mood really alters. We are comfortable as a three, we always have been.

'Eli was just talking about his boss, Sam.'

'He's not my boss.' There's almost rapturous laughter. As if I am filming a sit-com in front of a live audience. 'I think my stories may paint him as slightly more entertaining than he actually is.'

'Oh, come on, he can't be that bad.'

'Honestly. He's a frightful, self-involved, hypocritical, racist, right-wing...' I swig my beer, '...and this is the good stuff—'

Jackie interrupts. 'All right, all right. We know what he's like. We've heard it every day for God knows how long.'

I resist a joke about what God *actually* knows because the atmosphere now is, thankfully, a lot lighter, even if it is predominantly at the expense of my own misery.

The rest of the evening flies by and I'm taken back to when we all first became friends, and it was new and exciting and innocent, and we all wanted to be alive and we all had dreams that we would ultimately never follow through and we all had a passion, not only for each other but for what we thought we had to offer the world. We had romance. We had romantic notions about art and democracy and music. We weren't concerned with money or material possessions. Basically, we were young, poor and we hadn't actually formed our own ideas yet and that was just fine by us. It was a simpler time.

Tonight is not simple. My therapist would even have a tough time with this small crowd and she – that's right, my fake therapist is a she – knows me better than I know myself apparently, so that's a third of the work done.

We've been reminiscing all night but I want to discuss the present.

'So, Mike, any luck on the job front?' I enquire, sipping at one of my beers.

'Not yet, mate. I'm holding out for something better.'

Evasive, but I pursue. 'Better than unemployment?'

'Well, it's going to be tough to compete with the current intellectual stimulation I get from daytime television, Eli, but I'm optimistic.'

I know he's mocking to avoid the subject. I move on. 'No new people in your life, then?' I pry.

'Oh, Eli, I love the way you tease me to breaking point with your probing questions.' I smile. 'I assume you are talking about women.'

Jackie takes this as her cue to leave. As if we are about to enter some 'male' discussion from which she is excluded. She stands up fairly abruptly, downs the last two mouthfuls of her wine, and kisses me on the lips.

'Speak to you tomorrow, Eli.' Then she kisses Mike on the cheek. 'Mike, as always, a pleasure. I'll leave you to it. I'm off to lie down.'

We both watch her leave, but this time it's more of a stumble than the angelic prance of before.

The Gospel of John, chapter 15, verse 11: 'Greater love hath no man than this, but to lay his life down for his friends.' A fitting epitaph, I think. While Jesus was washing the feet of his disciples, Judas left to betray him, just as Jackie is leaving to betray me. She may be off to lie down, but not in her own bed. So while I metaphorically wash Mike's feet using words of encouragement as water, with friendship as a sponge and alcohol as a gentle exfoliator, Jackie is ready to sully the evening with her penultimate act of malice that surely undoes all my hard work.

'None right now,' Mike continues.

'Sorry?'

'Women. None right now, I'm afraid.' Of course there aren't any women right now. Who is he going to meet sat at home watching another show about how nobody can make money from property development in the current climate and that we should all just be happy to be 'on the ladder'? The only people he gets to interact with are me and Jackie. No wonder he wants to kill himself.

Once Jackie has left we really start to drink heavily, but the discussion, in contrast, remains light. Nothing too personal, mainly comparisons of the latest cinematic travesties to grace our local screen. Mike likes his images to be generated by computer; I prefer real people with a narrative structure driven by dialogue. We talk about contemporary singer-songwriters and their inability to be implicit.

From my side this was certainly a regular evening in The Scam. Conversation didn't even veer towards contemplating one's mortality or being unemployed or a born-again virgin or Jackie or hands in legs.

By enjoying Mike's company was I failing him?

Woody Allen once said, 'Nobody in Brooklyn ever killed themselves, they're all too depressed.' So, by making Mike happier, am I partly to blame?

He comes back from the bar with four tumblers.

'So we're moving on to spirits, I see.'

'Thought I'd just grab two each so we don't have to keep getting up.'

We laugh.

Keeping him happy. Keeping him dead.

'Where was I? Yeah, the new idea. It's about a guy so obsessed by film that he tries to live his life like he's in a romantic comedy. With a blurred sense of what is real and what is fantasy, he creates a situation that ultimately results in his tragic downfall. I'm thinking of calling it *King Liar*.' I could talk about my writing all night. I ask him what he thinks.

'I think you don't need me to blurb for you anymore. I'll reserve judgement until I see the second chapter, eh?' He holds up his second vodka and tonic. We tap glasses in hopeful acknowledgement.

By the time the bell rings for last orders, I am in a comfortably drunken state and aware that another vodka will cast me into a less relaxed frame of mind, but I can't say no when Mike suggests a whisky to keep us warm on the journey home.

It's our last drink together.

And we are silent.

A silence that is only comfortable between close friends who don't really need to converse to be enjoying each other's company. A moment of reflection for me. I think about the possibility of a second chapter. I decide that I won't bother turning up for work tomorrow either, it's just not worth my time. It doesn't deserve my headspace.

I'm just content with the moment. At this point I can only guess that Mike's own thoughts mirror mine in some way. But they don't. The simple fact is, no matter what I do, no matter how great tonight is, or any other night, for that matter, my best friend, my apparent closest friend, wants to die.

We're the last two out of The Scam. I only have sixty-four steps before I collapse on my therapist's couch, but Mike has to fall onto a Tube, stagger home in what feels like Baltic temperatures despite the Glenn-something-or-other Scotch whisky we knocked back, then work his way through four different keys until he gets the right one that lets him into his flat where my girlfriend is waiting to have sex with him.

FAKE **THERAPIST**

INT. ELI'S OFFICE/FAKE THERAPIST'S OFFICE

    ELI
It was a great night at The Scam. We just work, you
know? As a three, I mean. We work as twos, too. In
every possible combination. But…
    FAKE THERAPIST
Go on.
    ELI
I don't know what it is but something tonight has
got my brain sparking. I love the idea behind *The
Principle*, but it needs rewriting. Same characters.
Same premise. Different take. I want to try again.
I know it's another first chapter but it'll be a
better one.
    FAKE THERAPIST
And you think this will work?
    ELI
I've never done this before. Usually, I finish, I
struggle with a second chapter, I give the idea to
Mike and he blurbs. Then it goes into the shop.

(He nods towards the bookcase behind his fake therapist.)

But I'm excited. This has legs, I think. Inspiration
is hitting me.
    FAKE THERAPIST
And why is that happening now?
    ELI
Maybe it's my life. Maybe it has always been within

me. Maybe it's the story that I'm supposed to tell.
Who knows? Maybe it's worth nothing, an exercise in
futility. Whatever it is, *The Principle* is dead.

(The fake therapist nods and makes notes on a pad.)

~~THE PRINCIPLE~~
KING LIAR
(WORKING TITLE)
BY ELI HAGIN

F I R S T **C H A P T E R**

No kid gets through high school unscathed. The cheerleaders are insecure, the dorks are constantly afraid, anyone who is part of a sports team feels alone.

High school even sucks if you're middle-of-the-road. Laney Boggs is that plain-looking girl, who always does well in class but not so well with the boys. But it turns out, without her glasses and with her hair straightened, plus a generous helping of mascara, that plain-looking girl is gorgeous.

She's all that.

She gets the guy. The captain of the football team, no less.

The problem is, she turns into the kind of girl she has hated throughout school. The seemingly confident cheerleader type. Popularity makes her into the monster she has always feared and loathed.

She loses the guy.

She loses her friends.

Her parents are worried.

Laney has to realise that her beauty comes from within. She just needs to be herself. That's the girl the football captain fell for. That's the reason he likes her.

This is how Bud Ellis wishes his secondary-education experience had been. But, of course it wasn't.

This isn't the movies.

University is more of the same. There's that one student who has spent seven years on a three-year programme. He loves the lifestyle, his popularity. But his father has spent too much on an education that appears to be going nowhere. He's cutting his son off.

But this guy has a very specific skill. He knows how to throw a party. He's been helping undergraduates have the best college experience for free but now he has to support himself for the rest of term and put in the work to finally graduate.

Along the way, he meets a woman. She wants to write an article on the legacy he will leave. She is also dating the captain of the football team, because somebody has to. There's a teacher that seemingly hates him but secretly believes in him and wants him to succeed. All of the things that Bud did not experience at university. He went to parties but his legacy is drinking a bottle of tequila one night and throwing up over his own shoes.

Real life is a let-down for Bud Ellis.

Until he falls in love.

He didn't meet her on a cruise liner that he won tickets for in a poker game. She isn't upper class, and he is not a poor, struggling artist, sketching one-legged French prostitutes. He never got handcuffed to a pipe as the boat snapped in half and began to sink. And he won't be forced to let himself drown. (Even though there was plenty of room left on that floating door, Rose.)

Bud wasn't married before Ashleigh came along. He didn't have a kid who called in to a radio station to find a new wife for his father. The radio presenter didn't fall for him and ask to meet on top of the Empire State Building on Valentine's Day.

Ashleigh was not part of a rival family to Bud's. Their love was not forbidden. They did not have to meet in secret. He did not declare his love by climbing Ashleigh's balcony. They did not have a clandestine marriage. They will not end up in some tragic suicide pact.

They didn't even meet at work.

Or out one night at a pub or club.

It was a dating website. For film fans.

She liked Tarantino.

He liked French stuff.

Somehow they were perfect. For each other, at least.

But theirs was a love that was undeniably instant and passionate and right.

A forever love that people dream about.

Bud Ellis does not like Candice. He watches her young, firm breasts move up and down as she works on top of him. He sees that perfect rectangle of pubic hair, as she puts her middle finger in her mouth and licks the tip before placing that hand between her legs. She is enthusiastic and energetic, and he should be turned on. She is vocal, and that usually helps him across the line quicker but he can't stop thinking about Ashleigh.

Because he loves her more than anything.

Almost anything.

Not more than the movies.

That's why he's doing this. To complicate things. For the chaos that comes before the order.

Movie love.

He's about to come but he just wants to cry.
This will only make them stronger.
The love of a lifetime.
When he wins her back.
When he gets the girl he already has.

Bud Ellis loves the movies.
He's an idiot.
Order is not always regained.

SUICIDE **THURSDAY**

As I'm gently ushered out into the night-time air by an uncharacteristically composed member of Her Majesty's police force, my recent realisation that Mike may have done this for me, and the subsequent epiphany that should follow, is delayed somewhat by a new recognition. I may now have a serious problem.

If the police interrogate me, possibly using a good cop/bad cop technique that I've seen in movies, they may eventually stumble on the questions they should be asking me about this situation; questions that may lead to me admitting that I do have some suspicion about Jackie and Mike's late-night rendezvous.

And that is an issue.

It gives me motive.

I'd never considered my own arrest before so I hadn't really thought about what it would be like. Would an officer cuff me and throw me over the bonnet like some supporting actor in *Serpico*? Or would he be a donut-guzzling stereotype who would be out of breath by the time we hit the ground floor of Mike's block?

Honestly, it is neither; and despite my lack of any expectations, it's still an anticlimax.

I am calmly ushered into the back of a Vauxhall Astra and we head off; the officers don't even push my head down forcefully to get me in.

They sit in the front, silently. No stories about recent collars or anecdotes concerning the day's events. No sweet pastries or street-talking wise guys or drug dealers, counterfeiters, money-launderers and certainly no Royale with cheese. Just two silent policemen and me, alone with my thoughts about my recently deceased best friend and the girlfriend who just tried to pin it all on me.

All I see is blurred lights on the way to the station, and I spend most of the journey speculating about how it will be possible for me to provide a convincing alibi that I was at my therapist's when I heard the news about Mike without them asking for her number to corroborate my story. That could open up a whole other area I am not willing to discuss. It may also dent their assessment of my sound character.

The officers are not even rough with me when we finally arrive at the police station. Where's the Bad Lieutenant? I'm just processed like any sixteen-year-old kid caught hitting wing mirrors on his way home from the park after sharing a two-litre bottle of cider with three friends.

I don't understand it. Aren't I being held on suspicion of murder?

I don't remember what they say, what is real. I have the right to remain silent, maybe...

After giving personal details to a guy on the front desk, about everything except the age I lost my virginity, I am led into my own cell. I suppose this is just their technique, to make me stew for a while and think about what I have done, and scare myself into a confession. If that's what they want, they should have roughed me up a little on the way here, not treat me like an in-law they are meeting for the first time.

They don't even get around to interrogating me. They just leave me to sweat.

I saw somewhere that if you place a bunch of felons together in a cell, it is the guilty one that gets the best night's rest. The innocent are so worried about being falsely accused that they can't relax enough to get any sleep. So now, even though I have had a long day at work, followed by a session of therapy and the emotional strain of finding my best friend sat with his hands in his legs, drained of life, not to mention my long-term girlfriend sewing a seed of doubt into the minds of the local constabulary regarding my innocence, I find it difficult to reject the modicum of comfort that a solitary mattress has to offer, because if I'm seen to be resting easy, I might implicate myself further in what may now be a murder investigation.

I remain standing so as not to incriminate myself in any way by succumbing to narcoleptic impulses, and lean against the cold white walls of the cell in an attempt to calm my new perspiration problem while also keeping myself alert and, more importantly, awake. As I torture myself in this North London dungeon, a more senior officer arrives at the scene, where Jackie is still in mild panic but the shock is wearing off.

Viewing what is a clearly successful suicide attempt, Inspector Brabham first questions the young, enthusiastic, if overly ambitious, Police Constable Taylor, as to why a man has been taken into custody over this. In further discussion with Jackie, he uncovers that her outburst of judgement was meant in a metaphorical and marginally hysterical sense; that I was at fault for not correctly carrying out my duties as a friend, boyfriend or respectable human being. Not, in fact, for being in any way responsible for Mike's literal ruin.

The flap in the middle of the door slides open, startling me from a standing nightmare, and an officer calls my name and tells me I am free to go.

Jackie has saved me.

I am freed without hesitation in order to avoid any embarrassment to the force and the possibility of a lawsuit. On the contrary: really, I think I was treated rather well.

Should I now feel thankful? Grateful to Jackie? She was the one that put me in here, for crying out loud. I have a flicker of appreciation that she came to her senses before I provided the law with a motive and no evidence of my whereabouts at the time of the crime, but I just feel that maybe this is all part of Jackie's bigger plan.

This seals the deal.

This Friday is our anniversary, and I am going to make sure we still go out, eat, drink and break up.

That can't be in her plan.

WEDNESDAY
(THE DAY BEFORE SUICIDE THURSDAY)

I know Sam is in early today because, well, he's in early every day. Part of it is for appearance; so that he looks keen or committed or something, but also because his youngest son decided that 4:20 was getting-up-while-singing-and-watching-a-DVD-in-the-hall time. According to the Sam Jordane school-of-parenting, the best way to deal with this is to leave your wife to sort it out while you depart the house for work two hours before you need to. It's worse than *laissez-faire*, but I don't know the French for 'I don't give a fuck'.

I phone the office at 7:30, and he's already there.

'I've been throwing up all night.' This is only marginal fabrication. I was sick when I got home from The Scam, but I shouldn't really drink on a weeknight and I certainly should never have tested the body-warming capabilities of a single-malt Scotch.

'Okay, Eli. That's fine. You get some rest. I'll finish off the campaign.'

What? There's nothing to finish off. It was air-tight apart from maybe a quick proofread, so what he really means is: *I'll pretend the majority had to be altered in some way and take all the credit.* Classic Sam.

I thank him for being so understanding about needing the day off. I don't bother arguing because I just can't bring myself to care.

'Ping me an email later if you feel any better.' Another Sam-ism.

Ping, fire, launch, catapult, shoot; why can't he just say send? Send an email. Jesus.

'Yeah. Okay, Sam. Will do. Bye, then.' He doesn't sense that I'm patronising him. I hang up and mutter the word 'idiot' under my breath.

Instead of getting up and taking advantage of my time off, I decide to take a longer rest on the sofa that I woke up on. I can't locate the remote control so fall asleep to the sound of the world.

MIKE

While Eli attempts to sleep off the beginnings of a hangover, Mike's alarm sounds, instructing him that it is time for the snooze tune. He rolls over to the middle of the bed, expecting to find an average-looking, red-haired woman next to him, but there is no one. Nothing. Not even a note. Jackie may be an immoral whore with a penchant for pseudo-nepotistic sexual relations, but she won't shirk the responsibility of her job. It's 8:52 and she is nearly at work already.

A radio presenter with a mildly annoying regional accent introduces the song Mike has momentarily woken for. 'Close to You' by the Carpenters. Yesterday's choice would have induced a sufficient level of guilt, but this morning's ditty reminds him that last night he had someone to be intimate with.

Well, Mike, you can't get much closer than being inside someone.

He goes back to sleep as he always does, only not with a feeling of sadness or disappointment, but with an aura of contentment and even accomplishment.

JACKIE

Jackie, as clinically cold as ever, manages to make it to work on time. The only thing she does differently is to have a green tea rather than her regular early-morning Earl Grey – or, as Jackie calls it, her early grey – as if this act will perform an adequate degree of cleansing before her midweek confession to Father Farrelly.

Her mood for the rest of the day is that of someone who only scraped two numbers on the lottery. Someone who was one number from winning the smallest prize possible.

Someone who is almost not a complete loser.

TEXTS

Do it today?

> *I feel too awful today.*

What?

> *I just feel so shit. I don't even want to get up.*

Get up.

> *It doesn't work like that.*
>
> *I can't just snap out of it because you tell me to.*

Get up.

> *Fuck you.*

Why are you putting this off?

You say you want to do it.

You're stalling.

> *My head is a mess, right now.*

You're overthinking it.

You can't do that.

It's best to just do it. Get it done.

You know?

> *I worry about my family.*

It's not going to be easy on them, I won't lie.

You've tried before. It's not as if they don't know how you feel.

> *They don't.*

Nobody does.

Except for you.

I feel like we keep talking about it and you just need to do it.

If you're not going to do it, then I'm going to call for some help.

Don't you fucking dare.

You promised.

You promised.

You promised.

Stop talking and start doing.

If this is what you want, if you want to die, do it.

I will. I want to. I have to.

Today?

Later.

WEDNESDAY
(THE DAY BEFORE SUICIDE THURSDAY)

Personally, I just need to get away for a while. Away from Jackie, from another first chapter, from Mike, from this trendy little North London back street where everyone is so pretentious they might as well all be wearing berets.

I shower, eat a piece of brown toast with peanut butter while I iron my clothes, then get dressed and leave, still in time to catch the tail end of the morning rush hour. I get on a train and I go.

Not that far, but far enough away to not bump into anyone I know; far enough away from this reality. Okay, I'm not Hemingway; I can't lock myself in my cabin by the lake. I need the city. Besides, it's an entirely different world across the river on the South Bank. An alternate reality.

If I get on the Tube at Finchley Road, I can take the Jubilee line right under London and straight to Waterloo; and it's only seven stops through Swiss cottage, on to St John's Wood, winding my way down to Baker Street, Bond Street, Green Park, Westminster and eventually London Waterloo. And it means I only need a ticket for zones four and five.

The reports claim That the Jubilee line is clear today; there are only delays to the Northern and Central lines. I file down the stairs like one of Hamlyn's children, blending into a crowd of nameless politicians who will depart one stop before me in their thousand-pound suits already smelling of cigarettes and stale coffee. It's almost a prerequisite for political success. These people pull eighteen-hour days for most of the week. Caffeine and nicotine are their drugs of choice. They choose bad breath and cancer, and all for a career with no control, no reward and little respect.

I'm relieved to just fade into the background and by Bond Street the tension in my shoulders is released.

I'm nobody now.

Hundreds of corporate robots surround me as we quick-step in unison towards the bottleneck at the foot of another escalator. It's so high that the top seems to disappear into a bright light, which, for me, signifies something pure and different from any other day. The light is cleansing me of my predictable, routine existence but, for every other lemming on this stairway, it submerses them in a warmth of security and reliability that makes people forget their dreams. They forget that they have given up, that they have sold out, that taking a job as a secretary for a newspaper five years ago still hasn't materialised into writing for that newspaper. You started at the bottom and haven't worked your way up, but that's okay with you now. It's not about that anymore.

So, while I am awash with optimism as I emerge atop this moving staircase, this procession of mediocrity, the flock around me, in front of me, behind me, are all numb with inadequacy. And they don't even know it.

And I think I'm nobody?

A quick left turn, through a walkway, down some stairs, fighting a vicious crosswind that blows the front three pages of a London broadsheet newspaper past my face, left again and I am walking along the Thames. It's early but I've already been asked for change and given a pamphlet that says 'Let Jesus Guide You'. I'm following my internal compass today, though, not Jesus or even an A-Z of London. I let my feet go where they want me to go.

The Dali exhibition at County Hall doesn't open for another half an hour, although the McDonalds inside is already serving up Happy Meals. I make a note of that and stare out across the water, towards Parliament.

While I think I look a little different, standing out from the crowd in my North London fashion, my jeans, trainers, retro T shirt and tweed jacket, a hybrid of styles and eras that I happen to think is the latest in metropolitan panache, I actually look remarkably like the forty-six Chinese tourists crouching in front of the Thames, the Millennium Wheel, that bastion of commercial architectural achievement, to their left and St Stephen's Tower behind. All this they capture with a sharp, deep focus that only comes with the latest in Eastern photographic technology. And, for a moment, watching them, I forget about Mike.

Nothing is open yet, so I walk. Soaking up the Westminster architecture and absorbing the plethora of personalities and individual characteristic movements of the horde, I salmon against this flow of people towards I-don't-know-where. I-don't-really-care.

Opposite Downing Street, an Israeli man in his fifties strips to his underwear and washes himself with a two-litre bottle of water; I suspect that it isn't from a volcanic spring as the partially picked-at label suggests. He takes his beige-with-age white T-shirt and dries himself with it, aggressively wiping away the liquid from his frail torso, then puts it back on. I worry for him. I can feel the breeze even through my tweed.

He takes up most of the pavement with his beaver dam of signs. Signs that say things like: *Stop MI5, they are the Mafia.* Not a particularly punctuating statement and I'm not really sure that I agree.

Another sign says: *Get K. Clark out of Iraq.* At least he has used a certain assonance with this one but I'm still a little confused at the point he is trying to make.

He wants his passport returned to him. I can't help but feel that stripping for the prime minister is not the best way to get it. This isn't America.

I keep walking, passing a statue of Field Marshall Montgomery; he looks like Jackie's partially demented grandfather. The resemblance is uncanny.

Perching on a wall just past heroes of British wars only the Teds would have heard of, I write down everything that has just happened. Maybe I'll get a chapter out of it. People walk past me and stare. They're thinking, *I wonder what he's doing? Maybe he's a writer.* And I'm suddenly starting to believe that I am again too.

I haven't felt this way for a long time. I've achieved so much already today and it's not even 10:00 yet.

So I write everything down, from the strength of the breeze to bus number plates, from the taste of pollution to the smell of fine-cuisine preparation. I write while I walk. For once, people are moving out of my way. I need to find somewhere to sit down, drink coffee and keep writing.

Even though I may waffle on about capitalist takeover and its effect on London's history and architecture, I really don't care that much. Everyone is angry about something, apparently, and we don't even need a reason anymore. I may think that I want to find and support a small, family-run, independent coffee shop in London but, really, isn't that exactly what I want to escape from? Secretly, I'm hoping to saunter by the magnet of a Starbucks so that I can enjoy a mug – not a cup, a mug – of their blackest espresso roast coffee, made from the finest Arabica beans, hand-picked from the trees found only on the highest part of the mountains. I prefer something from Sumatra, a bold, smoky flavour but still with a relatively light body.

So that's what I do.

The sixteen-year-old Portuguese exchange student doesn't know what I want before I've even said it like Ted would. The nineteen-year-old manager is out the back, checking her emails, stealing a portion of espresso chocolate brownie and marking it down as waste on her paperwork. She's not chewing on a biro and staring at a napkin like the other Ted would be. They are so normal, no novelties, no defining characteristics that set them apart from everyone else.

They don't know that what I need is a hot black liquid that will help perpetuate that wonderful British stereotype by rotting my teeth; it will also dissolve my liver and ultimately cause an addiction that will give me a chronic headache if I do not consume at least one litre per day.

And that's when some diluted form of realisation hits me. Things have got to change.

I push the hair away from my eyes and look at the kind of people that I'm sharing my morning with today. It's not just a glance or a perusal; it's become an exploration, a scrutiny. Not examining midgets or the homeless; there are no conjoined triplets or thalidomide homosexuals, these people are real. Four students in designer clothes obviously funded by Daddy's credit card; six middle-aged men who keep saying the words 'net' and 'gross', one of them asking me if he could borrow a chair from my table. A perfectly tanned Mediterranean couple have the only sofa, and I'm sure the girl is playing to an empty crowd, posing for pictures that aren't being taken.

The only other person on their own, apart from the espresso drinker by the window shouting at his mobile, who, on any other day I would have had down as a paedophile, is a twenty-something sporting the latest in boho-chic sartorial elegance. She looks, well, arty; like she could tell the difference between Yeats and Keats.

Another suit walks in with a tablet computer and sits with her. They clearly don't know each other, he just decided that her empty seat was a lot more appealing than mine.

This club, all of these suits and ties and granola bars and £150 plain-white T-shirts with the designer label pointlessly on the inside and electronic personal organisers and mobile phones and glossy magazines … and me with my 20p biro and leather-bound notebook that cost more than my shoes, wearing my tweed jacket at twenty-nine years of age. I feel like I stick out, like I'm abnormal, an impostor, but nobody even notices me here.

And I don't know whether I really like it or not.

MIKE

Mike wakes up again at 11:08.

Phase 2.

He rolls over half expecting to see Jackie beside him then registers that he has done this once already today. He stretches ferociously, letting out a growl as he does so, then sits up.

The room still has a remnant smell of intercourse that Mike wishes he could just wallow in, but he needs to get up. The living-room floor isn't going to varnish itself.

Everything about his daily routine is marginally different today. His usual languid stroll down the hall into the toilet is a little more draughty with no underwear on, but his conquest last night means he is almost pleased to see his naked reflection in full splendour, rather than keeping his eyes closed and hoping to hit the bowl as usual.

Opting out of breakfast, Mike wades straight in and transfers the contents of his lounge into various other areas around the flat. His ghastly sofa, another large mirror identical to the one behind his toilet and the TV set are all that remains. Unremarkably, Mike doesn't have as much stuff as he thought he had, and this exercise only takes thirty-four minutes to complete. So, with the smell of sweat from lugging furniture around his tiny duplex and the stench of long overdue yet irrefutably disloyal sex mixing together to form a perfume known as *Delayed Guilt*, Mike takes an early shower.

While Eli uses his own distinct brand of therapy, and Jackie attends a masochistic ritual of confession, Mike, simple as he is, opts for the shower as both a literal and emotional cleansing tool. Some days this occurs in the form of high-volume weeping; on others it involves almost violent masturbation; and on the truly taxing days there is a strenuous fusion of both activities that has proved to be cathartic, albeit exhausting.

But today is different.

Masturbation would tarnish the events of the previous evening and, instead of crying, there is singing. Songs like 'Celebration' by Kool and the Gang, with extra-loud 'wooo-hoos' to emphasise his elation; or 'Walking on Sunshine' by Katrina and the Waves – the most obvious opening exposition of Mike's Wednesday.

Suicide Eve.

He hums the latter tune while washing his hair using the Lynx shower gel that he got in a gift-box set from his aunt last Christmas. He's twenty-nine years of age and his fragrance of choice is that of a desperate, rampant teenager. Still, his aunt will save £5.99 this year.

He finishes, dries himself, wraps the towel around his waist and heads for his near-deserted living space for breakfast and a hot date with a talk-show host: Winona or Edith or Donovan. Meanwhile, Jackie queues up to be branded a harlot, and Eli is being talked at by an illiterate pedant struggling with Italian for beginners.

At 12:05 on Wednesday, Mike looks least likely of the three friends to over-step a cry for help.

The toast burns and sets off Mike's overly sensitive smoke alarm, but he still butters both slices, adds peanut butter – the crunchy kind, of course – and drops on chopped banana to add a dash of health. He then cuts each slice into four triangles and sets down to watch the latest instalment of Nadia or Remington or Persephone.

Ingesting the carcinogenic snack, Mike finds himself getting angry at the inbred trio on screen.

It looks as though Stacey is with Matt and has been for several years; they even have a two-year-old child together. Matt and Andy have been friends almost since birth but it turns out that Stacey and Andy had a thing for about a year behind Matt's back. To make things worse, this was going on about three years ago so now Matt wants a paternity test to uncover whether the child he has been raising and caring for is actually related to him by blood.

This is a fairly standard tale on the show and every time he sees it Mike gets angry at the people on screen for being so underhand and treacherous towards one another. This morning's airing of Andre or Lawrence or Naomi reverberates through Mike with a resounding boom of hypocrisy, and he is finally forced to deal with what he has done.

A dumbed-down epiphany.

Some reach a turning point in their life when they open themselves up to religion or philosophy or any of the arts. Some even find enlightenment through science. But Mike, simple, one-dimensional Mike, is almost ready to make a radical, life-changing decision based on the ramblings of three degenerates from the West Country in their early twenties on job-seeker's allowance with child in tow who are being paid £500 each to ruin their lives further when the kid would have had more chance had they just succumbed to their usual ignorance.

Euphoria is replaced with culpability, triumph with blame, and song with regret.

Go on, Mike, take another shower, but you can't scrub or wank away what you have done this time.

Entering the first stage of melancholy, Mike takes out his tools to start varnishing the floor. The floor has been sanded and the dustsheets are back in the cupboard; all he has now is a large brush and a polyurethane sealant that produces a tough, durable finish resistant to oil, water and other chemicals – it is touch dry within two to four hours.

This job takes hours, but Mike is determined to get an entire coat down today, so that he can create something to be proud of, so that he can achieve something worthwhile.

Unfortunately, his current deteriorating state of mind proves so distracting that he starts varnishing at the doorway; his only exit from the room. And, by the time he realises that, he has literally started to paint himself into a corner, he has completed too much of the floor and can't get out. Carl Lewis couldn't even make it out without a decent run-up. This forces him to continue the floor all the way into the kitchen and use his sink as a toilet should the need arise.

Not wanting to step on the wet floor, Mike hangs over the cupboards, lying across the kitchen tops in order to reach down and finish the last parts of the floor. His sense of accomplishment is subdued by thoughts about Jackie and how he has deceived Eli, but now he has two to four hours to continually go over this in his head while his first coat dries.

He lies down on his back, stretched out along the kitchen surface. He's able to reach for an ice-cold beer from the fridge and a packet of cheese and onion crisps from the cupboard above his head.

And that's lunch.

Another distraction.

The time spent in silence proves too loud in the mind of Mike, and he decides to make a call.

'DoTrue UK, Sam speaking, how can I help?' He picks up within the designated two rings. It's company policy to do so. To ensure that customers feel that there is always someone available to answer their queries.

'Hi. Can I speak with Eli, please?' His timidity lets Sam know immediately that this is not a business call, but he's as professional as ever.

'Unfortunately, Mr Hagin is not in the office today, can I help or take a message?'

'Er, no. That's okay. Thanks for your help.' And Mike hangs up. Now he is worried about Eli. What if he is sick? What if he is not sick?

What if somehow he knows about what went on last night?

He calls Eli's mobile.

But Eli doesn't answer because he is off on his pilgrimage to South London in pursuit of creative salvation, and is subsequently screening calls he does not consider to be of value to this quest.

This frustrates Mike even further.

It's necessary for him to converse with Eli, to gauge his emotion. That way, he can make a decision as to whether he should confess his sins or compartmentalise them in his brain, forcing himself to believe that nothing happened.

Eli would always opt for the second option, but Mike is too honest for his own good. He waits seven minutes and tries to phone again, but Eli has it switched off by now because he doesn't want it going off in an art gallery. Someone might confuse him for an installation.

He leaves a message this time. 'Hi, mate. Mike here. Just wondering how you are feeling after last night. I called your office and they said you weren't in today. Give us a call back when you get this. Cheers.' It sounded fairly natural, not too concerned and not too jaunty either. Just the way one friend speaks to another.

But now all he has is more silence.

More and more silence.

So he waits.

He occupies some time by making patterns with his eyes on the Artex ceiling, folding his crisp packet into a neat little thimble, tapping this cheesy thimble on the work surface in time with the hum of other 1980s power ballads. He even dedicates some time to reviewing his bedroom performance.

Then he calls Eli again.

He's on the Tube so it goes straight through to voicemail. Again.

This is the last straw for Mike. His frustration at not being able to confront his guilt by talking to the person he has wronged boils inside of him, erupting into irritation that manifests itself in Mike throwing his phone across the room, hitting the mirror on the opposite wall and smashing the majority of it onto the only section of the floor that has dried.

Right now, he has no idea that two of those pieces of glass are going to be used to pierce through the skin of his thighs, shred through his sartorius muscles, and rip apart some fairly major veins and arteries, causing him to panic and die on the floor he is afraid to touch.

He's got less than a day not to come to that decision.

Mike deals with this in the only way he knows how: he lies back down on the kitchen surface, crunches on another packet of crisps, despite the fact his mother told him not to eat while lying down and against the wishes of Bethyl or Dorian or Sebastian who showed him only last Tuesday that comfort eating is a short-term solution to a long-term problem.

And he cries.

Not the kind of vocal, hysterical crying an infant does when they lose their mother in a supermarket; not the controlled crying that a girl does on a first date to the cinema when she doesn't want to look ugly as she weeps to the rom part of the rom-com; not the kind where you make the noises, the sharp inhalations, but no tears emerge; and certainly not the manly cry where you open your eyes as wide as you can and puff out your cheeks in disbelief that something like this has happened to you.

No. It's the kind where you lie down on a kitchen surface after creating the weapon for your ultimate demise in a spasm of rage and tears silently fall from your eyes. When your facial expression remains fixed and motionless but water still drops out of your ducts, sliding down your cheeks and onto the surface of the floor that you need to wait another 150 minutes to dry.

Even though Mike's day began a little differently than it usually does, and even though many moments throughout the morning may have pointed to a turnaround in fortune, Mike has still ended up where he always does at this time of the day. Alone and crying.

There's no use feeling sorry for him.

It's too late for that now.

TEXTS

It's later. What are you doing?

Are you there?

> **I'm here.**

> **Sorry.**

Why are you sorry?

> **For still being here.**

> **For still being alive.**

What are you doing?

> **Lying down.**

If you want this as bad as you say, tonight could be the night.

Do you want to keep living this way?

> **Of course not. That's the point.**

Then stop stalling.

Stop hesitating.

> **I know. I know. Thinking makes it worse.**

Exactly that. You need to just do this.

> **Getting the pills wrong that time was awful.**

> **A couple more and it would have worked.**

You need something you can't get wrong.

Something that you can't back out of.

> **I know what it is.**

I stood with a rope around my neck for forty minutes once and couldn't go through with it.

I just cried. I stood on a chair with a rope around my neck and cried.

Maybe I'm not strong enough to do this.

You are. You know it's the only thing for you now.

First thing you need to do is get up.

Get out of bed, okay?

I will.

Promise.

I promise.

Text me when you're up and ready.

Sure.

JACKIE
(THE DAY BEFORE SUICIDE THURSDAY)

In the same way the gym is always busy on a Monday after people gorge on fast food and alcohol over the weekend, there always seems to be a queue for confession on a Wednesday evening.

A midweek declaration of guilt seems compulsory to ensure full purification and thus a stress-free end to the working week in preparation for another weekend of sin. It's also perfect if you deliberately missed the spinning class you booked for the beginning of the week but didn't attend because you thought there would be too many people at the gym.

Jackie knows this and decides to beat the crowds by going on her lunch break.

There are four people lingering in front of her when she arrives.

She waits patiently in the arctic confines of the church aisle. Ahead, a middle-aged man is contemplating cheating on his wife with a journalist he has recently met in the city, a twenty-something woman needs to discuss the ethics of abortion one more time, and two elderly ladies merely need an excuse to get out of the house.

It feels glacial in the church this afternoon. Around her, choir boys sing without the menace of Father Farrelly to distract their thoughts. Their harmonies are so close and haunting, Jackie feels colder just listening to the melody.

This makes her even more nervous.

It was only two nights ago that she was falsely confessing to impure thoughts about a mystery man. Initially she will have to explain that this was no spectre, that he is alive and exists – for the next twenty hours at least – and that in the time between this and their last meeting, she has followed through and was delivered unto evil with this person, making her dream seem all the more prophetic.

Last night, she dreamed that he died.

The three confessors in front of her in this queue of sin, this line of ordinary human behaviour, this file of honest mistakes, all receive the 'God wants you to be holy and free from sexual immorality' speech. But for Jackie, Father Farrelly reserves his favourite 'adultery is a trap – it catches those with whom the Lord is angry' diatribe.

Jackie knows this is coming, though. She already feels the guilt and senses the burning stare of the pale, skinny Jewish man nailed to a cross above the even paler, ghostly altar boys. She is afraid to look at him directly.

Although she may want to cry, she believes that what she is doing is necessary.

Adulterous male finishes and exits the booth with what he thinks is a free licence to fuck anybody. The way he likes to keep his original sin literally original is to perform a succession of lurid acts, each more devious than the last, until his hunger for abnormality is so insatiable that he has to commit a heinous sexual crime to get his kicks and is ultimately punished by law, which proves to have a more lasting effect than reciting a Gloria Estefan, or whatever it is.

But finally, Jackie gets her turn in the upright coffin she calls confession.

Before she even has the opportunity to ask for some degree of forgiveness, Farrelly intervenes.

'Jacqueline.' It's not so much a question as it is an affirmation, and he manages to sound authoritative and composed at the same time.

'Father,' she acknowledges like a toddler who has drawn on the living-room wall in dark-purple crayon. 'Please forgive me, for I have sinned. Ignoring the advice of the church and my own conscience, I have been led into temptation and acted on these wicked urges.'

'Go on.' This request from Father Farrelly for Jackie to continue the exposition of her sensational exploits implies that this is the point at which he will commence judgement; but, in truth, judgement began as soon as Jackie perched herself within the fear-scented, guilt-soaked mahogany of Farrelly's two-room torture chamber.

She explains who Mike really is, how Eli is, their relationship, her growing feelings towards Mike as a confidante, her despair over her boyfriend, the possibility of loving two people at the same time. She really opens up in what actually sounds like honest confession this time. Farrelly's idea of help is to advise that God is angry with her; that she is essentially nothing more than a whore. It actually sounds remarkably similar to the advice he gave twenty minutes earlier to the twenty-something woman's abortion queries.

A lengthy one-way discussion ensues in which Farrelly passes judgement, hurling a barrage of demeaning prose camouflaged by the poetry of New Testament scripture, and doles out his sentence.

Jackie thanks the priest, who closes the divide and heads straight for his choir.

She remains seated for a short while, afraid to emerge under the watchful eye of Christ; she takes a second to reflect and compose herself. Once again, not everything Jackie told her counsel was entirely true. When lying becomes habitual, it is possible to confuse stories and convince oneself that the lie you are telling is true, ultimately persuading others towards the same conclusion.

Before sloping back to the office, Jackie lights a candle for Mike, as if she knows something that nobody else does. Eli is still enjoying some prolific note-taking in a coffee chain, and Mike is munching on a couple of slices of burnt toast before he settles into staining his living-room floor.

It's as though nothing important happened today.

WEDNESDAY

I start to question what is actually important.

My relationship with Jackie?

No.

My entry-level job in the marketing team at DoTrue?

No.

That my best friend is going to smash his mirror and pierce it through his thighs tomorrow night?

No.

Although, according to Jackie, that will definitely give someone seven years bad luck. And I don't think Mike needs that right now.

I've got to reassess my priorities in life. My best friend isn't going to make it past thirty; my relationship isn't going to last past the weekend; my job is just a simple waste of fucking time; and the only real thing I have left is my writing and maybe the reason I can't finish that is because I have to put an end to these other areas first.

After the third bite of my low-fat chicken and mixed-pepper panini with crème fraiche, I have an idea. I'm not sure whether it would be for a short film or the opening scene to a feature. It begins with what seems like an innocent exchange between a couple at a train station, proclaiming their love for one another before the man embarks on a journey.

A moment of reflective silence ensues between the couple only to be broken by the sound of a train horn, signifying that it will pass straight through the station.

The couple step back from the yellow line.

I stop for a second and take a sip from my venti Americano. Someone was trying to be clever at the counter when I bought it by saying that 'venti' means windy in Italian, so I was actually having a windy coffee. I fake laughed; if it was Jackie I probably would have corrected her, stating that it actually means twenty, which refers to the fact that this particular size is twenty fluid ounces and that she was actually confusing herself with '*vienti*' which does mean windy in Italian. Idiot.

I continue to write:

```
As the train approaches the platform, girls hold
their hands between their legs to stop their skirts
rising, old ladies cling to their husband's arms,
the couple embrace each other and a man appears
suddenly from the right side of the picture, running
at full speed, not stopping. He jumps. Launching
himself off the platform, he hitch-kicks himself in
front of the locomotive, instantly dissolving into
particles of blood and entrails, spraying the
oblivious patrons on platform five. Almost in
unison, the entire platform turns their wrists
towards their faces to take a glimpse at the time.
The man turns to his partner saying, 'Looks as
though there might be a delay.'
```

I know. My therapist would be telling me that this particular chapter has a glaringly obvious undertone, reflecting my flippancy when dealing with suicide and my reluctance to discuss death in depth with anyone other than myself and her, my imaginary therapist – I can't wait to see her again. She would say that the man's deadpan reaction is a direct manifestation of my relationship with Jackie; that I remain removed from her but ultimately want her around. Perhaps it is merely a cultural critique of British attitudes and aloofness.

Jesus, I wish she would just blame it on the abandonment issues I have with my mother/Jackie/Mike/God.

Jung would obviously interpret it as an attempt to find spiritual and emotional wholeness; that I use these dreams and fantasies to get to know my shadow. He'd be wrong: these are what I use to suppress my shadow.

It's simple anxiety, I'm sure.

I slam my notebook shut and throw my partially-chewed-with-frustration biro towards the coffee-shop entrance. Still nobody notices; even the Mediterranean girl has lost interest in me.

I've lost interest in me. I can't write. I'm a freak show. A one-trick pony. Okay, in a way, I'm a writer, but not really. I write first chapters that can't possibly lead anywhere because the stories are full of Dutch midgets and suicide and homeless people and lobotomised transsexuals and superstition and mirage and paraplegia and nothing that's real and little Italian sociopaths and coffee and venereal disease and lack of substance and pathetic ten-page novelty tales to hide the fact that I actually have nothing poignant to say and, well, maybe that's the answer.

I bound out of the coffee shop spelled the old-fashioned way with one P.

Instead of turning right and heading back the 486 steps towards Trafalgar Square, I head straight, wondering how many steps it would have taken me at this pace. Maybe 262.

So now I'm running. I head down a cobbled alley that wouldn't look out of place in a Florentine back street, but it smells dank with pungent animal urine rather than tomato-heavy gastronomy.

The path leads to a public garden that I never knew existed and, even though I can see where I want to go, the fence seems perpetual. It's empty here, like nobody knows of its whereabouts – or cares. On any other day than this, it would have been like finding a fold in time or space that allowed me to enter Eden, or at least the Chelsea Flower show.

It reminds me of Central Park and how you can still see the sky-scraping buildings through gaps in the foliage even in the centre of the undergrowth. It's like Central Park but on a far more British scale. The fact that this can exist, unspoiled in the heart of one of the world's most polluted capital cities, a city that can turn a person's nasal mucus black from one day of inhalation, is astonishing. Its existence suggests that the world might not be as infected as I thought it was; empty benches and vacant public paths reaffirm the appreciation that we have of our planet. That sounds like something Mum would say.

I don't notice any of this, though. The garden could have been packed with hallucinating morris dancers and I wouldn't have seen them. I am too busy torturing myself.

How could I say that I'm not a writer?

Of course I am. It's the only thing I know anything about.

I am a writer. I've just been writing about the wrong things.

I don't remember crossing the road, or walking up the stairs to the bridge. I do recall that there were thirty-seven steps, though, and that my left foot touched nineteen of them. A train above me is slowing down, or maybe it's another illusion because I am running so fast now, despite my arms being constricted by tightly woven tweed.

I feel my phone vibrate in my jean pocket. The name flashes blue-white: *Mike Home*. I stop, not wanting to appear out of breath, and the train snails past me overhead. But I just let the phone ring.

I'm sure he really needs to talk to me, that he has problems or a confession that he would like to make; and, normally, I would play the role of the concerned guy. But I have my own things to think about. How I get past a first chapter; how I can afford to quit my job; how I get rid of Mike and break up with Jackie; whether I am even thinking straight.

Right now, I just want to spend a couple of hours wandering around the Saatchi exhibition, soaking in the second part of *The Triumph of Painting*, and put off these thoughts for a while.

The call goes through to voicemail.

And that's how it happened. A deliberately missed call between two apparent friends. Something as arbitrary and everyday as that. Something any person wouldn't give a second thought about. This phone call was as good as signing a hit on Mike.

Maybe Jackie was right. That's how I did it. Maybe that's how I killed Mike.

The nail in his coffin.

The mirror in his thighs.

JACKIE

Descartes hears the key turn in the door and rolls his eyes.

She's home.

Early.

'Hello, boy.' She speaks at a higher pitch than usual. Descartes turns his back to Jackie, lifts his tail and walks into the kitchen, where he knows she will head, straight away. He doesn't like being spoken to like a dog.

'Lovely to see you, too.' Jackie kicks off her shoes and follows the cat into the kitchen. She opens the fridge and takes out the half-empty bottle of Chardonnay from the other night, gives it a sniff and pours it into a large glass.

'Are you hungry?' She looks down at him.

Descartes looks back. He won't rub himself against her ankle. He won't wind himself around her legs. It's degrading. He settles for a purr.

Jackie finds a tin of cat food and a clean bowl. She peels the lid from the tin and keeps talking, much to the disdain of her apparent companion.

'So, work was shit, thanks for asking. I lied to my priest about what's going on in my life, too. So it hasn't been the best day.' She mashes the food with a fork. It's the bent one. So she knows not to ever use it for herself. Even when it goes through the dishwasher.

Jackie drinks.

'And I have to go and see Mike later to sort things out.' She places the bowl on the floor and Descartes dives straight in. The quicker he is finished, the less he has to listen to this. 'Because I slept with him last night. That's right. Fucked him good and proper. Fucked him up, too, no doubt.'

Her phone vibrates.

'Here he is now. Again.'

If he wasn't so damned hungry, Descartes would take a shit in the flat, somewhere discreet, and head out for the evening. Maybe if he eats quickly enough it'll make him throw up a little, so she has to get on her knees and clean it.

Jackie types a message and throws her phone onto the kitchen counter. She picks up her glass, takes a swig and crouches down next to her cat to stroke him.

Descartes expects to bristle at her touch but is instead comforted as he licks the last morsels of lamb-and-spinach-cake meat. He turns to her.

'Sometimes I wonder if you're the only one I can rely on.'

He can tell from her tone that she's getting desperate. Descartes takes a drink of water from the other bowl, turns to display his anus to his owner again and languidly struts towards the open window before disappearing.

Jackie watches him leave. The nonchalant little prick.

'You'd be dead without me,' she mutters under her breath.

The phone vibrates.

Mike again.

Jackie ignores it, finishes her glass of wine in record time, tops it up and rinses Descartes' bowl under the tap before placing it in the dishwasher.

Another buzz.

And another.

And another.

'What the fuck does he want now?'

TEXTS

Maybe I shouldn't.

This is getting out of hand.

You need to make your mind up.

How is that helpful?

How is going back on what you said helpful?

I can't have doubts about killing myself?

You can question anything you want.

It's not healthy to keep swaying like this.

It's a big decision.

Today it's a big decision. Last night it was a certainty. Yesterday you were going to do it.

You're mean today.

And you're indecisive.

So pick one. Choose to live or choose to die. But choose one.

I'll support your decision, either way. But fucking pick one.

Maybe I shouldn't talk to you today.

Another maybe. Message me when you're ready to put on your big-boy pants.

You're being a dick.

Can't you just tell me what to do?

You can't put that on me.

Take a moment. Breathe. You'll know what's best for you.

You're right.

So, you're gonna do it?

WEDNESDAY
(THE DAY BEFORE SUICIDE THURSDAY)

The room appears to be filled with crude oil. It smells like oil too and it certainly looks like that may be the case, but I'm not allowed to touch anything to verify my suspicions and satisfy my curiosity because that would ruin the illusion. But that is art, I suppose.

My phone would be ringing right now had I left it on, but I am preoccupied figuring out whether there may in fact be a sophisticated use of mirrors and a single line of paint in this grease-scented room – an installation, they call it. To me it is more concerned with physics than actually holding any artistic pedigree but it's interesting all the same, thought-provoking even.

Certainly a more appealing alternative to listening to Mike drone on about his infantile problems. I'll probably miss that when it's gone, though.

I leave the Saatchi exhibition after using a room that said 'toilet' on the front, which may have been a real lavatory but may well have been another piece of art, judging by the standard that was on display in the rest of the building. 'All a little derivative,' I heard someone say. Another proclaimed that 'it lacks a certain oneness' or that it had 'a marvellous negative capability'. Nevertheless, I urinated in it whether it was art or not. How very post-modern of me.

Stepping outside, it's already turning dark, which makes the lights of Parliament all the more spectacular from my elevated view. Even the Millennium Wheel has majesty about it as night draws ever closer. I decide that enough is enough for today; I opt out of food or a quick pint in order to avoid another journey with the socially lobotomised office robots. I willingly pass up my opportunity to mingle with mobile phones and Filofaxes and buy, sell, trade, rip off, consolidate, accumulate, and start walking, finding myself in a world of people who seem a little bit more like me.

A couple of guys holding guitar-shaped cases who I assume are musicians rather than pantomime gangsters. There's a man in his mid-thirties who has spilled coffee down the front of his white shirt; he is jogging to get somewhere, a rather tattered and overflowing Hessian satchel over his shoulder, and I can only presume he is a journalist on a deadline. There are still a few suits around, hopping from one agenda-less meeting to another, sipping their tenth cappuccino of the day and fake-laughing it through the pain of their own insecurities.

In the midst of this potpourri of civilisation I spy a female battling with herself to stay on her feet.

She has hair that falls down way past her shoulders. Blonde, which isn't normally my thing, but this woman certainly stands out. She appears to be carrying some kind of portfolio that is bursting with paper. Flared jeans with a purple dress over the top. I never really understood this look but it is certainly working on some base level for me today. She is also sporting a bandana that, as it clearly isn't holding her hair back, I guess is a fashion accessory. It's such a contradiction to anything Jackie would wear. She is so plain. So predictable. Dowdy, even. This girl, this magnificent creature stumbling before me, is funky, bohemian, just more interesting than other women.

She drops everything. Her bag, her portfolio, some chalk drawings that wouldn't fit into the folder, and the bagel that was being held in her mouth while she scuttled along. The only thing left intact is the take-out latte in her left hand.

Of course, I move over immediately to see if I can be of any assistance.

'Get your hands off my work,' she says sternly.

'I'm sorry?' I'm so shocked I don't think I've heard her correctly.

'Get your filthy hands off my fucking work.' I hear her correctly this time.

I was hoping to maybe spark up some mutual interest. Perhaps even dispute some modern art, if that was her bag. Personally, it leaves me cold for the most part, but debate can be healthy.

I even allowed myself to contemplate for a second that she may be the catalyst for change, an interesting complication in the six-year saga of the Eli and Jackie Show. Now I just feel lucky to have a woman like Jackie, and I don't want to feel like that at all. It's not helping.

Surely it's not stable to be that precious over your work.

I just walk on. Mum used to say that rejection is a huge part of life.

Mike thinks it gives you cancer.

A tramp asks me for some spare money to get into a shelter for the evening. He needs another £1.48 to get a roof over his head for the night. I give him enough for the shelter and perhaps one can of lager to help him on his way. It's unlike me, but I have just met someone more deplorable than a scrounging peasant, so this brief encounter with a stinking drunkard seems like a Disney parade in comparison.

The escalator down is more depressing than the light I mothed towards this morning. A light that signified change and opportunity; that allowed me to hope. Now I plunge into that dank abyss of swirling underground rail network, where you can always spot a rat on the tracks and always have to consider that a backpack may contain a bomb and you have to fear for your life just to take a shortcut to get to a job you hate or to return to a home life that offers no sanctity, reward or justification for you putting yourself through this ritual each and every weekday.

And you're stuck doing it.

And you'll always feel like this. The temporary job you took to earn money while you looked for something you really wanted is now your actual job; and, in some way, you have actually started to care about what you do. It's at this point I think about the best way for the back-to-school campaign to be implemented on the internet.

My carriage is fairly empty and I manage to get a seat for the duration of my ride home. Six Eastern European men in leather trousers and Motorhead T-shirts board and are fairly rowdy but not offensive. One is clearly morbidly obese and the tattoos on his arms just draw attention to that, while the pointed biker goatee gives the illusion that his face is fatter than it actually is. He might die way before he should, but something tells me he's fine with that. He's living and he's enjoying it. This is more than can be said for the array of docile iPhone zombies peppering the remainder of the carriage.

The train comes to an abrupt stop and the doors automatically open, making the noise you only hear on *Star Trek* when a door slides open on the Enterprise.

'Mind the gap.' And like some Pavlovian stimulus, a spark flies to my brain telling me that I am home. I won't start salivating until I smell the pretzels, though.

MIKE AND JACKIE

As Eli minds the gap, Jackie is shouting through Mike's letterbox trying to get him to let her in. But he's worried. The floor looks dry but if he touches the one section that isn't it could ruin the entire look.

'Come on, Mike. I know you're in there. Let me in. Don't make this more awkward than it has to be.' Jackie makes her point with a tender raise of the voice.

The pressure is too much for Mike to handle. Does he stand up and risk destroying the floor he has been working on for weeks? Or does he save his floor and risk the woman he has waited so many years for leaving, never to be seen again? The frustration of this quandary induces yet more tears.

Obviously, he knows that the floor isn't perfect anyway and he knows that if he dies tomorrow, which he definitely will, his last moment with Jackie will be a delicately intimate exchange of one another's deepest emotions and not an uncomfortable, embarrassing vocal rehash of the previous evening exchanged through a brass letterbox at distance.

'Miii-iiiike.' Jackie gives him the double-syllable treatment. 'Let me in. Please. I need to talk to you, we need to talk.'

He knows that she has a key. They all do. For each other.

But Mike can't resist this. He's waited far too long to be in this position.

Taking a deep breath he lifts himself to a seated position on the kitchen work surface looking out over his dark-tan masterpiece, his legs dangling down the side of a cupboard. Another deep breath and he elevates himself off the side, but doesn't jump, just hovers, supporting his weight on his arms. He drops back down again. One last, deep breath. The floor looks evenly dry-ish, so maybe if he is fast, it won't make a difference.

He drops to the floor and bounds to the doorway like a club-footed ballet dancer. The floor remains unaffected; it has actually been dry enough to walk on for forty minutes, but as Mike reaches his goal he forgets that the room divider that used to hold the carpet in position is yet to be replaced and a spike goes through his big toe on the right foot, causing him to shriek and bleed all the way down the hallway carpet to the door.

Jackie has gone.

'FUUUUUUUCK.' But just as he starts to shout, Jackie's head pops into view as she makes her way back upstairs. She was on her way back up anyway when she heard the painful yelp a few seconds earlier. Miss Fagan appears in her doorway.

'Everything alright, Mike?' she enquires, genuinely concerned.

'I'm fine, Miss F. I just stubbed my toe.'

Jackie smiles as she heads towards him.

'You're bleeding,' Miss Fagan observes in concern.

'Don't worry, I'll get him fixed up,' Jackie reassures Mike's elderly neighbour, who takes the hint and retreats into her lonely Port-soaked dwelling.

'Hi,' Mike says affectionately.

'Hey,' she responds, giving him a peck on the cheek. 'Let's get that wound seen to, shall we?' And she walks through the door as if she has lived there for years.

Mike is happy.

Eli is not.

WEDNESDAY
(THE DAY BEFORE SUICIDE THURSDAY)

When I get home I can't find my keys and when I phone Jackie to come round with her spare set, she doesn't answer. Neither does Mike. I text Jackie to inform her of my predicament and head to Gaucho's for a coffee while I wait.

Ted greets me by shouting my regular drink order at me; the other Ted taps his head with a pencil in his usual salute to acknowledge my presence. I don't hang around for a story as it seems to be getting busier towards the end of the working day, and I've already done a lot of soul-searching by myself this afternoon, so the Teds' attempts to uncover some intuitive leap of understanding will be futile. I just want to smell my coffee and allow the steam to hit my face while I hang my head over the mug and wait for a response from either my best friend or girlfriend.

I have some time to kill because, as far as I know, Jackie is still working, and I have no idea where Mike could be. Luckily, I am perched next to a mothers' meeting of middle-aged to slightly older women all discussing their triumphs and failures this week regarding weight loss. I jot down some interesting ideas that I might be able to use in a future chapter.

Initially it would appear that a majority of the women are called Val, but names aren't really that important at this point. I hear one lady talk about being in counselling for the last two years. She is going to report herself tomorrow as she feels that she has used food as a reward several times this week. Another opens up about her two children being delivered by Caesarean section and the scarring on her stomach looks awful but how plastic surgery is not the answer and it would just make her feel worse even if her stomach looked really good.

I'm still waiting for a genuine comment.

'The other day I sat down in front of the TV and had a Kit Kat. It was fine because I haven't really had one in ages,' one of the Vals trills on.

'I was the same last week with a bag of Wotsits, but I hadn't touched crisps for nearly a week.' I feel like they might be getting somewhere until another overweight liar says that making an event of it and actually sitting down to enjoy the chocolate is much better for you because if it's more of an event – you know what you are doing rather than mindlessly snacking and not keeping a record of what you eat. The whole gaggle squawks in agreement, even though they virtually banished one of the group for rewarding themselves with a food they enjoy not sixty seconds earlier.

A slender woman pipes up, saying, 'I just tend to eat what I want.' This strikes me as funny because obviously it is the first true comment, which means it is something that the rest of the pack does not want to hear. The fact that she isn't even overweight just adds insult to her apparent blasphemy. She clearly has some kind of eating disorder and has just as much right to be there and offer her thoughts.

I'm forced to laugh in my head.

I check my phone even though it hasn't made a noise to indicate that a text has come through. A phantom vibration. Mike and Jackie are deep in discussion, so I am going to have to wait a while longer for rescue.

JACKIE

A man jumps out of a plane at five thousand feet.

At three thousand feet, as the earth below edges ever closer, he pulls the string to release his parachute, but nothing happens.

At two thousand feet, he pulls his emergency cord for the spare parachute with the same result.

At one thousand feet, he passes a man in blue overalls with a spanner in his right hand and asks, 'Excuse me, can you fix my parachute?'

The man replies, 'Sorry, mate, I only do boilers.'

This is a key joke in Mike's adult life with regards to women. He can't alter the direction he is headed. It's come to a point where he can no longer even slow down the inevitable. He's unable to deviate from this path.

Yes, he has finally taken the plunge with Jackie but at three thousand feet I ignored his call, at two thousand feet he cuts his toe open and, at one thousand feet, when he courageously attempts to take things to a new level with the woman of his dreams by leaning in for a kiss, he finds out that she only does boilers.

He's been dumped before it's even started so, to Mike, it doesn't matter now that his parachute won't open, because he'll already be dead before he's even hit the ground.

'I can't do this, Mike.' This is Jackie at her clinical best. Succinct. To the point.

'What?' And Mike at his inexperienced worst. Idiotic. Blathering. Innocent.

'This. This whole sneaking-around thing. Infidelity. Betrayal. I mean, both of us, we *both* shouldn't be doing this. He's your best friend and my—' He cuts her off.

'Ex.'

'No, not my ex at all. He's my boyfriend. My current, long-term boyfriend and, with all his faults, he doesn't deserve this, Mike. Not from us.'

Guilt makes him react in a less-than compassionate way.

'Oh, well, that's fucking great, isn't it?' He raises his voice a little. Jackie doesn't respond particularly well to this when Eli does it, so she certainly won't take it from Mike.

'Don't raise your voice at me, Mike.' She's like a stern schoolteacher.

'Look, I'm sorry. This is just a bit of a shock. You know? I mean, last night was great, wasn't it?'

Jackie remains silent.

'And you obviously went through with it for a reason. So what was it? An experiment? To see just how much you could fuck me up?' Hysteria creeps in.

'It wasn't like that, Mike, and you know it. Look, I didn't come here for an argument. I was hoping we could be grown up about this.' She doesn't mean to but she is placating him.

'Grown-ups? You want to act like a fucking grown-up?' He gets to his feet and momentarily doesn't feel the blood rushing back to his injured toe. 'Well, try looking at yourself, Jacqueline. What are you doing that's so grown up, eh? Playing games. Messing with people's emotions. Playing out some schoolgirl fantasy. You're trying too hard, Jackie. Trying to be in an adult relationship, trying to be an upstanding Catholic, trying to do the right thing by everyone.' Then: 'Aaaaargh.' Suddenly the adrenaline is overtaken by pain, and he drops back onto the sofa as his toe throbs and pulses with blood and antiseptic.

'Are you okay?' She drops her guard for a second and smothers him a little.

'I'm fine.' He brushes her off, embarrassed.

'Look, obviously you're upset, I don't blame you. But I think I should leave, before one of us says something that we will end up regretting. We can talk again tomorrow.'

This is not what she said.

This might sound like something that Jackie would say in her annoyingly diplomatic and coldly removed manner, but she is less than perfect. Why else would she spend so much time in confession? Eli would tell himself that she is manipulative and everything she says or does is for a reason. A reason that proves to serve only her self-interest.

'I'm sorry, Mike, this is as hard for me as it is for you. You're lucky that you are only in love with one person, because it's complicated in my head, I'll tell you.'

She starts to cry. Now Mike is forced to be the giver of comfort and uses the situation to his advantage while she is in such a vulnerable state.

Within seconds they are kissing and this soon turns into yet another tender lovemaking session right there on his horrendous puke of a sofa while his toe drips the first few droplets of his blood onto the floor and Jackie cries silently through the ordeal.

But this isn't what she said either. This didn't happen.

Unfortunately for Mike, Jackie has arrived at the flat with a clear objective: to call it off with Mike and screw him up in the process.

'Are you okay?' She drops her guard for a second and smothers him a little.

'I'm fine.' He brushes her off, embarrassed.

'Good because listen to me, you pathetic little boy. What I have with Eli is real, okay? We'll have been together for six years on Friday. You and I aren't anywhere near that, and I assure you, it's no teenage fantasy of mine to screw around on the man I love with someone like you. And don't you ever question my religious convictions again, you hear? You wouldn't understand.'

She said this.

'Okay. I'm sorry, calm down. Please.' He has basically just been told off and now he is pathetically whimpering to her.

'I'm just not in the mood now, you've upset me. I was hoping we could come to some amicable decision today but clearly you're too immature to do that right now.' She is clever. She insults him on the most fundamental of levels and then makes him feel guilty about the way that he has acted.

'Please, Jackie,' he whines, lightly tugging at her arm.

'No, Mike. I need to get out of here. I'll come by tomorrow. Hopefully you'll have had some time to cool down.' She just gets up and leaves and she won't return to the flat until the early evening of tomorrow – Suicide Thursday.

She waits until she gets to the Tube before breaking down in tears. She's lost and is now out of her depth this time. Even with all of this going on she is thinking of Eli and how he cannot get into his place because he misplaced his keys.

Once again, she is Eli's saviour.

WEDNESDAY
(THE DAY BEFORE SUICIDE THURSDAY)

By the time I finish my third cup of dark, malevolent, espresso roast Americano, I am really aware of my breath and need the toilet, but it's so busy in here now and I don't want to lose my seat.

Where the hell is Jackie? It's been nearly an hour.

I can't take it anymore and, almost as soon as I stand up, sure enough someone jumps on my chair. I squeeze past the queue that seems never-ending and think about how long I've been holding this in. I remember an article saying that doing this can damage your prostate, making it difficult to become aroused; this just makes it feel even better when I finally release. Standing over the toilet I groan with pleasure, not caring about who might hear me, it's almost the highlight of my day.

With one problem solved I grab a tin of mints from the front of the counter. Not wanting to queue, I hold them in the air and shake them. This is a good enough indication of my intent to the Teds; I'll pay for them tomorrow.

The wind is getting brisk outside so the eight steps to my door is actually quite awakening, especially after my recent caffeine infusion. It's not that long until Jackie turns up; not enough time to promote the onset of haemorrhoids from slouching on my temporary concrete couch.

'God, where have you been, it's freezing out here?' I could be more grateful, I know.

'I had my phone on silent. Sorry. Why didn't you just wait in the coffee shop?'

I brush this off. I'm just being difficult and I'm annoyed I've had to call Jackie to my rescue. It's even more annoying that London looks entirely washed out and grey, while Jackie seems to glow with colour.

My angel.

She opens my front door and I follow her in.

MIKE

He's been working on his living-room floor all week. Mike doesn't have the funds to get a tradesperson in, with their dust-free sanding techniques and professional tools. He doesn't want a stranger in his flat, chemically stripping the wood or applying low-maintenance lacquers to protect his surface and prolong its life.

Mike has time, which is an odd thing to say about somebody ready to kill themselves, but he has no real job, so he has hours in the day that others do not.

He has been sanding by hand. First with a coarse grain and then with something finer, to achieve the smooth finish he wants. There have been several deliveries of something called pumice powder. This is what he uses to fill the gaps in the wood and the grain, working it in with a damp cloth, applying pressure in small, circular motions, just as it said in an article he found online.

The living room isn't huge. There's room for a television, coffee table, two-seater sofa and bookcase. There's even a little room to walk between the furniture. But the size of the floor can grow exponentially when applying the shellac for your French polishing technique with a ball of material the size of a golf ball.

Apply in long, sweeping motions in the direction of the grain.

Do not break in the centre of the wood as this will create imperfections.

Mike has lost count of the number of coats he has applied to his floor, but there's something therapeutic about the process. When Jackie leaves, he takes his wad of material and adds a couple more.

He thinks about Eli and wonders what he will think when he sees what Mike has done.

Mike eventually falls asleep on his couch with his injured foot slightly elevated, and settles down for one, final dreamless night.

TEXTS

I've finished the floor.

Okaaaaaay.

It's taken me ages but it looks really great.

I'm pleased for you.

Is that it?

What?

That's all you're going to say to me?

You've finished staining your floor. I don't know where I'm supposed to take that.

Every day you're asking me if I'm going to do it, when I'm going to do it.

Have you given up on me?

No.

It's okay. Everyone has.

Hey, fuck you. I ask you because I haven't given up on you.

I'm supporting you.

You want a way out. You want to stop the pain.

It's the only way.

I'm the person who is always here.

So don't you dare.

Okay. Okay. I'm sorry.

It's just that, well...

The floor is finished.

I'm ready.

You're going to do it?

Everything is in place.

Where?

It's best that I don't say.

It's happening.

It is. I want this.

I love you, you know.

I know.

SUICIDE **THURSDAY**

I'm dreading hearing Sam's pontificating already, and I've only just passed reception, Jackie is halfway through her *early grey* and Mike will be asleep until the snooze tune kicks in. We switch ourselves to automatic in preparation for another routine weekday cycle.

But today will be different from any other weekday.

It's Suicide Thursday.

Sam has already been here for ninety minutes. I'm sure I'll find out at some point this morning what catastrophe ensued within the Jordane household to prompt another pre-breakfast exit. Maybe his kids set fire to the dog.

I grunt something that sounds vaguely like 'good morning' but his head remains behind the monitor, his eyes fixed to the screen. He doesn't even have the courtesy to ask how I am feeling after my day off sick.

I drop heavily into my chair and turn on my PC. It starts up with a loud whir of the revolving hard-drive to let me know that I am now in a place of work. I slump into the seat, put my right hand on the mouse and wait patiently for a screen to appear asking me to enter my password.

It takes a little longer than usual this morning.

'Wow, Sam, my computer is running like a dog.'

No response.

I type in my password – DoTrueIsHell – and wait for all the programs to click into place. It shows just how important my role is here at DoTrue when I open my inbox to find a puny twelve unopened emails from my impromptu day off yesterday. Four of these are from Sam, too, who appeared to be posting a running commentary updating me throughout the day on his activity.

Hi Eli, just spoke to you on the phone, looks like you won't be in today due to illness. I'll take care of the back-to-school campaign and fill you in on any major events on your return.
Kind Regards,
Sam.

He sent that at 9:03.

What does he actually do?

It takes me less than eight minutes to weave my way through the myriad of worthless droning prose that Sam sent me while I was off, and I delete, unread, the two emails advertising cheap Viagra. Another tells me I have won a lottery that I never bought a ticket for; and another is from an African man who wants my bank details so that he can put $30,000,000 into my account until he gets over to this country. I delete both.

With that covered, I need to make myself busy, but, just as I am about to get a cup of coffee to kill some time, Danny walks over to Sam and makes him feel worthwhile. He leans down to him in his seat like a teacher or parent. 'Sam, can you round everybody up and get them into the boardroom? I need to make an announcement.'

It will be a real pick-me-up if he is leaving the company.

'No problem, Danny. I'll sort that now.' I wait. I know what's coming. 'Eli, can you make your way to the boardroom now, please? We have a meeting with Danny.'

I sit directly opposite Sam – our desks face each other; they touch – so I hear their conversation in its entirety, but it's another excuse for him to exert some authority over me, and if that's what he needs to get him through the day then I can just about live with that.

I watch him scurry around the office like a child with ADHD on a sugar high, bolting from person to person, from drone to drone, from robot to robot, from corpse to corpse. I see the procession of zombified graduates snail towards the boardroom while I have an existential debate with the coffee I have just poured to take into the meeting.

Sam will be last into the room. He always is. That way he can make an entrance. That way people will think he must have been doing something important.

He comes in late, of course, and exchanges a glance with Danny, who has taken his seat at the helm of the boardroom table.

'Thanks, Sam,' says Danny, fuelling Sam's ego even further. Sam smirks at me when he sits down to let me know that he is still the favourite. In forty-five minutes he will still be asking pointless questions and agreeing with every pathetic little yarn that escapes Danny Elwes' lips, while I will be quietly wishing my life away and envying the existence of a dung beetle.

I couldn't tell you what the meeting is about because I switch off from it entirely, instead deciding to utilise my time to formulate possible plots to include in my next first chapter.

Something is said about the company being in trouble in the UK. Something about margins. Something else that I don't really hear or care about. Something about getting up and leaving now with 'no hard feelings' if you don't believe you have the passion for the company and its product.

In my head, I run a daydream of exactly how I want to act to that offer and maybe how I should act. It's the best I can do right now because I'm too lazy to actually do something about it myself, of my own accord. Besides, when I do decide to leave, I want there to be a lot of hard feelings. A plethora of ill emotion. I want them to curse the day they ever hired Eli Hagin.

Maybe next week.

Our less-than-inspirational meeting leaves me feeling discouraged about my own part in this pan-European price-driven market and how my contribution, no matter how small, helps to perpetuate the stranglehold that organisations like DoTrue have over consumers. And that's when Danny talks to me.

'Eli, can I have a word?' I wonder whether Sam has said something about me calling in sick and now I'm in trouble. Maybe he'll sack me so that I don't have to think of a way to end the contract myself.

Everyone else leaves the room, including Sam, who manages to give one nervous look back before exiting.

'Hi, Eli, everything okay?'

I'm not really sure how to respond. ' Yes. Er ... fine.' I shrug my shoulders a little to appear more matter-of-fact.

'Well, I've been talking to Sam.' My shoulders tighten. 'He says that you have really had a huge amount of input on the "back to school" campaign and have risen to the challenge that such a difficult project can bring. I'd like you to work a little closer with Sam over the next six weeks on a retail project that will go live over Christmas.' This is worse than being told that I'm sacked.

'Oh, right. Er ... thanks, Danny.' This comes across as more of a question than gratitude.

'Good. Good. Now, don't let me down.'

This really is a kick in the face for me. What do I have to do to just be left alone? Jackie and Mike will laugh about this for hours when I tell them. Except I won't be able to tell Mike because he'll be dead before the early-evening news.

I leave and head straight to the kitchen for another coffee. This is one of my worst fears realised. Moving up within a company turns my position into something that vaguely resembles the beginning of a career rather than a stopgap job, and that scares me. What if I start to actually care about what I'm doing? What if they offer me more money?

Mum always said 'once you work for the money, you can never not work for the money'. She's right. She always was. If I do well, there is a chance that I may become accustomed to a certain standard of living, which will make it harder to quit this place and it's difficult enough for me to do that already.

This is a clearly deranged way of looking at the situation, but nonetheless, I conclude that the only way out is to do my job badly. That way, this kind of 'opportunity' won't arise again. Granted I formulated this plan in the twenty-one seconds that it took for the espresso to fall into my polystyrene demitasse cup, but it's the best and only strategy that I have right now.

I return to my desk, and Sam is busy typing away – he's worked in the industry forever but can still only manage to type using the forefinger of each hand. He is unbelievably slow and hits the keys as hard as you would have to on a typewriter.

Still watching his hands hammer the keyboard, we begin the day as normal.

'Soooooooooooo, do anything good last night?' Surely he's not trying to catch me out. He knows I was off ill yesterday. Obviously I can't tell him that I lost my keys otherwise he'll know I was out of the house.

'Not really, Sam. I was ill, so just lying around. Sleeping. You know?' I think I answer him in a sufficient timescale so as not to arouse any suspicion.

'Yes, of course. I hope it isn't what Charlie has.' Charlie is one of his sons. 'He's had it coming out of both ends.' I can already tell that this is a mess that he has left his wife to clear up, and I'm worried at how graphic this pithy story is going to get.

'Sounds terrible. I think mine was just some twenty-four-hour thing. It doesn't sound the same.' Please let that be the end.

'Yes, last night he threw up at dinner. We were having tuna pie. It went everywhere. I couldn't tell if the corn in my pie was actually corn or he'd hit my plate.' Oh God, Sam, no more, please. 'To make things worse, he woke up at 4:27 crying after finding that he'd shit the bed.' Surely the poor kid would be embarrassed if he knew that his father was bad-mouthing him like this. 'I'll be lucky if I don't get it now. Maybe I'll need a day off too this week.'

He laughs, believing that there is some molecule of comedic merit to his statement and that he has made a subtle comment regarding my time off yesterday. Sadly, Sam himself is the joke. He will never have a day off sick. He could be diagnosed with a rare form of cancer that can only be treated effectively by staying at home and showing your family that you love them and he would still come in to DoTrue. He could have a gangrenous appendage that required amputation and he would still schedule a suitable time for the operation that did not interfere with his marketing assignments.

This is his life.

And I won't let it be mine.

The rest of the day is filled with nothingness. Sam tells me to look through the previous festive-period campaigns to familiarise myself with style and content. I make this activity last for the entire day, feigning enthusiasm and marvelling at Sam's inefficiency as my apparent mentor.

21, 20, 19...

'How are you finding the previous articles?' What a time to ask me a work-related question. He's doing it on purpose.

'Yeah, great. I'd like to see more when I come in tomorrow morning. Just to get a more informed perspective.'

9, 8, 7...

He bought it.

'I'll hunt out a few more for you.' He smiles. I stand up ready to leave on the dot.

2, 1...

My breath smells like coffee and, in my haste, I have forgotten the mints in my top drawer, but I make my usual bus in time. It's as silent as ever on my multi-cultural, double-decker think-tank, and that's just what I need.

I arrive home to the sound of Kirsty McColl, turn Jackie's key and enter my therapist's office. I'm not going to write tonight, I'm not in the right place mentally, so I choose strict analysis over creative freedom.

MIKE

Jackie has left work and is making her way to Mike's for what she hopes will be the last time she breaks things off with him. Mike has left his front door ajar so that she can walk straight in. He drinks some more whisky, grabs two shards of mirror, sits down on his polished floor against his used-to-be-pea-green sofa and takes a deep, brave inhalation.

FAKE **THERAPY**

I'm not here.

I have an appointment.

Like I do every Thursday. And just because it's Suicide Thursday this week, that doesn't mean I can miss therapy.

I pull the chair from beneath my desk in the first-chapter library and move it to a position where it can face the couch – my £2000 black, leather, archetypal therapist's couch. It's on a slight angle, a classic psychoanalyst's trick to avoid eye contact, allowing me to overcome any inhibitions I may have. I place the Dictaphone on the seat, lie back and wait for the first question.

This is always the toughest part.

Today there is just silence. And that forces me to talk first.

About work, about Mike, about Jackie, about my writing, but not, as any normal therapist able to take corporeal form would want, about Mum. I'm not ready to talk about Mum just yet.

```
     ELI
Work is still getting me down. I just feel that I'm
not achieving anything of worth, you know? That what
I'm doing just doesn't matter.
```

She's heard all this before. It's symptomatic of the early stages of each session. I speak superficially, regurgitating the same old fables, then we move on to views concerning those who are actually close to me, which basically incorporates Mike and Jackie. I try to justify my feelings of dismay towards Jackie but I'm always corrected and convinced that I am still in love with her. Then, finally, we try to uncover the subconscious elements of my psyche and work on rehabilitation of the mind, but that is always when the session ends, time runs out and I'm forced to wait another week just to repeat the very same futile process.

But I do find this helpful. There are no interruptions. Nobody ever talks over you because they believe their own problems are far more interesting to discuss. It's like real therapy, only better, because I have admitted there are issues myself and I am attempting to rectify them of my own volition.

That's got to be healthy. Surely.

I speak first.

> ELI
> My colleague is the most pathetic man I have ever seen but in a way I'm glad he is there. Not for companionship; he doesn't act as a parental figure either. He reminds me every day that I will end up the same as him if I give up. He is the constant figure of failure and disappointment, the living embodiment of everything I stand against, a man so empty of substance that the only thing in his life that holds any weight is his own deluded view of self-importance. My pity for him acts as a stimulus to ensure I refrain from ever caring about a career in marketing or what Danny Elwes might think of me. I suppose that's pretty reassuring on a day-to-day basis.
> FAKE THERAPIST
> Mm-hmm.

(She writes a note then clicks her pen twice.)

> ELI
> I have been practising that little speech all day in my head so that I could deliver it correctly in this session.

I know. Not so healthy.

The phone rings.

I ignore it.

It can't be anyone who knows me otherwise they would realise that I'm not here.

I have an appointment.

Like I do every Thursday. And just because it's Suicide Thursday this week, that doesn't mean I can interrupt therapy.

    ELI

I'm almost certain that Jackie is cheating on me.

(He waits for a response.)

    ELI (CONT'D)

We all went out a couple of nights ago. To The Scam. It was awkward at first, with Jackie, but ended up being really enjoyable, and it was great to see Mike so … well … together. You know?

(The fake therapist nods to signify that she knows.)

    ELI (CONT'D)

Jackie left early saying that she had to go and lie down, but I'm thinking that she didn't mean on her own. Now, when I get home I find my mobile has a text message. I didn't take it out because everyone I wanted to speak to was with me that night. And so was Jackie.

(He laughs. His therapist does not react.)

    ELI (CONT'D)

Well, let's just say that the message suggested a meeting that night and her waiting somewhere. It was only sent a few minutes before I returned home. Obviously an indication of her guilt. She was

thinking of me and how what she was planning to do
would affect me and how wrong she was being toward,
that's right, me. So, with thoughts of me
monopolising her brain, she mistakenly sends the
message to the wrong person. She doesn't realise,
though, because I haven't mentioned it and her ill-
fated suitor turned up shortly after the message was
sent.

(Silence. The phone rings thirty-seven times before
it stops. They watch and wait.)

    ELI (CONT'D)
Where was I? Yes. So, I'm fairly sure she has been
unfaithful.
    FAKE THERAPIST
And … how does this make you feel?

(Eli tries not to roll his eyes.)

    ELI
Well, obviously I feel…

I don't really know what I should be feeling. I suppose, in a way,
I'm glad. It will certainly give me a real reason to break up with her
on Friday, or maybe sooner. But that's not what my therapist wants
to hear.

I tell her that I feel hurt and betrayed. That Jackie is the one person
I'm supposed to be able to trust. She let me down. Blah, blah. It's
irreparable if it's true. Yada, yada. That should do it. Show that I do
care about her but also give just enough information to reinforce that
I have a valid reason to end it next week, or sooner.

I'm the good guy.

This goes on. I've managed to open up about the infidelity, and that paints me as a willing subject. I've deconstructed the mundane activities of my common day and reduced them to pop-psychological Western wish-wash. I've even feigned optimism for my own imminent destiny; all this without even mentioning Mum.

As any decent therapist would, mine picks up on this. She always does.

```
    FAKE THERAPIST
How would your mother feel about your decision to
end things with Jackie?
    ELI
She's dead.
```

(He cuts her off. They stare at one another.)

They always want to discuss your childhood or your parents or your dreams or evaluate your emotional functioning with a Rorschach test or plot you on some continuum where one end is Buddhist and the other Ted Bundy.

I've encountered this with my current therapist and others in the past.

A quiet ensues, but my moment of reflection is disrupted by the echoing chime of my replica 1950s telephone. I remain as calm as I can, sit up gracefully, lean over to turn the tape recorder off, get to my feet and stroll over to the inanimate object that is causing me so much grievance. I then proceed to pull both the telephone line and the plug out of the wall in one aggressive swoop, wrap the wire around the body, trapping the receiver in the knot, then punch the plastic five times, walk over to the bin and throw the phone into the rubbish bag with some scrap paper that never made it to a finished first chapter.

With that done, I regress back to pacifism and redress the first-chapter library so that it vaguely resembles my therapist's office again.

Lying down on the couch once more, I momentarily forget what we were discussing. Nietzsche would say 'the existence of forgetting has never been proved; we only know that some things don't come to mind when we want them to'. I'll have to say that, on this occasion, a certain thing didn't come to mind because I *didn't* want it to.

Really, nothing has been achieved in this session and I begin to wonder whether this is actually working.

Not enough to make me speak anyway.

I take the recorder off the chair, lie down on my couch so that the back of my head is resting where I should be sitting and my legs dangle over the arm, which is a lot higher than my head. I will get a pins-and-needles sensation in both calf muscles when I finally get up.

With the recorder balancing on my chest I drift towards sleep. Whole metres of tape are eaten by the diegesis of my street: the traffic, children joking, money rattling against plastic as someone collects for another unheard-of charity, and the semi-constant spray of the steam wand in Gaucho's next door.

The timer on the heating clicks into place and heightens the scent of pretzels, which I find truly comforting but, instead of completely succumbing to my idleness and adopting a foetal pose, I decide to rectify my recent actions.

I don't need to say anything to her now. This is all she needs to see.

With the tape recorder back on her seat, I raid the bin for my phone. I unwrap the tight wire of hatred and place it back on the desk. As I plug the connector back into its socket, a spark ignites a vibration in the headset and the phone starts to ring again. It's as if it has been left ringing since I wrenched it out of the wall, strangled it with its own limbs and abandoned it into a stainless-steel sarcophagus.

I snatch the receiver and shout, 'WHAT?' A short moment of peace, then a sniff, then a woman's voice.

'Where the fuck have you been?' She dribbles the words out in what sound like a drunken gargle.

'Hello?' I can't decipher through the tears.

'He's fucking dead.'

What?

'You arsehole. Mike ... He's fucking dead.'

Jackie hangs up on me now that she has delicately broken the horrific life-altering news. I place the receiver down calmly this time and finally press stop on the recorder. My session is finished.

And so is Mike.

But for some reason, and not through any altruism on my part, the person I feel most sorry for is Jackie.

FRIDAY
(THE DAY AFTER SUICIDE THURSDAY)

'I'm sorry to hear that, Eli, but you are going to have to clear this with Danny.'

Apparently, as this is not an instance involving an immediate family member, Sam has no jurisdiction signing a couple of days off for me. It's Friday, the Friday after Suicide Thursday, no less, and I am exhausted. I've been standing in a damp jail cell for part of the night; before that I almost fell back in love with a woman I have been trying to break up with for the last third of our relationship, and this all took place after a truly agonising day in the office that I desperately don't want to go back to today.

And sandwiched somewhere in the middle of these events was the elaborately inventive self-culling of my alleged best friend Mike.

The worst part of it isn't the decay of my relationship with Jackie or even the horrifying discovery of Mike's exsanguinated corpse; it's the realisation that I have to grovel to Danny for a couple of days off, at his discretion, so as not to hinder any further holiday entitlement.

I tell him that, since Mum died, Mike *is* my immediate family and I will need three days minimum and I need to help with funeral arrangements and I go on and on until he says yes.

So now it's like I owe him.

And I hate that.

The showers at Dachau in the early 1940s, perhaps, or a visit to a Cambodian optician in 1975, maybe a weekend babysitting Sam's hyperactive, ill-disciplined offspring: it's difficult to think of a worse place to be than in the debt of the young Mr Elwes.

I accept his offer of conditional kindness for now because I have too much to think about, and I'll deal with it properly next week when I'm feeling more self-destructive. This should peak around Wednesday.

Maybe Thursday.

I replace the phone receiver and lie back down in bed, staring at the ceiling. I didn't see Jackie after my visit to the police station so I spent the night alone. I do still live on my own and have done so for quite some time now, but the fact that I know I'll never see Mike again makes this place seem emptier somehow.

I flip the radio on and manage to catch the snooze tune. When Mark Knopfler starts drooling out the sublime 'Brothers in Arms', for just that short span of time Mike is with me.

And I don't feel so alone.

JACKIE

Jackie does.

Descartes is irritated by her suddenly increased tactility and incessant desire to be close to something living. He works his way through a gap in the window and sits outside, where his morning cannot be disturbed by drama and melancholy.

Jackie can't seem to stop crying: for how she treated Eli; for what she did to Mike; for how relieved she feels, and for how guilty she is about feeling such relief.

Her eyes are red and bloodshot but she may as well be crying grains of sand because the noise and emotion is apparent even if the tears are non-existent.

All cried out.

She runs herself a bath.

This is Jackie's first day off work since Eli's mother died.

FRIDAY
(THE DAY AFTER SUICIDE THURSDAY)

It's difficult to know what to do with myself. Before this happened, at least I had a museum to visit or a coffee shop to dwell in. Right now all I have is an image of Mike. Not the picture of him shrivelled and bloodless, hands in legs, but how he was only two nights ago at The Scam. He even demonstrated some kind of ambition then.

I think about the time I first met Mike.

I can't quite figure out the point at which his decline may have started.

JACKIE

Jackie's head is pounding from some fairly expensive wine that she consumed last night, and her own misery over Mike's suicide only exacerbates this. In her hungover state, the sound of the water running into the bath is like an elephant stampede across her laminate-wood living-room floor, and the heat from the water steams her face until she feels on the brink of explosion. She feels stressed. Weighted. She thinks this will eventually relax her.

But, first, she needs to know what it's like to burn.

She wipes the sweat and tears from her face with a hand towel and moves the water in the bath back and forth with the swish of her hand to create waves and test the water. The motion appears to cool the bath but realistically it is only that her hand is now used to the temperature. She de-robes and lifts her right foot into the tub, sinking it up to the ankle. The water is excruciatingly hot and she can only hold it under for a few seconds before taking it out.

As if she needs a stimulus to feel real pain.

It's not even that she is numb, it's that she can't get past the pressure. The crush of knowing what she has done. Mike is dead. Eli doesn't have to ever know what happened. But Jackie knows. She will always know. And there is no way to relieve that burden. But, maybe, she can trick herself into feeling something else.

She repeats the process with the left foot. Doing this twice with each foot has the same effect as the waves did on her hand. She stands in the bath with the water almost to her knees, burning the skin above the ankles slightly. Gently, she lowers herself into the water, steadying herself with her hands on the side of the bath and supporting her entire weight on them.

It hurts her legs but she continues. The temperature has the greatest sensitivity on her most private of areas, but the sensation is equal levels of pleasure and pain. Once her stomach is under the water she takes the weight off her hands and slides down to cover her breasts. The heat makes it difficult for her to take deep breaths at first but, once immersed, she lies there until the water eventually turns cold.

Jackie knows that she wants to feel something, she just doesn't know what it is.

FRIDAY
(THE DAY AFTER SUICIDE THURSDAY)

I lie in bed with thoughts of Mike raging through my mind. My laptop is switched on and perched on the bed next to me, where Jackie would be lying had she stayed the night with me. I move the cursor over to my documents folder and open a file entitled 'Beach '04', which contains photographs of me, Mike and Jackie in Bournemouth from a few years back. We look like a small gang of beaming delinquents, living life and enjoying the sunshine and each other's company. I pause when I come to a photo that Jackie took of us posing behind a painting of a lifeguard carrying a woman to safety; it had two holes where their faces should be, and Mike and I filled these with our own heads. As pathetic as it was, we both found it hysterical.

I try to remember the last time it was like that.

JACKIE

Jackie wakes suddenly to the bang of Descartes flying back into the flat through the open window. Sitting up in her now-cold bath she notices her wrinkled skin and sighs. The sleep has left her feeling refreshed.

'Descartes,' she calls.

He languidly plods to the bathroom doorway and gives Jackie a look that says *don't treat me like a dog*. Then he leaves, turning his back and lifting his tail to show his disrespect. He jumps onto the sofa to relax as another act of disobedience.

Jackie feels slightly rejected and slumps back into the cold filth she has been stewing in for over an hour.

FRIDAY
(THE DAY AFTER SUICIDE THURSDAY)

I'm still in bed and have run out of photos to look at. I've been scouring them chronologically over a four-year period, trying to determine a change in mood, but Mike, unlike me, always manages to look great in photographs, whereas my smile always seems fake and the bags under my eyes tend to be the focal point. I feel like I'm missing a clue.

After realising that Mike left no suicide note, I decide to check my emails. I hope that I might find an explanation somewhere, but there is nothing new apart from my credit-card statement. Of course there wouldn't be. Mike's demise was anything but conventional.

So I think about what I might say at the funeral if asked to speak. Something Mike would like.

MIKE

Mike doesn't care.

Mike is dead.

Eli could stand in front of Mike's family and friends and blame them all. He could call them names. He could insult them. He could hire a group of morris dancers to shake their bells around Mike's coffin. He could learn a song on the piano. He could recite some meaningful poetry or spit out a limerick.

'There was a young woman from Hever, who could pick up a pencil with her...'

It doesn't matter.

He could put on a Scottish accent and recreate the Auden speech from *Four Weddings and a Funeral*. Sure, nobody there would know why he did it, but Mike will not be affected.

Because there's nothing he wants from a speech at his funeral.

All he wanted was not to feel that pain every day. He just wanted not to be alive with the torment of existence. He longed for self-worth. He craved direction. And love. And to feel content with himself for a moment.

Not once did Mike consider what Eli would say at his funeral.

That wasn't important to him in any way.

So, Eli can do what he wants. He probably will, anyway. Make it about him, somehow.

Mike isn't thinking this. He's not bitter. He's not angry at Eli.

He's just dead.

He always thought that everybody would be better off without him. And maybe they will. But he won't know. Because he's gone. And that's what he wanted most.

JACKIE

Jackie is forlorn. She wonders whether going to work would have been the best thing after all, to keep her mind occupied. She's cried as much as she can over Mike today and is now lost as to what to do. At least when Eli's Mum died she could aim her attention at him to feel useful, but with Mike's death she feels as though she is suffering more than anyone.

And she's probably right.

Nevertheless, it makes her remember Eli's mother. They had a great, albeit short-lived relationship – she got ill about a year after Jackie and Eli had been together – and it brings a smile to her face to think back to some of the more embarrassing stories she would tell. The memory inspires her, finally, to give up her affectionate advances towards her weary domesticated feline and head for her wardrobe to find a suitable outfit to go and visit Jesus. Her other dead boyfriend.

FRIDAY
(THE DAY AFTER SUICIDE THURSDAY)

I haven't been to Mum's grave since we put her in the ground. I'm still not satisfied with the way she just seemed to give up. She was out of fight. As if there was nothing or no one else to consider. She said the chemo just made her feel worse; sick and tired. I told her it must be better than dying but clearly she disagreed.

She let herself die. That's the same as killing yourself, surely.

This Thursday, before Mike's funeral, a week after Suicide Thursday, four years after Let-Yourself-Die Sunday, will be the first time I have seen her since I threw a handful of mud at her tiny ivory coffin.

The crash of the letterbox jolts me back to the present as one of the Teds drops a card through to console me for my loss, but I can't force myself out of bed to retrieve it. The bed is safe. Nothing awful can happen if I just stay here for the day, wallowing in my own self-pity.

All I want is some time alone to regroup. To think about Mike and wonder what Jackie is doing but, for some reason, I start to think of the best layout for the back-to-school campaign I have been working on for DoTrue.

JACKIE

Mike wanted to die.

That's what Jackie tells herself.

It wasn't her fault.

He'd been planning it.

All those other times, he was half-arsing it. Crying for help, people would say. But it wasn't that, it was just a lack of commitment.

The floor polishing, the sanding and staining and buffing, and then the mirror, and the hands in legs, that is not impulsive. That is not someone reacting badly to a break-up and deciding, in that moment, that life was not worth living. Whatever had happened between them, Mike was going to kill himself.

Jackie reassures herself.

The first time he tried to do it, neither her nor Eli really understood it. They hadn't seen it coming. They were best friends. Three musketeers. Eli took it the worst. Blamed himself. Couldn't write for months. Then he got angry with Mike. They got through it. And, when Mike did it again, they understood a little more. They supported him. Sat with him in hospital.

Somehow, it brought them closer.

And the opposite happened to Eli. He hit a purple patch. Pages of work. Artistically, he flourished. Maybe because he was more open, emotionally.

This was planned.

Written in the stars.

Nothing to do with what Jackie did or said.

She stands outside the church, looking through the doorway. Another day in that booth, pouring part of her heart out to her priest, reserving the really bad stuff for her cat. She didn't want to do it. What would she even say? She has nothing to feel guilty about. Mike wanted it. He wanted his pain to end. He wanted to leave everything behind. The people he loved, the home he had painstakingly decorated, the family who had always worried about him.

She cries. The silent kind. The tears just fall. Her expression doesn't even change. She didn't think there was anything left.

Jackie is sad. She misses Mike already. But she doesn't feel guilty. So she keeps on walking, hitting the high street and browsing the windows and clothes rails for something new.

Mike is dead. His life is over. It doesn't mean that Jackie has to stop living. She needs to grieve properly, but not today. It's her anniversary with Eli. They should be together. They should find a way to celebrate their love, even through this. She can't let Mike ruin it.

He wanted to die.

He got what he wanted.

And, as hard as it seems, perhaps the weight of Mike's friendship will lift from their shoulders and allow Eli and Jackie some respite, more time for one another.

Mike's death is significant, of course. Epic, even. But Jackie won't allow it to kill her relationship with Eli or his relationship with his words. Mike has found an end but, for Jackie and Eli, it can't be. At most, the emotional chaos that will undoubtedly ensue must be seen as nothing more than a stumbling block on their path. A tragic but inevitable complication.

FRIDAY
(THE DAY AFTER SUICIDE THURSDAY)

This is so fucked up. Our best friend killed himself yesterday, and we have kept our reservation at À La Gare.

But, if it's still the plan, then I'm still on plan.

Of course, it doesn't go that way.

It can't.

I am supposed to be breaking up with Jackie after this course and finally drawing a line under this charade. But now I'm drunk, which means that I will inevitably mess this up somewhere along the line.

How did I get back to this place? Am I my own complication?

I picked Jackie up in a cab about an hour before we were due to eat because she said she wanted to go for a drink before the meal. I can't personally understand this. If we are going to a place that serves us food and drink, is it not more efficient to do it all at the same venue? Still, I oblige. This is her anniversary, her last supper – with me, anyway.

She ordered a Pinot Gris and explained to me that it is essentially the same as a Pinot Grigio. Either way, her choice of aperitif signals to me that I could almost definitely indulge in sexual relations with her at the end of the evening, and, as it is a celebration, maybe experiment with something a little more risqué. If that was what she wanted.

I ordered a Brazilian bottled beer that astoundingly cost more than a pint of lager. It arrives with a wedge of citrus crammed into the top of the bottle. I'm not sure that this is necessary as Jackie explains that the function of this is really to keep flies away from your drink – a problem that is prevalent in South America but probably not in London, on an autumn evening surrounded by pollution that should act as a barrier to a majority of wildlife.

I think Jackie is nervous. It does feel awkward to be out so soon after Mike's death. But I don't know where all these facts are coming from this evening; it's like being on a date with Google.

We take a seat in a shadowed booth. Jackie with a bottle of wine in an iced bucket and a solitary glass, me with an overpriced *cerveza* that is blocked by an oversized lime. It's almost as if the dark wood of the pews in this secluded, shadowy corner vestibule have calmed Jackie down. She feels more comfortable in this environment.

So tranquil in fact, that she forgets why we are here and brings up Mike.

'Look, Eli, it was really tough yesterday.' I throw her a look. 'I just wanted us to do our own toast to Mike.'

'Jack-eeeeee.' I elongate the *ie* to *eeeee* to show her that I am not impressed by this comment.

'I know. Tonight is supposed to be solely about us. I just wanted to say one last thing and now we can concentrate on us and enjoy the remainder of the evening.'

For a split second I picture something sexually exotic that we have never done before.

It's the little things with Jackie. These tiny sentiments that don't mean anything to anyone really, but she has to do them because it makes a huge difference to her, I find them so endearing. It makes me wonder whether I'm doing the right thing here.

My first mistake of the night is to aid in the consumption of the Pinot Gris or Grigio, I forget which one it is, but apparently that doesn't matter anyway. We leave and walk the rest of the distance to À La Gare. Jackie has no idea where we are going; this is my first surprise of the night, but as we draw closer she realises exactly where I have booked. Immediately embracing me, she kisses me flush on the lips in four quick successive movements to convey her excitement. She then tells me I am 'soooooooo sweet' and that she loves me.

And it feels great.

Oh, God. Why does it feel so great?

I am instantly intimidated by the place. In the same way that I hate going to a 'proper hairdresser', I just don't feel that I belong. I'm getting really paranoid that everyone is staring at me, and even my waiter looks me up and down as if I'm not good enough. I would glean less attention had I arrived giving a bloated Elvis impersonator a piggy-back.

So, when we are seated and the waiter asks me if I want to see the wine list, I take a short glance at it and order a £350 bottle of Champagne as if money is of no consequence. Jackie knows how expensive it is, even though it is one of those restaurants where only the man has a price on his menu. She probably even knows the grape variety and is prepared for the delicate notes that will undoubtedly compliment the sea bass – £34.95. Her level of joviality is heightened to a new level.

This makes me more anxious. She has no idea what I am going to say to her before dessert. And neither do I.

We talk; as couples do, I suppose. Mainly reminiscing over the times spent together over the last six years and, don't get me wrong, there have been some great times. Like the time we went to Rome and I got my pocket picked by a vagrant at the Colosseum. This directly affected my entry into St Peter's because I was wearing shorts and had to have my legs covered. With very little money left the only thing I could afford was a pair of women's leggings, which we bought and I wore because Jackie didn't want to miss this opportunity to see that ceiling.

You'd have thought she would have known about this custom, being a religious lady and knowing that we were going to the epicentre of her chosen faith.

But at the time I thought it was funny and I did it because I loved her and didn't want to ruin anything for her.

It hasn't been like that for a long time.

I question whether my plan is the right thing to do tonight. Am I wrong? Could we feel this way again? Is nostalgia a bogus remedy?

Should I make huge decisions while grieving?

Maybe it's just my third glass of Dom Perignon but now I wonder whether what we have is some kind of sibling devotion and that's why we can't be apart.

I just have to keep telling myself what I know is true in my head, that I don't like Jackie, that I find her manipulative, merciless and governed by self-interest.

Is that really true?

Although only my menu has an indication of price, Jackie manages to select the most expensive main course – the sea bass. Of course, when our waiter suggests a delicate Italian Pinot Bianco as the perfect accompaniment for this course, I agree to add this to our ever-growing collection of liquid depressants without batting an eyelid. I start to wonder whether Pinot is the wine word for expensive. I don't want to ask, though, because she probably knows the right answer.

Her starter is fairly modest for a decent helping of king prawns in some kind of garlic, chilli and tomato sauce. She has already decided on dessert even though she doesn't have to; a lemon soufflé that you have to order fifty-five minutes in advance. Well, she can wait on her own for that.

We get through the meal and order something to raise our blood-sugar levels and break the lethargy of a post-meal comedown. I think to myself that ideally I will be back at home when Jackie's arrives in just under an hour. She should be left here, sat alone and unloved while tears of isolation spiral down her lush cheeks and drip onto her dessert, dissolving the icing sugar on top of the soufflé.

I'm going to hell for this. It's got to be better than where I am now, I suppose.

'Eli?' She makes my name last a little longer than usual to let me know something is on the way. 'I've been thinking...'

'Yes.' She pauses, I take a quick swig of the wine, then grabs my hands tenderly across the table cloth and looks sweetly into my eyes.

'Thank you so much for this. I know that it has been a really hard time for you, for both of us, but the fact that you arranged all of this for us, well, I can't thank you enough.' This is either one of her beautifully pithy sentiments or yet another manipulation. And this is the difficulty with loving Jackie.

'It's no trouble, really.' I attempt a tone close to humble.

'Don't brush it off to be modest, Eli.' She starts rubbing the backs of my hands with her thumbs. 'It really shows me how much you care and that no matter what life throws at us we know that we'll always have each other.'

I feel like scum now. Is this real? Is she intoxicated? Is this fiction?

'Er ... well...'

And then our waiter unexpectedly appears next to our table, as if the restaurant is built on a labyrinth of waiter-sized meerkat tunnels with an exit at every table.

'Can I pour you some more wine?' Perfect timing. I could kiss him. But I won't. Instead, I allow him to fill our glasses again. I made the mistake of pouring my own top-up earlier and you would have thought I'd mugged his grandmother by the look he gave me.

I'm saved. For now. But it won't last long.

Either the bubbles from the extortionately priced Champagne, or the alcoholic content of the cocktails mixed with lager and a sweet after-dinner wine, are beginning to take effect on me. I sense the rise in my inebriation and am alerted to the fact that some basic motor skills are escaping me.

'The thing is, Jackie, there comes a time in every relationship when—' I'm interrupted once more.

'Was everything all right with your meals?' Oh, would you please just fuck off.

I hate the way that waiters and waitresses do this. I would say that on average we tip at about ten per cent in the UK. It's not as big a culture as it is across the Atlantic. Not for me. I start at eighteen per cent and knock off one per cent for every time someone asks if everything is okay – within reason. This essentially means that staff at TGI Friday's should give me back six per cent of my final bill for the amount of fake glee they dish out.

I don't make an issue out of it this time, though, because I am still trying to fit in.

'Yes. Everything was perfect, thank you.' I hope that deep down he can tell I would rather the Gestapo instruct me line up next to that pit rather than go through the ordeal of another arbitrary conversation passing as a less-than-amateur critique of modern French cuisine.

I down the remainder of my wine.

That was a mistake.

So I pour another. And I take a rather large gulp of that too.

It's all downhill from here.

'Where was I?' I'm slurring more now, but in an endearing way, I think.

'You were saying that there comes a time in every relationship...' She moves forwards on her seat a little as if she's anticipating something. She grips my hands a little tighter to remind me that we are still in contact. 'So, go on. There comes a time in every relationship...'

'Yes. There comes a time in every relationship when ... when the love you have for someone isn't the love you initially had when you first started out as a couple; it evolves into something else. Does that make sense?' Her eyes widen as if she understands my point. She is thinking of love transforming into adoration while I am reminiscing over love deforming into abhorrence. Her face lights up.

'I know exactly what you mean, Eli.' She doesn't.

She has no idea.

'Well, that is something that I have been thinking a lot about recently and not just because of Mike – since before that.' Before you slept with him. 'I just think that maybe we are at a stage now ... in our relationship ... we have been together for six years.'

I can't believe I am actually going to do this. Break up with my long-term girlfriend on our anniversary in a packed, fancy London restaurant, the day after our best friend killed himself. I can feel the tremors of excitement coursing through my body as I contemplate the exact words I am going to use to terminate this farce.

'I think that, in a way, our relationship has been building to this moment for far too long now, waiting for one of us to do something, so I'm just going to come out and say it.'

You're dumped, it's over, fuck off out of my life, drop dead, I never want to see you again, you treacherous two-timing whore, we're finished. Any of those would have done but, of course, that's not how it goes at all.

I take one last swig of Jackie's Pinot Bianco for a boost of courage and take a deep breath; I am suddenly more nervous than I have ever felt before. As I am about to let rip with my onslaught, Jackie distracts me with yet more hand rubbing and her foot even touches my leg, making me jump and knock some cutlery onto the floor.

The next part all happens very quickly.

I grunt at my own inadequacy and the interruption that killed my confidence. Sliding across my chair sideways I drop to the floor to pick up the cutlery. I find myself on my knees, dizzy and seeing everything in a blurred double, and Jackie doesn't want me to worry. She swivels her legs around so that they are free from the constraints of the table and looks down at me crawling about, fishing for knives and forks.

I don't know what I'm doing. I can't break up with her now. The opportunity has passed.

On my knees, I put the cutlery back on the table without looking at what I'm really doing, then, as I go to get up, Jackie's face comes into focus and she looks radiant. In a moment of lost time I find that I am still on the floor, looking up into Jackie's eyes, my hands holding hers, resting on her lap, the restaurant seems quiet and Jackie leans delicately down towards me and whispers.

'Go ahead.' It is fairly sultry and suggestive.

'Will you...' I don't actually get to finish this sentence but to be honest I'm not sure how it would have ended anyway. Will you help me up? Will you pass me a napkin? Will you please just leave me the hell alone? Will you tell me how I got back to this place?

'Of course I will.' She jumps down to my level and kisses me, and the restaurant is suddenly full of noise again and this is worse than last year and what have I just done?

Am I now engaged to someone I've been trying to break up with?

That was manipulation; leading the witness, and it has made it ultimately more arduous to put a stop to this relationship.

But, my God, she looks so happy.

I smile without thinking.

The thought of this impending misery should shock me back into sobriety but, instead, I'm pensive. I think about Mike and the evermore that is death and I wonder whether it is less painful than a lifetime of monogamy.

Which one feels more like eternity?

What hurts the most?

Before I can fathom an answer, the soufflé arrives. The waiter gives us two spoons because, apparently, Jackie and I share everything now.

How am I going to end things now? I haven't even given myself time to breathe. Where will I get the strength to quit my awful, demoralising job? Am I writing about the wrong things, is that why I can't get past a first chapter? How am I supposed to finish all the important things when I can't even get through my half of the dessert?

Jackie is going to want to go back and celebrate. I guess if I am going to fake real life for a while, then I should probably make my fiction more real.

WEEK TWO

FIELDING
(WORKING TITLE)
BY ELI HAGIN

F I R S T **C H A P T E R**

She says they nearly called me Barley. Then she
laughs.

Cue sense of self-loathing.

Cue overwhelming feeling of inappropriateness.

My mother signs at a ferocious pace when excited.
I only manage to decipher the words 'writhing' and
'orgasm' before despair sets in. My father views her
every gesticulation with the same loving intensity
he showed her over thirty years ago.

I watch her hands: she says there was a light, and
then came the silence.

Cue drama.

Cue family tradition.

We go through the story of my miracle conception
every birthday, as if my parents' condition is not
a constant reminder.

Twenty-nine years ago my parents were the same love-
struck puppies they portray themselves as today. They
even look the same on the surface, though their bodies
are withering inside. A side effect of radiation they
say. Eternally youthful yet terminally troubled.

My father had finished playing an intimate set at
a folk club in Avebury and had taken my mother for
company. After the performance, a sell-out my father
assures me, they throw the guitar onto the back seat
and load the amp and cables into the boot before
setting off on their drive back to London.

Along one of the dark, spiralling roads that intersects nothing but crops and open land, my father's car splutters, jolting back and forth for several seconds before every light on the dashboard illuminates and the car rolls to a peaceful stop at the side of the road.

Cue my mother's ability to be irrational.

Cue panic manifesting itself as sexual tension.

After waiting for twenty or thirty minutes my father realises that the chances of a Good Samaritan passing them on this particular road at this late hour is minimal. In order to help my mother, he opens the boot and perches himself on the back bumper with his guitar and knocks out a melody in an attempt to quell her anxieties.

It works.

She grabs a tartan blanket from the boot and runs off towards a field of oil-seed rape.

It wasn't even barley. The name would have romanticised the situation somewhat.

My father follows her, leaving the boot open with the guitar on display to only the elements.

He chases her through the crop, which breaks like giant sticks of celery, leaving a path of destruction behind them, to a spot around two hundred yards in, where the blanket is laid down.

Most people can't imagine their parents being so frivolous and sexual but my parents have remained this way since that day. I know no different.

Mid-coitus my father notices a small light, not above him but coming towards him. This is the point that my mother signs 'writhing' and 'orgasm'.

This is the point before the *silence*.

To this day, neither of them could identify nor disclose what they saw that night. In the height of passion your judgement can be untrustworthy so they have never mentioned this to anyone but me.

As they lay there, my mother on her back with her legs wrapped around my father's torso, her heels digging into him like pincers, him pumping away in a press-up position resting his entire weight on his large, musical hands, the crops around them begin to fold down into a perfect circle. Outside the large circle are six smaller circles, which form the points of a geometrically perfect hexagon, and outside one of the smaller circles are three very small, randomly scattered circles.

Grapeshot, they call it.

The stalks lay down around my parents undamaged. Unlike the crop, which snapped and crunched under their footsteps on entry, the stems around them are bent, as if they have been heated to an extremely high temperature in a very short space of time. But my parents are not concerned with this. In fact, they do not notice at first.

My father has catapulted his seed into my mother, unknowingly sending some of his greatest swimmers on a journey that will result in the creation of another life.

An accident, they call it.

Not a mistake.

Basking in the afterglow, they stare up at the stars. It's May and good weather is on the way. There are no clouds to block the tiny flecks of white light, but the crickets do not croak, the planes do not roar, the wind does not howl.

My parents stand up to find themselves in the

centre of a crop circle that has formed around them. The engine doesn't purr, the birds do not sing, my parents do not hear.

Cue hysteria.

Cue silent wailing.

My mother always sheds a tear when she tells this story. She says that it was a gift. The situation gave them a child.

But it took away their hearing. So, whenever they look at me, they don't think about what they have gained, they think about what they have lost.

Mother hands me a gift that is quite clearly a book. It is meticulously wrapped in black paper with the words 'Happy Birthday' emblazoned on it in golden glitter. I find it hard to get in because she has used enough tape to cover every possible entry into the package. I bite the top and tear at the hole I have made.

It's not a book. It's an anthology of CDs in a presentation set that looks like a hardback book yet actually contains a decade of music and accompanying literature about the band. Steely Dan is the band. My father got me into them from an early age.

Cue memories of school teasing.

Cue foot tapping to a catchy jazz progression.

'Thanks, guys. This is great.' I speak the words while I sign. A habit I have so that I don't have to repeat myself if we have company.

It does mean a lot. I know that they have difficulty with the speed that technology moves in the current climate and CDs, DVDs, the internet, all carry a certain degree of mystery and trepidation for them. It's even more embarrassing

that they are approaching sixty, yet, due to the
event of my conception, have not aged a day in
twenty-nine years.

This time next year I will probably look older
than both my parents. People are already getting
suspicious and asking questions.

Olive oil, they say.

Plenty of sexual interaction they say.

They are still ageing inside though, so, as such,
tend to stay indoors the majority of the time now.
But they don't mind, as long as they are together.

The doorbell rings, but only I hear it.

'That'll be granddad,' I sign, standing up to
answer the door. They follow me.

I see his silhouette through the mottled glass of
the door. He's looking around for anything out of
place, as inquisitive as ever. It brings a smile to
my face.

I open the door to find him fingering one of the
bricks while balancing his weight on his walking
stick.

'Oooh,' he says. 'You frightened the life out of
me.' He has become accustomed to signing while he
speaks for the benefit of his deaf son and daughter-
in-law, but he can't manage it while standing up as
he needs one hand on his stick at all times. My
parents understand from his expressions most of the
time anyway.

'Happy birthday, old boy.' He hands me a card as
he hobbles in. No doubt it contains a twenty-pound
note. This is his usual offering for annual events.

'Thanks, Granddad. How are you?' I take his coat
off and hang it in the hallway while my father
despairs at my enquiry.

'Oh, don't get me started,' he replies, exhaling to signify his exhaustion with the modern world.

My mother quickly flaps her hands round in front of his face, asking if he would like a cup of tea.

'That will be lovely. Thanks, dear.' And he wanders over to my father's chair, continuing his story. 'Well, you know about my war with Tesco…'

Cue thirty minutes of your life passing by.

Cue passion against corporate hegemony.

He always starts his stories with such punctuating resonance but will undoubtedly recount several other irrelevant stories from bygone years, the nostalgia making him forget his original yarn. But that's why I am here. I pull him back into a linear narrative.

He tells a story of how they mis-priced some soup this week. How he always buys the chicken because the vegetable is two pence more but this week there was a sign saying that they were both the same price so he bought two of each. However, when he got to the counter they still charged him the extra two pence.

That's not right, they say.

They're not the same price, they say.

All Granddad hears is a spotty checkout girl calling him, a man who fought for his country, a liar.

He tells her there is a sign.

She calls him a liar.

He asks her to walk with him and check.

She calls over her manager.

So now he is riled that he has to repeat himself. He offers to walk the manager over to the sign. The manager obliges with a sense of indignation and powers ahead of the elderly man, who trails behind with his battered knees and walking aid. But when he rounds the corner, the store manager stands rigid in embarrassment with a fluorescent yellow sign in his hand that says something about price cuts.

Unapologetic, the manager whooshes past my grandfather without acknowledging him, goes to the till, takes out the four pence he owes and places it in my grandfather's hand, saying something like 'There you go.' Then he disappears among a sea of citrus and a miniature forest of broccoli.

His gripe is not that he is a pensioner that has been short-changed by four pence, it's that he worries about the amount of people that this happens to and the stack of four pences that a large corporation receives that 'it darn well shouldn't'. That one in every eight pounds spent in this country goes to one company. That just by getting the price of soup correct, it might only be one in every £7.98. That he might be able to make a difference.

That he actually cares.

Cue my father's rolling eyes.

Cue Mother's timely entrance with the tea.

I don't even have time to respond to his political tirade before he has moved on to yet another conversation.

'So, Oz,' that's my father's name, short for Oscar, 'Alan,' my dead uncle, 'Max,' my grandfather's dead dog, 'Grace,' my mother's name, 'oh,' he stutters. It can sometimes take a few attempts before he gets to the name he wants. I give him a clue.

'Ffffiieee,' I drawl out so as not to give

everything away and make him feel completely inadequate or worse, insane.

'Fielding. Fielding, my boy.'

My parents opted out of calling me Barley, mainly because I was conceived in a field of rape, so chose to romanticise their night of unbridled passion by referring to it as 'fielding' rather than fucking.

They fucked, therefore I am.

It's cute, they say.

Original, they say.

Cue more playground teasing.

'Fielding, my boy, how is the love life? You're not getting any younger.'

This is the part that I always hate. I have too much to live up to.

My grandparents were married for fifty-two years before my grandmother died. That was nine years ago. It is a great tale of spirit and triumph in a world of divorce, infidelity and man's alleged predisposition to procreate. He still kisses her picture goodbye every time he leaves the house and tells her that he loves and misses her. They were the poster couple for the perfect relationship and my parents have followed closely in their footsteps with their eternal honeymoon period.

I am slowly descending into the realm of *black sheep*. The disappointment.

Some say I'm looking for something that doesn't exist, but I see that it exists every single day. When my parents finally fall from this mortal coil, I have no doubt that a one-hundred-year spell of true love will perish with them.

The line stops here.

With me and my string of could've, should've, would've.

'Nothing to write home about.'

'But he is seeing someone,' my mother interjects with a frenetic flapping of fingers and thumbs.

'Yes, but it's early days yet.' I attempt to combat her enthusiasm with something close to *laissez-faire*.

'Well, I have some news myself.' Thank God for my grandfather's minuscule attention span. He already has another anecdote to share.

We are all sitting to attention now. My father even feigns interest on this occasion. My mother perches on the edge of the sofa with the steam from her tea slowly clouding her glasses as she takes a sip. I lean back in triumph that the focus has turned away from me.

My grandfather steadies himself, edging to the front of the couch. He stands his stick to one side, rubs his hands together and starts to sign to all of us without actually speaking the words.

'I've met someone.'

My parents clearly hear this like a foghorn.

What? They say.

Are you joking? They say.

It's true. He has met somebody at his retirement home and believes that she may be the woman he was supposed to spend his entire life with.

Cue stunned silence.

Cue my father's heart attack.

I wonder what my therapist will make of this new first chapter. My best friend dies and then I write something about two people who won't age, who will stay the same as they were in that one perfect moment where they conceived their child. A child who is forced to grow up, move on, go beyond a place the other two people in his life could ever have imagined.

And then there's that love-story element. Why did that come up? Apparently I'm engaged now. Secretly. It seems insensitive to share the news with anyone, on account of Mike's untimely yet deliberate demise.

The sex has been great all weekend. And it has certainly served as a welcome distraction to Suicide Thursday, but the plan was to end things with Jackie. Mike's death was showing me how to end things.

Quit my job.

Write a second chapter.

Get to the end of a book.

Dump Jackie.

I've screwed up that last one, it seems. At the very least, you'd think that Jackie would have broken it off with me when Mike had finished slashing at his thighs. She seems keener than ever.

The words are flowing, though. Not quite moving into second-chapter territory but I'm not short of ideas. Whether I'm drawing from reality or not, they're coming thick and fast. And I'll take that.

Maybe I should start with DoTrue. Rip the plaster off. Tell Danny Elwes to go and fuck himself. Slap some sense into Sam Jordane. Go out in a blaze of glory. Do something memorable. Leave a goddamned legacy of some kind.

I don't even get paid loads of money for my job. Is that all I'm worth? How much does it cost for someone to give up on their dreams? It must be different for everyone. The fact that I am still at that place means that for me, it wasn't much.

If I can somehow compartmentalise the horror and guilt surrounding Mike's death, if I can park the confusion I am feeling towards Jackie for a week, at least until Funeral Friday, perhaps I can focus on the anger I have with myself and with DoTrue.

Rage. It gets things done.

I'm not there, yet.

Still in the *denial* phase.

I'm pushing the printed version of Fielding into the first-chapter library when I hear Mike's voice.

THE **NOTE**

It doesn't make sense to people when you say that
you want to die. They don't believe it. How can you
feel that bad, right? What about all the things I
have? Friends, family, somebody to love, somebody
who loves me. I know that. I know all of that. But
I also know that you will all be better off without
me here. I'm a drain.
The only way I can stop the pain I feel each day
is to not exist.
I've tried the counselling. The drugs don't work.
I can't get level and stay there.
It hurts. It physically hurts me to be alive.
This is not about anybody but me.

If it doesn't make sense, it doesn't matter. This is how Mike felt.
This is what he believed. He believed it enough to do what he did.
He wasn't thinking about anybody else because he truly felt that they
would move on quickly. That it might not even affect them.

I don't have a choice anymore. The only way I can
make things better is to die. I can't get life
right. I need to get out but I don't know how. I
can't even do that properly.

Mike was in a state of despair. Disrepair. He had been trying for
so long to 'fix' himself that he became even more lost than when he
started. It got easier to give up on things.

There's very little food in the cupboards, no real
job, no prospects, so there's just no point. Having

```
a freshly polished floor isn't enough to keep me
going.
```

All true.

```
The messages didn't make me do it. I want to do it.
But I'm a coward. I need the strength, a push. Okay,
maybe they were the push. Today I have it. So it
has to be now. Otherwise I will back out again. Or
I will only half kill myself. Again. I know I should
be sorry. But I'm not. I'm just not. I want some
peace. I need it. I need the quiet.
```

Nothing is more damaging to a human being's sense of self-worth than a lack of identity. This can be taken from a person through abuse or neglect or failure or fear but, for Mike, there was none of that. This was just the way he felt. The way he had always felt.

```
I do love you all. Dad, Eli, Jackie, Ralph. You are
my friends, my family. But that is not enough. My
world is small and I still can't handle it. So, now
I have to sleep and hope that I never wake up again.
It's the only way I can rest. It's all the help I
will ever need.
```

And he doesn't say that he will see God or meet up with Jesus. He doesn't ask people to remember his qualities. The laughter. The fun. The positivity. The drinks at The Scam.

Because he doesn't ask for anything. He doesn't write a note to leave behind for his friends and family, to help them understand the intricacies of his state of mind. He doesn't give a reason. There is none of this insight into Mike. He doesn't feel like he owes anybody an explanation because he has been telling them how he feels for years. He slices the glass across his legs so that he can be in death the way he felt in life. Completely alone.

FUNERAL **FRIDAY**

I made a promise to Mike's dad.

He's such a sweet old guy and he has already had to suffer his wife leaving him after thirty-five years of marriage, and today he has to bury his only child. The wife part can, just about, be handled – and at least she has enough respect to turn up here alone today – but no parent should have to go through this.

And I'm not about to make it any easier.

Father Farrelly takes to the lectern as we all sit down after droning out another hymn for which nobody really knows the melody but which everyone somehow manages to muddle and moan our way through like good little pretend Christians. The Father says a few kind words about Mike, and the congregation responds accordingly with looks of recognition, nods of agreement or a politically correct laugh at the whimsical yarns shared by childhood friends.

He mentions some of Mike's failed home improvements, much to the pleasure of the crowd; it even brings a wry grin to his dad's dour face. But I can't help noticing that most of the sentiments he imparts, lifted directly from scripture, seem to be aimed directly at Jackie alone.

Then he introduces me.

'Now we shall have some words from Mike's closest friend, Eli, which he has prepared himself.'

I stand and everyone turns toward me. Jackie grabs my hand in support as I get up, and mouths 'be strong' at me before letting go.

God, she can be so patronising. I should try to remember that.

I mentally run through everything as I edge cautiously toward the lectern: Mike's memory, his father's wishes, Jackie's feelings, my job, my evening with Kate ... but I have to do this. For me and for Mike.

Of course, it's mainly for Mike, and, as his 'closest friend', surely I know what is best and what he would have wanted?

I step up to the lectern and open with some words to draw everyone's attention.

'Hi, everyone, thanks for coming today. I'm Eli Hagin, and Mike was my best friend. And, like all of you sitting here today, I wasn't there for Mike when he needed me the most.'

A silent gasp of discomfort washes over the congregation. I see them looking around at each other as if to say 'surely he doesn't mean me'. They know that I'm right, and now I have their undivided focus.

'I know why everyone is here today. It's for Mike. We want to commemorate Mike. We all know what a kind-spirited, benevolent guy he was.' I'm killing them with convention here. 'He'd always think how *his* actions would affect *you*. How he could somehow help anyone else before himself. It wasn't until the end that he finally did something for Mike.'

From my elevated position I look down at Mike's dad at this point, to reassure myself, and I can see that he is welling up. Whether this is due to feelings of aggression or disappointment towards me I just don't know. Perhaps he understands the truth in my words more than anyone else here. Or maybe, just maybe, he's a little upset that his only son hated life so much that he stabbed himself through the thighs and bled to death on his newly polished living-room floor and his bloodless corpse is lying in a wicker basket ten feet in front of him ready to be dropped into a hole in the ground for all eternity.

The coffin is apparently environmentally friendly and biodegrades at a faster rate. 'What Mike would have wanted,' everyone says.

I don't think any of these people knew him at all.

'Mike was great. He was my best friend in the world and I loved him. I loved the fact that he would stay at home during the day to find a cheaper way of shrink-wrapping things merely by using cling-film and a hair dryer' – they laugh – 'instead of going out and finding a job.' Only Jackie laughs at this point.

One of the reasons I first fell for Jackie was her wicked sense of humour. I glance towards her in gratitude, but Father Farrelly peers on in contempt.

'I loved the way that he would drop anything if he thought you needed him.' This is the part I'm most afraid of. This is how I truly feel about Mike but didn't realise until recently. 'The way that your problem was always his problem and he would do whatever it took to fix it. The fact that your goals in life were always more important to him than his own. I'm not sure that anyone here could honestly say they knew or had even asked what Mike's own ambitions were. He would make mix-CDs of songs that you might enjoy, or record a programme that you might find interesting, and even though you never returned the favour for him or bothered watching a four-hour Swedish documentary about Nazis, he didn't mind. If only we could all be so selfless.'

I know that these are really miniscule gestures in the grand scheme of the world, and I know that the loss of Mike isn't going to impact our planet in a cosmic sense, but the loss of *all* Mikes would surely make everyone sit up and listen or chaos would most certainly ensue.

I'm working myself into a state with the thoughts crowding into my head about Mike and the speech I am trying to deliver, and I have to take a long, deep breath otherwise I will cry.

I should have taken the drop of Rescue Remedy that Jackie offered me to remain calm.

Or I could have started drinking when Ralph did.

'I could go on and on about the great traits of Mike and still not pinpoint what it was that made him so loved. I thank Ralph, his childhood friend' – he nods towards me – 'for making such asinine comments about a puzzle-loving boy with the clichéd "zest for life" that we hear about in so many textbook eulogies.' I make the speech-marks sign with my fingers as I say 'zest for life' to accentuate my insult. 'I find it odd that Mike has never even mentioned you over the last half-decade.'

Ralph stands up in disgust.

'Stop tarnishing his memory and sit down,' he shouts, without the support of the crowd. I can see that he at least cares and is remorseful, but I am beyond that now.

'Sit down and stop embarrassing yourself.' A childish remark that achieves my goal of making him withdraw, but makes me blush somewhat. 'What I am trying to say is that, yes, Mike was a beautiful baby, an elegant child, a giving man, an altruistic human being, we all know this. But he didn't just die. He killed himself.'

Farrelly looks at me, shaking his head, and then stares at Jackie with intent.

'Is it Ralph's fault for falling out of touch with him? No. Is it his mother's fault for running off and neglecting him in favour of her own sense of deluded happiness? I'm not so sure.' This comment was a gift to Arthur – Mike's dad. 'Was it Arthur's fault for being a perfect, loving, supportive father until the very last day and beyond? Not a chance.' My final gift to him. I've done what he asked, now I need to say what Mike really would have wanted.

'We are all to blame. Me for being so fucking self-absorbed not to notice the peril in my best friend's eyes. Ralph, for quitting on him. You' – I point at his mother – 'for abandoning him through his formative years.' My finger moves towards his father. 'You, for being just like him and blinded by the reality of it all.' There's a stir and a nervousness in the pews as if I could pick anybody out and declare their failings to the congregation in front of God. 'ALL OF YOU' – my sweeping gesture encompasses the entire church – 'for being fake friends and family. We are all to blame for letting the kindest guy in the world feel so worthless that his own death was the only exit.'

My mouth feels particularly dry at this point, as if I've been talking for hours, as if I'm in an interview with a panel of ninety people trying to nail the position for idiot of the year. I swallow because I think that might help.

'Look, I'm not really here to point the finger at one person in particular, in the same way that I'm not trying to reduce a complex individual like Mike to a pithy anecdote. Mike was a lot of things. Caring, understanding, giving, but he was also irritating, childish and lazy. He was funny and charitable but also depressing and selfish. I can't stand here and pretend to understand Mike fully, and I won't cherry-pick his best points so that we can all insincerely reminisce. That's not how I am going to remember him.' After my outburst these words seem to win back everyone's attention.

The inside of my mouth is now so arid that I cough into the microphone, making a horrendous high-pitched, feedback-like squeal that nearly ruins the end of my sermon.

'I'll remember Mike as someone with a gift for giving, as a Good Samaritan.' Father Farrelly finally agrees with me on something. 'But I'll also remember the image of him sitting there in his own blood, his fingers buried into his thighs, and the pain that his actions have caused. I'll remember that I wasn't there when he needed me and that I let him down in the worst way possible. I will for ever wonder whether there was anything that I could have done to prevent us all having to go through this ordeal today, whether we could have stopped Mike from travelling the road of his own harrowing torment each day. I'll wonder whether anyone else here could have done anything more than tell the story of when he first fell off his bike. And I hope that everyone here, like me, will forever feel completely devastated and utterly ashamed at what transpired last Thursday, because that's what we should feel. Shame.'

I take a last gulp and look at the bemused pew-folk before I descend from my mount and head down the steps, walking up the aisle to the large, heavy oak doors of the church and out into the smog of our nation's capital.

I can't even hear a murmur inside. Maybe they are expecting me to come back in.

I'm not going back in.

I button up my jacket and look up at the sky. It looks like it might rain. It's bright but brisk. I feel that now would be a great time to light up a cigarette and walk off into the distance. But I don't smoke. Instead, I fixate on a grey cloud in the sky and say out loud, 'Well, Mike, I think that went pretty well.' And I smile to myself, knowingly, before wandering around for the next hour trying to remember where I buried my mother.

JACKIE

It's Monday and Jackie slips effortlessly back into her morning routine.

She's mourned enough.

At 6:45 her alarm sounds. She uses her mobile phone as an alarm and the default setting is the echo of waves crashing against rocks. Eli has learned to loathe this sound from the numerous occasions he has had the displeasure of waking to it when Jackie stays over. It vexes him.

The snooze function is warped too and gives her a nine-minute rest on the first press and a six-minute break on the second. This means she arises at exactly 7:00 each morning. She showers even though the previous evening, before retiring to the couch for an hour with a glass of wine and a pre-recorded soap opera or a magazine full of celebrity skin and gossip about mating habits, she had a long bath. That's another twenty minutes.

Luckily today's outfit was prepared the night before so as to keep her morning free from decision and as efficient as humanly possible. However, it took almost an hour to choose a skirt-and-blouse combination that was appropriate and entailed many revisions paraded in front of the mirror and many more questions of 'So, Descartes, what do you think?'

She leaves food for the cat and downs a glass of fresh orange juice on her way out the door, leaving for the Tube with plenty of time to spare. This way she is never late and feels justified rewarding herself with a cup of Earl Grey on arrival.

This strict, regimented daily plan means she can keep her head clear of any impure thoughts or irrelevant dreams. Everything is covered.

Everything is calculated.

It's how Jackie works best.

It gets her through part of the day without succumbing to regret. It doesn't allow her a moment to feel guilt about Mike. Or Eli.

MONDAY

I've dropped out of routine. I don't even know where the weekend went. I've fallen into a waking coma of indulgent self-loathing, which can only lead me down a path towards a darker place. I believe it was Camus who said, 'God put self-pity by the side of despair, like the cure by the side of disease.' I don't feel desperation right now. Self-pity is my new drug of choice, though, and it acts like a bulletproof cashmere comfort-blanket, protecting me from the reality of the world outside. It's addictive and intangible, and is the mysterious, invisible wasting disease that chews you up from the inside, leaving you as an embryonic version of your former self.

For me, despair is the only cure.

I can't even escape to the reality of another first chapter. But I try.

With the quilt wrapped around me, I waddle down the stairs to the first-chapter library. It's still safe under here but the aroma is becoming more noticeable with every passing hour. Three nights of nightmares resulting in profusely cold sweating added to a morning of masturbation mixed with tears, snot and dribbling. I'm aware of what is happening but it's like I don't want to stop feeling like this just yet.

I want to hurt.

It takes an age for my laptop to boot up. I have been offered a discount from work on a new one but I don't really want any of the DoTrue products in my house. I don't want them to cross over the barrier between home and work. My job, a thing I hate, must remain separate from my home, a thing I love. In the same way that Jackie should have remained separate from Mike.

I double-click on the file entitled 'King Liar', the idea I had last week about a character who wants to live his own life like a movie and forces himself to sabotage his relationship for some foolish romantic ideology that winning the girl back is the ultimate commitment to a relationship.

Scrolling up and down the pages I start to get bored of the story. This happens a lot when I repeatedly read the same part over and over again. I sterilise it. I mentally shrug and open a brand-new blank document. With my fingers poised I stare at a white screen for six minutes, almost tapping keys at several points but withdrawing in disappointment.

I close my eyes and tilt my head back in resignation, sighing as I do so, hoping that my fingers will move on their own and type something worthwhile. Like a psychic demonstrating automatic writing, I hope that something can be channelled through me onto the display so that I can get through the next couple of hours as a normal person.

Help me, Mike.

He doesn't help me. Much like I didn't help him.

I don't think that makes us even, though.

I can't conjure any words and my themes appear to centre on death or Mike or betrayal. I'm not a non-fiction writer. I need to make something up.

With all of the letters, languages, words, combinations and structures that exist, I should be able to come up with something original. It must be an endless pot of wonder. You can do so much with just words.

They have power.

There is a knock at the door.

I creep towards it and listen, remaining quiet so as not to arouse suspicion that I may actually be at home. Carefully picking up the card that Ted posted on Friday, I sneakily edge closer to the peephole in an effort to discern who is attempting to disrupt my lament. As my eye reaches the hole a louder knock scares me and a reflex makes me shout in shock and fall back over my putrid quilt.

'Eli? Are you there?' It's Mike's dad.

Mike's dad is a lot like Mike is, or was. He's genuine. He's lovely. He's the man that makes all your friends think that their own parents are rubbish. His son died four days ago and he is knocking on my door. He has already had time to buy himself a paper and he has brought round some pre-filled croissants. And he's wearing a fucking tie.

I've shouted now. It's a clear indication that I am, indeed, here. I open the door.

'Morning,' I say. I'm not sure what else I can say. If I ask 'How are you?' that just sounds pathetic, like I don't actually understand what is going on. I can't apologise for his loss because I know him too well for cliché. I can't put my hand on his shoulder and say something like, 'He was a great man,' because I'm not sure I truly believe that at this point and I can't lie to a grown up. So I innocently offer some exposition in case he has lost some time over the weekend, as I have.

'Can I come in?' He's acting as if everything is normal. Like nothing has happened.

'Of course, of course. Come on in.' I already sense that I, too, am being somewhat jovial. He steps in and kicks off his shoes.

He's a short man with a marginally heavier frame than Mike had. I assume he is in his sixties as he has that distinguished grey hair that only newsreaders seem to get. He, of course, wears trousers, a shirt and a tie, but has taken to walking in very expensive Nike trainers. He does a lot of walking and he dresses for comfort. Jackie would describe him as cute, I just find him to be cool.

He places his shoes neatly by the door and clearly takes in the scent of my quilt as he bends down to straighten them, because the look on his face suggests he doesn't have full control of his gag reflex.

'I brought some croissants. Mike always said you liked bagels, but I couldn't find any that were pre-made and I figured these were just the same.' He hands me one in its polythene packaging and wanders into the library, looking for a seat.

'What can I do for you today?' I'm speaking so informally – to appear unaffected or something – that it just makes things uncomfortable; for me, anyway.

'Well, Eli, I need to ask you something. I need a favour.'

'Anything. What do you need?'

'The funeral is this Friday. It means that I have four days left to get everything arranged. I'm almost there.' This can't be easy for him. Of course I want to help.

'What do you need from me? I'll help in any way I can,' I reassure him.

'That's very kind, Eli. Thank you. I have already spoken to Ralph.'

'Sorry, I don't know who Ralph is,' I interrupt.

'Oh, well, Ralph was Mike's closest friend growing up. I have asked him to say a few words on Friday and I was hoping that you would do the same.' This makes me nervous because I don't particularly enjoy talking to crowds of people. That's why I like to write. 'You are his best friend; I know that, I just think you will have the greatest knowledge about Mike and you can do him justice. You are a great writer, according to my son, so I am sure that you can write something great about him.' I can't say no to that. Even though it will be a personal struggle for me to talk about the greatness of a man who takes his own life, I can't let his father down. That's not fair. It's not just about me.

'Consider it done. I would be honoured.' This sounded like the right thing to say in my head but in the open air it comes over as moronic. That should be the thing you say when you are asked to be a best man at a wedding or a godparent. Not for a funeral.

'I wasn't sure whether Jackie would like to say something too. I know they were very fond of each other.'

'Oh, I don't know if that's such a great idea.' I have to cut him off at this point and I become temporarily lucid. 'She is taking it harder than most, I don't think she could handle it up there in front of people.'

'Yes, yes, perhaps you're right. Well, thank you. Eli, that is a weight off my mind. Look, I have to go as I need to visit the florist to confirm arrangements.' He gets up and heads slowly but fluidly to the door and replaces his high-end sporting footwear. 'Just a few more things to get confirmed today,' he mutters to himself.

I open the door for him.

'You make sure you eat that croissant. You could probably do with some food.' Like Mike, he is more worried about me than himself.

'Do you need any help with anything because I can be ready really qui—'

He cuts me off. 'No, thank you. I'm nearly done. You just get to work on your speech and that will be enough.'

I'm glad he said no because there is no way that I am ready to venture out of the house just yet and it might take me longer than I think to get rid of my personal odour.

He seems to be counting on me to put in a good performance on Friday, and I don't want to let him down the same way I have let his son down. So I drop the quilt to the floor in a circular heap, step outside the ring of filth and head straight to my desk to write.

I'm no longer in self-pity mode but I haven't advanced to despair yet. It's like a pleasant purgatory that I can enjoy for the next day and a half before returning to the office.

JACKIE

People deal with death in different ways. The obvious reaction would be utter devastation. Tears. Alcohol. Buckets of ice cream and boxes of tissues. Distancing yourself from everyone so that you don't have to explain yourself or listen to the platitudes like, 'If there's anything I can do...'

Then there are the people who laugh at a funeral. Or smile when they have to identify a body. Or tell themselves that a person who took all of their own anguish and insecurities and lack of self-worth and focussed that negative energy into a deliberate, shocking suicide, actually killed themselves for the greater good of somebody else.

And there's Jackie. All cried out on day one. Loved up on day two. Sexed up on days three and four. Back to normal by Monday.

It's lunchtime. She's been at work all morning. Liz, the office manager, was the only one to offer condolences.

If there's anything you need.
Anything I can do.
We're all thinking of you.
Thoughts and prayers.

Jackie just wants the mundanity of her regular life. She requires no sympathy. She's not even allowed to tell anyone that she got engaged on Friday because she'll look like a fucking psychopath.

So she takes her apple and her coffee cup and leaves the office. She's not thinking, she's just walking. And naturally, her autopilot directs her to the church. She doesn't want to go in there. She doesn't want to see Father Farrelly's smug face. She has nothing she wishes to confess. But this is her routine. This is what she normally does. So this is what she will do.

But she should check in with Eli. Because he won't be taking things so well. He's not as strong as she is. She knows that. She hopes he is putting the tragedy to good use. Like he did when his mother passed away.

She also just wants to hear his voice.

Jackie finishes her apple, throws the core in the bin and looks into the church. Farrelly catches her eye and makes to walk towards her. She lifts the phone to her ear and puts one finger up on the other hand as if to say, *Hold on, I need to make this call.*

Jackie dials Eli's number.

And it rings and rings.

It takes Jackie back to that night, blood on her hands, crying, trying to get hold of Eli. She shakes it off and hangs up.

Eli can see that Jackie was trying to reach him, but he is doing exactly what she wants him to do. He is writing. So he ignores her.

He has already forgotten; the last time he ignored a friend's phone call, they died.

MONDAY
(FOUR DAYS BEFORE FUNERAL FRIDAY)

There are five stages to grief.

Denial. I've done this. I did it all weekend. Sticking my dick into Jackie whenever I could. Apparently celebrating our impending nuptials. We hid away in my flat to avoid the world. It would be insensitive to discuss our love and commitment to one another straight after our friend had killed himself. So we decided to ignore that.

It didn't really happen.

Mike is fine.

He was probably at home, putting up some shelves or upcycling a chest of drawers. Or something.

It was easier than you'd think to live in denial of the horror. To float through a weekend of sex and booze and ordered-in food. And Jackie would give me an hour or so in my office to tap out some words and she would sit on my therapist's couch wearing just her underwear and one of my T-shirts that was a little too big for her and she would read through my creation. And she would um. And she would ah. And she would laugh in the right places.

And it made me feel proud.

And then she left here on Sunday night while I wallowed on my own. And I couldn't help but think about Mike. Sitting there. Hands in his legs. And all that hard work I'd put in to denying that he was gone, it just evaporated. That wonderful sense of numbness had vanished.

Mike was dead. He was never coming back.

But I started to hear his voice.

He was telling me to write.

Begging me to finish something.

Anything.

And then his dad shows up. His delicate, caring and trodden-on father. The corners of his mouth trying their hardest to turn down but his optimism was more powerful.

He is like Mike. Simple and caring. Just the sweetest old man.

And he pushed me into another stage of grief.

Anger. Mike's death was cruel. It was unfair to have him taken at such a young age. We had so much left to do and see. But he did it to himself. That was his decision. Not mine. Not Jackie's. Not God's. I don't even believe that there is a God but I am angry at Him, too.

I can't stop myself thinking about things that happened weeks ago, months ago, last year. Signs that he wasn't feeling right. Events that could have been altered, things I could have done to make a difference to Mike. Things that would have altered his path so that I wasn't here, on a Monday morning, trying to write a fucking eulogy for my best friend, who decided nothing was worth living for anymore.

Where is Jackie now? Where is the glorious vagina she has been tempting me with all weekend to put me off the scent of Mike's betrayal.

I'm angry. And there is no greater creative lubricant.

I type:

```
Hi everyone, thanks for coming today. I'm Eli Hagin
and Mike was my best friend. And, like all of you
sitting here today, I wasn't there for Mike when he
needed me the most.
```

And, damn, it flows. Words spill out of me with ease. I'm not holding back. It's true. It's honest. It's brutal in places, but my fingers do not stop moving until I reach the end of my speech. A perfect first draft. No edit required. I hit print, collect the papers, tap them against the desk like a newsreader and place them neatly in the drawer for Friday.

I stare at the couch, but it's not the right time to talk to my fake therapist. I'm getting it out in other ways.

The clock tells me it's not even noon, so I feel like I'm achieving something.

I pour myself a whisky. It's not measured. Two large glugs. A 'house single', as it is known. And I continue to let it all out.

Whisky and anger. My favourite cocktail.

I open 'King Liar', select all, and delete.

Then...

```
Someone once said, 'Things turn out best for people
who make the best of the way that things turn out.'
I got a phone call a moment ago telling me that my
best friend has just killed himself and, in a way,
it has filled me with hope.
```

I lift the glass, smile, take a swig and look over again at the couch.

Mike looks back at me and nods.

This is it.

I'm shitting gold.

RALPH

He's good with technology but you don't have to work for MI5 to find out about somebody in this age of humble bragging and photographs of the meals we eat.

The first-chapter library has its own social-media page to promote it. The page is followed by hundreds of locals and wannabe writers. There's a picture of Eli outside the building with Gaucho's next door. So, when you go to another social-media platform and look up Eli Hagin, you know that you are viewing the correct one. He likes The Royal Scam pub and Gaucho's Coffee Shoppe and Furry's Vinyl.

Stupidly, there's a post where he talks of his birthday plans. You know how old he is and can now calculate his date of birth.

There's a link to family members. His mother, who is dead, still has an open profile. So open that anyone can scroll through her photographs. She has even put her maiden name in brackets so that people she went to school with, who she has lost touch with, can find her if they do not know that she was married.

This took Ralph less than five minutes.

He knows what Eli looks like, where he lives, he has his date of birth and his mother's maiden name. If Ralph was inclined towards a life of crime, taking Eli's identity would not be the greatest of efforts. In fact, he suspects that his password for almost everything will revolve around the words 'first' and 'chapter'.

F1R5T CH4PT3R.

Perhaps.

Ralph, too, is angry. Not at Mike. Not because his best friend from school sliced across his legs and bled out. He is angry that Eli Hagin gets to make a speech at the funeral while he only gets to 'say a few words'.

He knows nothing more about Eli than the things he found from scouring the internet for a few minutes. But he feels certain that Eli did not know Mike as well as he did.

Mike was hurting.

Always hurting.

He wasn't crying out for attention.

He wanted to die. So that his pain would go away.

Ralph knew this for certain. Because it was almost all that he and Mike would talk about. Years had been spent on the subject. Several failed attempts. And it was heightened near the end. Mike was gearing himself up for it.

Mike wanted to die. Ralph knew this. And when the news broke that Mike had tried again and been successful, Ralph was pleased. Pleased that the pain was over for Mike. Pleased that they could stop talking about it.

Ralph, with little grasp of mental-health issues, but with a deep affection for Mike, was happy when he heard that Mike was dead. He thinks that it was the right thing for Mike to do.

Maybe that's why he wasn't asked to deliver the eulogy.

MONDAY

I don't know why I find myself drawn to the whole Mike situation with my writing. And I don't want to get bogged down in that 'life imitating art/art imitating life' debate. Besides, Mike seems to approve.

I know that the original idea is to have Bud Ellis ruin his relationship on purpose and try to win the woman back, but the death of a friend just makes the story richer. I hope.

Mike thinks so.

He sits on my couch, nodding along. He's there to support but I also get the feeling that he is blocking my therapy. He thinks I'm using it to procrastinate, to not finish.

Look, I know that he's not really thinking that. He's not thinking anything. Because he's dead. I'm through the denial phase. I've used the anger. But he's there. I can see him as clear as day. I don't know if he is on my shoulder, or in the back of my mind, or I'm too close to the bottom of the whisky bottle, but Mike is here with me and, if he is thinking something, then I am thinking it, too.

I place my new first chapter for *King Liar* down next to him and say, 'I'm going upstairs for a bit. You read.' And I imagine his ever-enthusiastic face. The way he would smile. Or how large his eyes got in the excitement of receiving a new chapter from me.

It didn't seem fake then and it doesn't seem fake now.

Even though it is.

Upstairs, I flick on the television. Somebody has upcycled an old armchair with some printed fabric of the *Mona Lisa* that they have splashed neon paint over. And it looks annoyingly stylish.

My phone vibrates, and I wonder if it's Jackie after I ignored her call earlier. But it's an email. I got caught up in the world of social media for a time and registered for everything. Facebook. Twitter.

Friends Reunited. Vine. YikYak. MySpace. A few of them have shut down now but I still exist on things like Reddit and LinkedIn. And that is why my phone vibrates. It's a notification from LinkedIn. Somebody has looked at my profile – a profile I forgot I still had.

Ralph Levi.

Never heard of him.

I swipe to the right and delete without reading.

There's half a bottle of wine in the fridge that has been left over from my debauched weekend with Jackie – the future Mrs Hagin, apparently. I chug straight from the bottle and I think about my character, Bud Ellis.

What would he do in my situation?

How would he complicate things to get me out of this?

Do I even want to get out of this?

I start to wonder whether my life would be better as a movie. Would it even be interesting?

And that's when I hear the gunshots.

THE **TEDS**

Five minutes earlier:

One of the Teds has scribbled a line drawing of a horse on a Gaucho's napkin.

'Very good,' says the other Ted. 'They can be tricky. Especially from memory.'

Artistic Ted turns down the corners of his mouth as if to say, 'I guess so.' Then he opens his mouth to ask for a cappuccino.

'Make it yourself, you layabout. I need to go out the back for some clean cups.' And he walks out towards the kitchen and the dishwashing cycle that has recently finished.

Then:

INT. GAUCHOS COFFEE SHOPPE. DAY
The sound of a coffee-machine steam wand whistles above the bubbling of customer chatter.

    TED 2
  Howdy, stranger. What can I get for you?

(He shakes chocolate powder over a fresh cappuccino.)

    STRANGER
You call everybody 'stranger'?
    TED 2
I mean no harm, friend. We know most people who come in here and I'm very good with faces. And your accent tells me you're not from around here.
    STRANGER
It is true. I am from a small town in Italy called Loreto Aprutino.

TED 2

The name alone … sounds like a beautiful place.

STRANGER

Oh, it is. You've never been?

TED 2

To Loreto…

STRANGER

(He laughs.)

To Italy.

TED 2

I'm sorry to say I have not. Can I get you something to drink?

STRANGER

Double espresso. Thank you.

TED 2

To take out or are you staying?

STRANGER

Staying. But not for long. Is this the part where you ask me my name?

TED 2

(Smiling.)

That's a different coffee place. But I will tell you mine. I am Ted. Very pleased to meet you.

(Flips a switch on the machine and waits.)

STRANGER

Ted. Ted who has never been to Italy.

(Ted 1 emerges from the kitchen with a tray of clean cups and saucers.)

TED 2

It's true. But this man has, haven't you, Ted?

TED 1

What's that?

STRANGER

Ted?

        TED 2
  Yes. Confusing at first, I know.
  (To other Ted.)
  I was just saying that you have spent some time in
  Italy.
        STRANGER
  Ted who has been to Italy.

Ted 2 hands the espresso across the counter and takes
a swig from the cappuccino he made for himself. Ted 1
looks the stranger in the eyes, recognises him and
drops the tray. Before it hits the floor, the stranger
has put two bullets into Ted 1's chest. He drinks the
espresso. Turns, and leaves.

Of course, this is only one version of what happened. A romanticised version perhaps. How it might play out in a movie. But, still fairly accurate.

Ted did emerge from the kitchen and he did look deeply into the eyes of the stranger. Those deep-blue, brave eyes. The eyes that refused to cry.

But he didn't recognise him straight away

The stranger told the other Ted that he was from Loreto Aprutino. That his family had lived there for generations. His father before him. And his grandfather before that.

His grandfather: Anastagio Calvano.

Ted never used the name of the town when he told that story, he always said, 'No Man's Land'. Again, to romanticise the situation. Taking something true, turning it into a story so that the truth remains but the reality is blurred.

One detail that Ted always relied on was the name of the grandfather who had exploded into a million particles as a result of that ill-conceived snuff-box bomb. Anastagio Calvano. And the grandson who had watched him die but refused to shed a tear in front of the British soldiers.

That brave boy. Ilario.

Who became a man. A beautiful but vengeful man. A man who had tracked down the soldiers present on the day that had been scorched on his memory. A man with a list of names, the first of which says 'Ted'.

A name he can now cross off.

One witness says that there were two gunshots and then a crash of plates. Another says that the plates crashed first and then there were two shots. Another said it all happened in slow motion.

But it didn't.

This was not the scene from a movie.

Ted is Dead.

FUNERAL **FRIDAY**

I can't find Mum. It all looks the same. To make things worse I have found a wall covered in brass plaques that conceal miniature sarcophaguses for ash-filled urns to occupy. I'm temporarily distracted at the thought that perhaps the plural of sarcophagus should be *sarcophagi*. Then, when I lift my head away from yet another etching of the words 'devoted wife', I find that this wall is actually a building, a red-brick tomb. It's located in the centre of a crossroads that separates the graveyard into four smaller graveyards. There seems to be no theme or possible guide to navigating this without just simply remembering where I left her.

I know the congregation will be filing out of the church soon, bemused by my speech. I just want a moment alone before I have to face them again on a personal level, where it will only be awkward because people will think it's not right to discuss what I said in public at such a time. It's so British and politically correct it drives me insane. I'm sure nobody will think my eulogy was lifted from the page of some how-to-deliver-the-perfect-funeral-speech website, and I'm sure they will feel as though they should be angry with what I said but, inside, they will understand that you can't remain that way about something you know is true.

Some of the headstones around me are obscene. Fifty-foot-high angels that are reduced to the appearance of a gothic gargoyle through years of neglect. Family tombs ridden with damp rot and grass that is half the height of the building itself. Somewhere, beneath the moss, next to the broken beer bottles, covered in mould and decaying through lack of care and attention, will be Mum's grave, and I want to find it.

In the distance I can see people leaving the service, trying to appear casual as they look around in the hope of discovering my location. Everyone lingers, not knowing what to do. I try to conceal myself behind a black marble obelisk so that I may observe the proceedings like some kind of morbid voyeuristic necromancer.

Nothing really happens.

Once Mike's dad emerges a few people shake his hand or pat his shoulder or kiss his cheek, then they all disperse to their cars, trying to disguise their haste, but they all want a parking space for the wake, which is being held at The Scam, sixty-four steps from my house.

I wait until everyone has gone before emerging from the shadow of another memorial. The delay gives me time to read more epitaphs, noticing two with spelling mistakes. I get angered enough to pick up the pace to a brisk walk, maybe even a canter, and autopilot suddenly takes me back four years to the spot where Mum still lies.

It's not what I expected at all.

The stone is white. Brand-new-piano-key white. Not a dull, rain-cloud white as one would expect, but a brilliant, angelic white. The stone has a picture of Mum's face on it. One where she looked healthy and beautiful and exactly how I want to remember her. Not withered, haggard or allowing cancer to eat her from the inside.

There are fresh flowers in the plant holders at the foot of the stone.

Someone has been here recently.

Someone has been coming here for a long time.

I wonder whether this is a final message from Mike, but it's not. It's Jackie. Lovely Jackie. The same Jackie I fell in love with six years and one week ago. She has been tending to my mother's plot since she died, knowing that one day I would have to return here. This is not the same Jackie that I am planning on breaking up with. This is the woman who pulled me through the death of my mother when all I could muster was a feeling of despair and anguish. The same person who supports my dream of writing a book and quitting my job. The one constant in life, who is always there while those around me disappear.

But none of this matters.

She isn't this person anymore. Every action has a hidden agenda. Every word is carefully planned and articulated to achieve her desired goal. She is now the person that sleeps with my best friend and tells the police that it is my fault he is dead. That's what I have to keep telling myself.

So, thanks for keeping the place tidy, Jackie; thanks, even, for the tear-filled sex on Tuesday afternoon and thanks for laughing at my inappropriate comments in church, but tomorrow night, I plan to get you out of my life. I almost did it last week.

The inside of my suit jacket has a silky lining and I take the corner in my hand and polish up Mum's picture, and sit down on the marble. I kiss the end of my finger and touch Mum's face on the picture. It's then that I start to cry.

'I miss you, Mum,' I say out loud, and the eyes in her picture seem to stare at me intently. 'Mike's dead, but I guess you know that, right? I mean, Jackie has been up to see you.' None of the things I am saying make sense. I don't believe that she can hear me, but it feels right to let it out and not just think it. 'I let him kill himself. You know he was sleeping with her?' She's not saying anything back to me, of course, and it reminds me of the start of most of my therapy sessions.

'I'm sorry I haven't been up to see you lately.' I'm now lying to a dead woman who can't even hear me. I haven't been up to see you lately? Four years. Four years since I have been anywhere near here. I've made this step, why start lying now?

'I've just been really busy writing and my job takes a lot out of me too.' I pause after this lie to think about what I'm saying.

'Look, Mum. I'm sorry. I know it's been ages and I know I should have been up here by now, but I'm here, I've done it. I'll be here all the time, too, now, because, well, you see, Jackie won't be coming up here anymore.' I wait as if to hear her gasp in disbelief. 'We've broken up. Okay, well, we are going to break up. Tomorrow, actually. I think she might have slept with Mike. So, I hope you don't mind but it will be me that comes to see you from now on, and I won't let your stone get like some of the others I've seen here today, I promise.'

Who am I kidding? Even if I manage to go through with breaking things off with Jackie, it's Mum she has the relationship with, so even if we are not together she will still visit and maintain the site. I know her. That will mean I'll only have to come up here half as much.

I'll be back here again in two days to converse with my mother's soulless remains and inform her that what I have just told her is, in fact, another lie. Some more of my fiction.

This feels like the right level of closure for today so I say my farewells and head back to The Scam for the wake. I have to walk because I arrived here at the front of the motorcade with Mike's limited family and have no lift back now. The rest of the cars disappeared in a puff of exhaust fumes as everyone vied for the best parking space at the after-show location.

So now I have to walk, and it's a lot further than sixty-four steps but it should give me ample opportunity to work off some of the alcohol I managed to drink before Mike's environmentally friendly wicker coffin arrived outside the apartment block that Jackie found him lying dead in only one week ago.

TUESDAY
(THREE DAYS BEFORE FUNERAL FRIDAY)

I wake up early on Tuesday morning. Before my alarm. Before the radio dribbles out another easy-listening track to numb me once more.

There's no point going outside. There's police tape everywhere. Gaucho's is shut. The press are still stalking the place. Local news. National, too. I don't want to get caught up in that. This is my final day to mourn Mike. Tomorrow I have to return to DoTrue, and Friday is the funeral, so I need to make today different. A turning point. Full recovery.

I need to get myself out of this bed. I need to unwrap myself from this six-foot security blanket and get on track to putting my life back in some kind of order. I've lost all routine.

I sit up hazily with my eyes still sticking together, and peel my sweating back away from the rancid sheet beneath me. As I approach an upright position the quilt drops from around my shoulders and exposes my naked chest to the cold of my flat. I'm tempted to drag it up over my shoulders and drop back to the comfort of idle wallowing. I need to snap out of this. It's no longer fruproyance. I certainly believe that depression is taking a more active role in my condition.

Perhaps frepressance.

I can't allow myself to get like that.

The stench of solitude and depravity greets me as I eventually step out of what some might call 'found art' but what I would call an unmade bed. Dressed in only a pair of boxer shorts I stagger into the hallway as my skin starts to goose-pimple in the morning temperature.

For some reason I sit down to go to the toilet as if the journey from the bedroom to the bathroom was too much effort. I flush the chain to signify the end of phase one and jump straight into the shower to hose down my putrid body and warm myself up.

I feel somewhat revitalised and task myself with clearing the flat and returning to a glimmer of the normal life that I had before Mike so abruptly ended his.

Walking back into the bedroom after vacating it for twenty-two minutes only heightens the scent that I left in there, and I immediately feel myself becoming unclean just standing in the doorway. Aggressively, I attack the bedcovers and pillowcases, ripping them off and hurtling them down the hallway towards the kitchen. Once I have the sheet off I pace to the kitchen door, collect the linen and scrunch it angrily into the smallest ball that I can before catapulting it into the washing machine and kicking the door firmly closed. I put the washing powder and softener into their respective trays and slam the drawer shut. Finding two old washing tablets under the sink, I decide that it wouldn't be a bad idea to use these too. So I re-open the door and bullet them in with the dirty material and flip the switch for a deep whites wash.

Returning to the bedroom it seems fresher but somehow I have managed to mask the usual smell of warm pretzels that usually flows through every floor. I open the window to let some air in and proceed with collecting the gin bottles, beer bottles and glasses with segments of lime lining the bottom.

This is reality.

My alarm sounds with the introduction of the snooze tune but I decide to flick the radio off today so I am not interrupted in completing my task, but once I have remade the bed with fresh bedcovers and a sheet that isn't stained with a presentation of mine and Jackie's bodily fluids I feel exhausted, and lie down once more to regroup and reflect on my morning's achievements. And I don't wake up for another ninety minutes, until the washing machine buzzes to inform me that the cycle is over.

The buzz and click from the washing machine drags me back to reality and autopilot kicks in. Before I fully realise where I am the sheets are hung out on a clotheshorse in front of the radiator in the hallway and I am placing two pieces of wholemeal bread into the toaster and grabbing the peanut butter from the cupboard.

I settle down on my sofa in front of some daytime television. In eighteen minutes, Roberto or Parsemonial or Ingrid is going to be discussing binge-drinking and smoking while pregnant.

Jackie has the afternoon off, booked a couple of weeks back for some reason. She decides to move her usual Wednesday confession to today instead.

I pour myself a gin and slimline tonic.

'One step at a time,' I tell myself. One step at a time.

JACKIE

At exactly 12:30, Jackie slips her jacket on, puts her bag over her shoulder and exits her building. Circumstances have altered her routine but she is a woman who always has a contingency.

The church is quieter than it is during her usual visit on Wednesday afternoons, but still a gaggle of elderly Catholic ladies lines the space between the pews. It's a wonder Father Farrelly has time to do anything other than take confession and intimidate impressionable choir boys.

Jackie takes her jacket off and folds it neatly over her bag in the hope that this will cool her down and slow her sudden perspiration. The ladies ahead of her are very sullen, glum even. It comes to a point where the art of confession is only utilised for companionship, and for these women it is as everyday as buying a newspaper.

For Jackie, it's a ghost train. She knows what to expect, she knows it's not real, but every time she is shocked or scared in some way, and every time she leaves slightly unfulfilled.

She waits. It isn't cold like the last time she was here and the choir are not practising at this time of day to add to the bleakness of the situation. Instead, the sun shines in through a stained-glass window, creating a multi-coloured stream of light that reflects off the dust particles in the air right down to the floor, creating a pathway that Jackie would love to escape on.

The curtain slides back, and an old woman gingerly steps down from her mahogany confinement, feeling cleansed and wanted.

It's Jackie's turn now.

'Forgive me Father—' she starts.

'Jacqueline?' he interrupts. He recognises her voice from her first three words.

'Good afternoon, Father.'

'What are you doing here?' he asks.

'Sorry?' It seems obvious to her why she is there.

'I mean, I've heard about Michael.'

'Mike,' she corrects him.

'Yes. Mike. I was expecting to either see you a lot sooner or not at all. But you are here now. I'm sure there are things that are troubling you, and I know that faith can often be tested in times like these, but I am still your priest and we do not have to converse through confession if that will help. If you need to just talk then I am here.'

It sounds, actually, quite genuine, like he would like to help her through a difficult time. She can be spoken to on the same level with no judgement cast upon her.

'Thank you, Father, but I would prefer this format for today.' She speaks softly and quietly but is succinct and firm.

'Very well. Please continue.'

And the judgement begins.

'I miss Mike so much, already.'

'That's to be understood.'

Jackie pauses for a second, annoyed at his interjection. She doesn't want his input, she doesn't want his guidance, she just wants to speak about it with someone because she has no one else. She leaves the pause long enough that it becomes awkward and her point is made.

'He was a great friend to me and I wasn't to him. I...' She takes a deep breath. 'I do feel some relief, though. I'm relieved that he is gone and I don't have to explain to Eli what has been happening, and I know I shouldn't feel like that but I do.'

'Emotions ride high in these circumstances.' Jackie doesn't really have the time or the patience for such banalities. 'I understand—'

She interrupts: 'How could you possibly understand? Have you ever loved two different men at the same time? Have you ever had to make a decision between the two men you love, knowing that someone is going to get hurt in the process?'

'No, Jackie, of course not, what I mean is—'

'Please, Father, don't.' She tries to cut him off but he continues.

'What I mean is that I understand the turmoil that can be faced when you give in to temptation. You are being tested and you have the right to feel this way. This is why we have faith.' Of course, he doesn't understand at all. He tries to subtly imply that Jackie should feel guilt and that she should feel the need to atone, and he delivers this through his regular series of biblical platitudes, attempting to justify his point by making his references fit her situation: '...but Mike's death is not your fault.'

'Father, I thank you for your words and your wisdom, but this is not why I am here. I know that I can talk to you outside of confession. I feel like you are not listening to what I am saying.'

'What *are* you saying, Jacqueline?' he says, clearly vexed at her insubordination.

She breaks down a little. 'I loved him. I loved them both.'

'I know that you think that.'

'I know it, Father, I don't think it, I know it. But I made my choice. I chose Eli. I choose Eli over everything. I always have, and Mike had to suffer because of my decision.' Tears stream down her face as she talks. 'I don't want Eli to ever know that.'

'You understand that you were wrong, Jacqueline, and you have repented for the sin of coveting another, but Mike's sin cannot be passed on to you. It is not your cross to bear.'

'Of course it is, Father,' she objects, 'of course it is. That's what I have been trying to tell you. That's why I am here today. It's why we are not sat outside in front of Jesus and why I am in this box. It is my fault. I killed him, Father. I killed Mike. I broke his heart, and it killed him.'

And then she leaves. Pushing through the curtain at speed she darts up the aisle in her heels with her bag and jacket flailing behind her and the cries of her name from Father Farrelly disappearing in the vastness of the church.

She enters the light of the world outside and continues, running, running, until she reaches Eli's door, where she bangs on the letterbox before even attempting to catch her breath.

TUESDAY
(THREE DAYS BEFORE FUNERAL FRIDAY)

My time with Alvin or Floella or Marmaduke is gripping although moronic, and the three gins I have guzzled during the show have left me so lethargic that I don't even have the energy to masturbate to pass the time. This is not recovery. Sure, my bedroom is tidy, but I'm still searching for a level of despair that will alleviate my sense of self-pity.

Then someone knocks on my door with urgent force.

I stand to attention and rush to see what the emergency might be. My heart starts to pound and adrenaline kicks. Excitement. Trepidation. When I open the door I am attacked.

Jackie barges her way in, breathing heavily, and pins me to the wall, kissing me passionately. It's primal and animalistic and exciting and arousing, and I just go with it.

She starts to rip at my T-shirt, pulling backwards and forwards indecisively. I try to get my hands on her bra strap but she forces them off and bites down on my lip. It hurts and I push her away, but that just seems to make her stronger and more eager. She forces me to the floor and straddles me, hitching her skirt up. She reaches down and grabs me to make sure I am hard which, of course, I am. Pulling her underwear to one side, she forces me inside her. All the while she is still kissing me all over my face and chewing at my bottom lip.

With her head above mine and her eyes closed, she moves back and forth, and breathes heavily into my face. I close my eyes too and it's the first time I've done that in three days without thinking of Mike. And then, I feel the warm droplets of Jackie's tears falling from above me onto my face as she continues writhing on me until we are both finished.

She rolls off and lies next to me on the floor of my hallway, staring up at the ceiling. Neither of us tidies ourselves away or straightens our clothing, and neither one of us speaks for a while. We just lie there not feeling anything. Not reflecting or comparing, just vacuous beings.

And it is great for that short amount of time to seem, feel, think and be nothing.

Nothing but real.

FUNERAL **FRIDAY**

It is cold walking back from the cemetery but it has sobered me somewhat. It gives me some time to reflect on what I have just done. I went back on my word a little, at least in the eyes of Arthur – Mike's dad. I said some good things about Mike, but I'm sure that Mike would have wanted the truth so that his efforts to perish in such a horrific manner were not all in vain. Even beyond the grave he is passing on wisdom to his friends and family.

I did feel justified in giving such critical appraisal of the congregation in honour of Mike, but now the temperature is inducing something more serious and thoughtful in my demeanour, and I start to question whether it was such a good idea to have seen Mum after all this time. I certainly shouldn't have lied to her, whether she can hear me or not.

Then I round the corner to my street, I pass the front door to my flat and know that I am only sixty-four steps away from entering The Scam, where the wake is being held, and I am filled with unease at what is likely to be a very uncomfortable reception.

And it dawns on me: I've left Jackie to deal with this on her own. Yes, I have decided that I will end our relationship tomorrow, and yes, I have recently joined the hordes of unemployed, unskilled creative types that litter the restaurants and bars of London, but I shouldn't be leaving her alone to deal with this today. She's going through as much as I am, nearly.

'Thirty minutes,' I say to myself as I fold my arms even tighter to create the impression of more warmth, and with forty steps still to go, the heavens open and drench me.

I once read that running in the rain actually makes you wetter than walking because more of the surface area of your body comes into contact with the rain. That may be so, but I still decide that sprinting to the door would be the best option. It makes sense.

So I pick up the pace.

Unfortunately, I manage to hit full speed after about thirty-eight steps and can't slow down in time to stop myself crashing recklessly into the doors and causing a commotion that diverts everyone's attention away from what they are doing and unifies their focus on my dripping late entrance.

I don't know what to say. Hello? Sorry I'm late? I apologise for ruining everyone's service with my ranting? Nobody else really knows the best way to broach the situation either. You can't make a fuss at a funeral but you can't be seen to condone my behaviour. Of course, Jackie rescues me.

'Let's get you out of that wet jacket, eh?' She steps through the crowd, breaking away from a circle of people that neither of us knows, and heads straight towards me with clear intent to act 'normal'. She takes off my jacket, puts one hand on the small of my wet back and ushers me to the bar. 'I think something for your thirst and something to warm you up will do the trick.'

I nod at her as I start to shiver.

'What can I getcha?' the barman drools in an overly enthusiastic cockney accent that I would usually find irritating, but I am just glad that he doesn't know what I have done today and for the moment he isn't spitting in my glass.

'A large glass of wine for me and a pint of lager and a large brandy for this morose sap right here.' She smiles and strokes my back as if to say, *It's all right, Eli, I'll protect you.* I'm really grateful for her help, but it doesn't change my plans for tomorrow. Not in the slightest. I know that she is enjoying this way too much.

I'm supposed to finish everything.

That's what Mike wanted.

That's how I'm making sense of this.

I knock back the brandy in one go but it's so big that I have to gulp in the middle, and I grimace with disgust. It does make me feel warmer, though, but the saliva in my mouth feels thinner and I have to hold back from throwing up. The ice-cold beer follows. Two large glugs and I only have half a pint left, and this gives me just enough courage to think about mingling but not quite enough to face Mike's dad.

Jackie and I sit down by the fireplace. It's the same table we sat at eight nights ago with Mike when we all thought the world was perfect. It was the same night, I think, that they both betrayed me, and as long as I can keep that feeling as near to the surface as possible I know that I can follow through with all my plans.

'That was some speech today, Eli. I had no idea.' Well, she wouldn't, I never told anyone. 'What made you do that? I mean, I'm not saying what you said was wrong, but it seems a little out of character for you.'

'I'm not really feeling like myself since it all happened, you know?'

'Oh, of course. I've been trying to use my work to take my mind off it all, but I just find myself wandering off every now and then.' She takes a sip of the cheap white wine that has been laid on for free and concludes that she will be happy to pay for her next drink as long as she can get something with body and a less vinegary quality.

'I just thought that it might have been what Mike would have wanted. I mean, he didn't leave a note or anything. How are we supposed to know why he did it?'

Jackie looks a little distracted by that comment and takes a bigger swig of her supposed Pinot Gris and nods.

'None of us can say for certain why he finally snapped or when it all started. What we can be sure of is that we all could have done something to prevent this. So that puts everyone in the blame. That's the point I wanted to make, and there wasn't any other way of doing that than to just say it. So I did.'

'Well, it was very brave of you, I think.' She raises her glass. 'Cheers.'

'Cheers.' We touch each other's glass with our own and polish off the remainder of our drinks.

'Another?' she asks.

'Of course. But no brandy this time, eh?'

Jackie smiles and stands up. She takes both glasses back to the bar, leaving me alone by the fire to get more paranoid.

Jackie gets back to the bar and orders herself a decent glass of wine, a Merlot, to sink her teeth into. She looks back to check that I am okay on my own, but a vulture has already swooped in to start ripping at the meat of my conscience.

It's Ralph.

'So, Eli, I guess you think you are pretty clever ruining the service like that?' He has jumped into Jackie's seat and looks me straight in the eyes.

'Ralph, I don't want any trouble. I'm here for Mike. The same as you.' I don't have a drink so I'm not sure what to do with my hands and I'm scared that in my discomfort I might express myself in a manner that may be misconstrued.

'Not for the same reasons though, eh? I'm here to celebrate the life of my friend while you are here to question it.' I can see his anger rising.

'There are still questions that have gone unanswered.' I know that my calmness is going to aggravate him even more. I do the same thing to Jackie when she wants to argue with me. It doesn't help the situation.

'But today' – he raises his voice a little and checks himself before continuing – 'but today was not the day to be looking for those answers.' He says it through gritted teeth to give the same effect as shouting.

'Can't we just say that we disagree and leave it at that?'

'Look, I don't care if we agree or not. I don't think you should have said anything today but you did. I shouldn't be making a scene tonight but I am. I just wanted to let you know that I think you were also a crap friend to Mike and possibly the most deplorable excuse for human existence that I have had the misfortune of encountering.' He means it. I can tell.

'I can't disagree with you there, Ralph, I happen to think the exact same thing.' I mean it too, but he thinks I am ridiculing him.

'Oh, you sit there in your ivory tower, all smug, looking down on the simple folk who you think are beneath you because you are such a tortured soul, well boo fucking hoo.'

I'm bored of talking to him now.

'Look, Ralph. That's not the way I think at all, and if you are going to hurl clichés at someone you should at least have a mild understanding of the words that you are using. I can't help it if you feel guilty for being a generally rubbish friend, and I can't help it if your vocabulary is limited, so I will try to use words that I know you will understand. Okay?' He doesn't say a word, he just looks at me with his eyes getting wider and wider. I lean in to him and speak in a loud whisper. 'Nobody cares what you think, Ralph, so why don't you just fuck off and leave me alone.' I fall back into my seat to indicate that I am done and no more of my time should be taken up with this incident.

He stands up and knocks back the drink that he brought over, then slams the empty glass back on the table and says something even more clichéd like, 'It's not over' or 'I'll be back.' Either way, I don't care at the time but, again, he isn't lying.

He crosses Jackie's path on her way back with the drinks and acknowledges her with a subtle nod of the head. She sits down looking bemused.

'Everything okay?'

'Yeah, it's fine. He just wanted to congratulate me on the speech.'

'Oh. Well, that's nice. He seemed like a nice guy. Ralph, is it?' She clearly hasn't detected the irony in my tone, but it's too late to correct her now.

'Yes, that's Ralph. He seemed like a good guy.' No sense in dragging it out.

For the next hour Jackie and I continue to drink and reminisce about Mike, remembering some of the funnier things that he did.

Eventually I am brave enough to venture to the bar on my own as nobody else has confronted me.

We talk and talk about Mike's useless inventions, his ongoing battle with DIY projects, his talent for blurbs, but at no point do we mention his death, his night of passion with Jackie or his hands in his legs; we do what everybody wanted me to do in my speech and skirt along the surface of a very complex individual to make ourselves feel better.

TUESDAY
(THREE DAYS BEFORE FUNERAL FRIDAY)

We both lie there on my hallway carpet, panting, although Jackie's breathing is considerably heavier than mine because she did most of the work and is still trying to control her crying. My trousers are down by my knees and the draught from under the door washes over me, cooling me down. It feels great. I feel almost back to normality. The only difference is that I usually feel dirtier after having sex with Jackie, but it appears that she is taking on that duty today.

With her skirt slightly twisted and her mascara leaving filthy trails down her face, Jackie lies there gazing at the ceiling. She is lying on my arm and would usually roll over towards me, resting her head on my chest, but not today. I turn my head to the side to look at her but it's as if I'm not even there; she continues to stare up at who knows what. She can't be looking towards Mike, because he certainly didn't go *that* way when he died, I think that's fair to say.

I continue to stare at her, waiting for acknowledgement, but she doesn't falter at all and, slowly, I start to drift off into sleep.

JACKIE

Whether Eli actually fell asleep or pretended to doze a short time after he closed his eyes, Jackie doesn't know. She sits up. Quietly and steadily she pulls herself up to her knees, which crack rather loudly as she bends them.

Now she looks at him.

Lying there peacefully, sexually fulfilled and emotionally drained, Jackie takes a minute to absorb the image of his innocence, then she places her hands on the floor in front of her knees and leans over to kiss his cheek delicately. He feels her eyelashes touch his ear and shortly afterwards he senses her breath there as she whispers, 'I love you, Eli, I'm so sorry.' And with that she stands up, straightens her skirt, picks her handbag up from the floor and leaves. Luckily the front door is still open because they never had the time, nor the inclination, to close it after Jackie attacked him, so it is not a disturbance. She is also very considerate in closing the door with the deftness required to cause minimal disruption.

If this happened.

Grief acts differently with everyone. For Eli, who has always had difficulty separating fact from fiction, that particular trait could be heightened. It is just as possible that Jackie was never there. That she is a ghost, that this happened in Eli's head and he masturbated in the hallway.

When you are trying to cope with death, does it always matter what is true?

TUESDAY
(THREE DAYS BEFORE FUNERAL FRIDAY)

What is she sorry for? I ask myself. For loving me? If it makes it any easier I wouldn't mind if she stopped loving me. It would make the weekend go a lot smoother.

I sit up, bewildered. The last half an hour has been a shock to every sense. Essentially I have been sexually assaulted and then given a verbal apology.

I stand up with my trousers still down around my knees and waddle up the stairs to my bathroom. I don't want to put my penis away until I have given it a wash – it's good, I'm starting to feel the guilt and remorse that comes with copulation. This is normal. Everything is nearly back to normal.

But there are still some things niggling me. Why did Mike kill himself? Daniel Webster, former US Senator, once said: 'There is no refuge from confession but suicide; and suicide is confession.' Was Mike's death merely a confession of his feelings for Jackie? Is this what Jackie is apologising to me about? I'd like to think that Mike was stronger than that.

With so many questions rattling around in my mind I decide it is time to get out of the house. I feel too confined. I am back at work tomorrow so I need a taster of what the outside world is like without Mike in it. So I grab my wallet, mobile phone and keys, and step outside into the polluted London air and head straight for Gaucho's.

The Teds will have some answers.

Outside, I duck underneath the police tape and walk up to the front door. I raise my arm above my head and rest against the front door so that I can look through the window and imagine.

The shop is fairly busy as the offices start to empty on another uneventful weekday. Ted – the Ted who writes and usually salutes me with his pencil as I enter - uncharacteristically stands up and walks over to greet me. We shake firmly and he puts a strong military hand on my shoulder.

'Hagin. How are you, old chap? Holding up, I see?' Before I even have time to answer he is ushering me over to a table. 'Come, come. Sit down here and let me get you a drink.' He shouts over to (Dead) Ted at the espresso machine, 'Ted! One for Mr Hagin, please.'

'Already on it,' he shouts back, prioritising my Americano over the needs of the queue that is slowly forming. Once it is poured he brings it over personally and lays it down in front of me. 'How are you holding up?'

'I'm okay, thanks, guys. Thank you for your card, too.'

'Oh, that's no trouble,' says drinks-maker Ted.

'Anything you need. Let us know,' writer Ted chips in.

I sip at my coffee while Ted jumps back behind the bar to see to his patrons. The other Ted sits with me.

'I read about Mike in the local paper.' I nod as I sip my beautiful black liquid, and the heat feels as though it is forming condensation on my eyes. 'Did you find him that way?'

'No, I was at home. It was Jackie who found him.'

'Oh dear, the poor girl. That must have been terrifying for her.' He seems genuinely shocked and distressed for Jackie.

'We are helping each other through,' I lie. I am coping with it myself while Jackie uses me as a sexual toy to exorcise her demons.

'It's good that you have each other in all this. I know how hard it can be.'

Ted speaks for a while, but I don't really ingest anything he says. His lips are moving, but I am thinking about Jackie and just how she felt to find Mike sat there with his hands in his legs, pale and lifeless, and unashamed of how his actions would affect others.

This is not how I planned it at all.

I catch the end of Ted's story: '…and you see, Hagin, that is why I made it and am still here today.' Oh no, I have missed out on some Ted wisdom. I was so preoccupied with thoughts of Jackie and actually considering how she must feel at this time that I didn't really take any notice of this perfectly kind and serious old man. To be fair, I probably wouldn't have spaced out if the other Ted had been here; he is the real story-teller. This Ted should stick to the poetry.

Still, I don't want to upset or insult him so I blag my way through.

'Wow, Ted, I totally hear what you are saying. Thanks.'

'My pleasure.' Phew, he bought it. 'Now I'll leave you to finish your coffee, I think Ted could do with a hand.' And with that, he is gone.

I switch off. I don't want to think about Mike, his death, how Jackie might feel, how I should feel. I just want the numbness that Jackie clearly felt while we lay on my floor in post-intercourse purgatory. I look around the coffee shop at some of the solitary figures reading books or sketching or tapping away at a laptop, and I ponder what they might be thinking about as they enjoy their alone time.

It takes my mind off reality if only for a miniscule portion of the day. I stand up and take my cup back to the counter to help the Teds out, and fumble in my wallet for the usual £1.95 my coffee costs.

'Your money is no good here, Hagin.' And Ted shoos me towards the door in another act of kindness.

A car passes behind me, noisily changing a gear, and the image inside Gaucho's evaporates.

Back to reality.

I return to the first-chapter library and make some tweaks to my speech for Mike's funeral. I'm filled with a sense of fear as I realise that I have to return to the office tomorrow and have decided to terminate my employment with immediate effect.

I need to finish something.

FUNERAL **FRIDAY**

Eventually the moment comes when I have had too much liquid, too much of that sweet alcoholic anaesthetic, and have to expel some before trying to ingest more. I tell Jackie that I need the toilet and will grab more drinks on the way back. She gives me a thumbs-up with one hand while drinking to catch up.

I have to walk through a few cliques before I find the men's room and try to be as gracious as I can as I stumble my way through their circles of trust and into the lavatory. I choose to use the cubicle despite nobody being in there. I hate it when I am halfway through and someone stands next to me and starts talking. I'm perfectly fine if they stand there but once they start talking it's like a valve closes, preventing me from finishing the job at hand; it switches me into polite conversation mode rather than liquid-excretion mode. The safety of the cubicle prevents this. The walls are my protection. This is how I am able to continue to expunge the brandy and lager when I hear someone else come in through the main door.

I whistle the acoustic version of 'Layla' to drown out the movement of the person who has walked in.

After I have shaken off, zipped up and flushed the chain, I straighten my clothing out. Without noticing, I flip the catch on the cubicle door while still tucking in my shirt and tightening my belt. The door creeps open slowly and I don't have time to even look up to see who is stood there before my head is yanked downwards and someone knees me quite ferociously in the stomach, winding me. He then pushes me backwards so that I fall into the cubicle. I hit my back on the porcelain bowl and slide down until I am sat on the sticky-with-old-piss floor, leaning against the toilet.

It's Ralph.

It isn't the end.

He *is* back.

I've been undone by my own efficiency.

'I told you to go home.' He kicks my legs in a playfully aggressive manner.

'You never actually said that. You might have planned to, but you didn't.' I have no filter. He kicks me again, this time less playfully.

'Look, do us all a favour, Eli, and leave. Nobody wants to see your pathetic face here anyway. You're just embarrassing yourself.' Then, for some unknown reason, he spits on me. It's the kind of behaviour you see from a Hugo or Bertrand or Philomena episode. 'I hope this is the end of it now. I don't like having to do this.'

He straightens himself up and I hear him go to wash his hands before leaving.

I picture myself getting up and cracking him on the back of the head so that his face smashes into the mirror, then, as he is down on the floor, repeatedly stamping on his head until it is a bloody mess and someone comes in to pull me off.

But I don't do that. Instead, I continue to lie in a concoction of hundreds of men's piss and spit while he casually goes about his business.

I don't have the energy for this. Ralph doesn't know what it's like to have his best friend kill himself. He doesn't really know who Mike was.

And I probably shouldn't have said that to him.

Eventually I summon the strength to stand up. I head straight to the sink to wash my hands thoroughly, twice. Then I wash my face and dry myself using the paper towels. I tuck myself back in and use a damp towel to wipe the spit off my shirt and start to dry it off under the hand dryer.

Someone else comes in.

It's Mike's dad.

'Hello, Eli. Glad you finally got here.' I'm taken back by his unlikely glee.

'Really?' I ask, probing for a reason.

'Well, why ever not? You are Michael's best friend, of course you should be here.'

Mike's dad really is the best. It makes me miss Mike more.

'Even after my speech?'

'I must admit, it was a tad unconventional, and I know it has ruffled a few people's feathers, but we both know that what you said was true and that is what is getting up people's noses. We both know that it's what Mike would have wanted too. So get yourself together and come back out and get another drink down you, eh? For Mike.' And he taps me on the back as he exits the room and I am still drying saliva from my shirt.

He only came in to wash his hands.

I stand at the dryer for another minute wondering whether that incident actually happened or whether it was my imagination telling me something I wanted to hear. Still, it makes me walk out of the toilet with a modicum of pride that I have done right by Mike's family, and even though Ralph has no idea about what may or may not have happened after he vacated the toilets, I could now take Jackie home and leave with my head held high in moral victory.

I grab Jackie's arm.

'Come on, let's go back to mine and have a decent bottle of wine.'

She stands without saying a word, and we escort each other off the premises to bumble our way back to the flat for some more drinks.

I have it in my mind that even though it is late, and it's Friday, nothing is going to stop me going to therapy tonight. Not after the day I've had.

Jackie asks me why I'm wet and whether I've eaten a urinal cake. I tell her that Ralph is upset and an aggressive dick, and it's then that she realises she left her scarf inside.

RALPH

He's just so pleased with himself. A week has gone by without his friend Mike. He knows he took it badly, and he took it out on himself and then Eli, but a tension that has been stiffening Ralph's shoulders for a week has eased. He orders the most expensive whisky he can find from the bar and inhales with glee after a few days on the cheap stuff.

He has his closure. All that's left of Mike is a bag of ash and four fillings. Ralph has made his peace with Mike's father. And he managed to get out the last of his anger on Eli. He even knows that it wasn't Eli's fault he was picked for the eulogy.

Ralph can move on.

He can finally relax.

Mike is gone and Ralph is at ease with that, now.

Then he sees her walking towards him. The woman that was with Eli in the church. Who bought drinks at the bar. She is too good for that cretin, he thinks. She is beautiful. Classy. It seems like she is approaching in slow motion. Calm. Poised. Focussed.

Before he has time to take a sip of his drink, Jackie is in front of him.

'Well, hello the—'

'Think you're some tough guy, huh?' She's not mad but there is a quiet menace to her.

'Wait there. Wha…' He looks around to see who is watching. Nobody is. Jackie is not making a scene. This is private.

'I know about you, Ralphy.'

'And what exactly do you know about me, miss?'

Jackie leans in. She speaks just above a whisper.

'Forty-three messages, Ralph. You've been busy.'

Ralph looks around again, this time hoping that nobody is watching them.

'I don't know what you're talking about.' He does. His face is flushing.

'Glad he's dead, aren't you, Ralph?' She keeps saying his name and it unsettles him. 'Think he made the right decision, don't you? Mike was selfish, wasn't he?'

Ralph stares at her, regretting what he did to Eli. Cursing himself for the messages he had sent to Mike.

'Shall I go on?'

'No. No. You've made your point. What do you want from me?'

'Nothing. Your secret is safe with me. I just want you to know that I know. And I want your drink.'

'What?'

'The eighteen-year-old Macallan you just ordered. Give it to me.'

Ralph hands the glass to Jackie. She takes a mouthful, lets it coat her tongue, and she swallows.

'God, Ralph. That is a great fucking whisky. Thanks. I'll see you soon.'

She drops the glass on the floor, turns and leaves.

Everyone at the wake turns to look at Ralph.

Closure is fleeting.

TUESDAY
(THREE DAYS BEFORE FUNERAL FRIDAY)

Bargaining. This is another thing we do – apparently – when grieving. We try to make a deal with ourselves to act a certain way so that we will feel better. Maybe campaigning for mental-health awareness would raise my spirits about the horrific passing of my best friend. If I treat others more compassionately, they will pay this forward and it will help me to heal.

Maybe God can help. I could be a better Christian or Muslim or Buddhist. Or whatever.

Maybe that's what Jackie is doing.

I'd like to be a better atheist.

For me, I think it's something else. I think Mike wanted me to be better and do better, and in order to achieve this, I need to quit my job, sort my love life and write something worthwhile.

Something real.

I take a seat at my desk and talk to Mike about the blurb for *King Liar*.

'I'm not sure about the title anymore, Mike. If we are going to make this more true, if I am going to draw on real experience, it doesn't seem to fit.'

Mike doesn't answer. Instead, he does that thing my fake therapist does where she just sits and looks at me until I add another comment or come to some realisation myself. Which, of course, is what I do.

'But then it does work in some sort of ironic way, I guess. I'm telling the truth but it's only a version and it can't all be true, can it?'

Still nothing. I cued him up for that one, too.

I take the previous version of *King Liar* from the bookshelf and lay it down next to my laptop.

'Your blurb won't work now, Mike, because we've changed the bloody story to include somebody committing suicide at the start.' My eyes glaze. I'm trying to bargain my way out of this situation but

I feel utterly devastated that Mike's final blurb will not be used, and I can't remember the blurb he wrote before this one, so I have no Goddamned idea what his last words were to me because he couldn't even be bothered to blurb his own fucking death, and I find that I have come full circle on this grief journey because I'm angry again.

And that is perfect for writing.

'Don't you worry about the blurb,' Mike says. 'That's my job. You get on with the hard part. Get the words down. You have your main character, Bud Ellis, he wants to live his life like a movie, right?'

'Right.'

'You keep that going. He wants to end it with his partner because he thinks that winning her back will only make them stronger. He needs that complication. So what is it about the death of his friend that plays into this? Is that the complication? Is it the catalyst? What does it add? Is there some kind of mystery there?'

'I don't know.' I'm honest. I really don't know why I decided to bring this element into the story. It just came out.

'Maybe it will come to you if you sit at that thing and start typing.'

He's right. Of course. I'm not the kind of person to make a plan, that's more Jackie's area of expertise. We complement each other so well: she is methodical and organised, and I'm always late for things. She is loving and manipulative, and I don't know what is real anymore.

I double-click the file that I have saved as *King Liar* and delete that title. It doesn't feel right. I'm going with my gut. I read through the short opening I have now, which I have copied from the real-life death of my best friend, and then I turn to him and say, 'That was some crazy news about Ted, eh?'

'Shocking. But that doesn't need to find its way into the book.'

'God, no. That would be crass.'

'Indeed. We should probably send the other Ted a card, though.'

~~THE PRINCIPLE~~
~~KING LIAR~~
UNTITLED PROJECT
(WORKING TITLE)
BY ELI HAGIN

FIRST CHAPTER

For everyone but Bud Ellis, death was final.

To him, it was a gift.

Heartbreak was a gift.

Getting fired would be a gift.

Girls who grew into women, believing they were princesses because their parents had always called them that, were destined for defeat. It was unrealistic. They were doomed to failure because nobody would ever live up to their standards. They would feel entitled. Privileged. Lucky. And the real world has no place for that kind of delusion.

Boys who grew into men, having been told they could be whatever they wanted to be as long as they worked hard, would have to ready themselves for disappointment. It's not always the case. Talent is not equal to success. A strong work ethic could still lead down a long road to the middle.

You may not have been told, as a child, that your sex and race and social class would be a huge factor in determining your opportunities - unless you were male, white and wealthy. Either way, your goals would undoubtedly prove unrealistic.

Heartbreak, depression and loneliness. That's what life was about. And it was all over far too quickly.

Bud craved complication. Only by experiencing true hardship could one appreciate a victory.

I hold down *Ctrl*.

I press *A*.

I stare at the screen for a few seconds, shake my head, and hit *Delete*.

It's shit. I need to get to the point quicker, mention the dead friend. Pull that into the complication, somehow. Kurt Vonnegut said to 'start as close to the end as possible', but I'm not sure I know how to do that.

And what is my ending? The friend is still dead. The boy loses the girl and wins her back, while managing to quit his job and, as I'm pulling myself into this story, he finishes his novel. Who wants to read that? It's too tidy. Everything sewn up in a neat package.

There has to be more.

I try to start closer to the end:

```
He cheated on her. He could have broken it off with
her cleanly. He could have said that he wasn't ready
for things to go to the next level, that would have
made it easier to win her back. But Bud Ellis didn't
want things easy. If he'd wanted that he would have
just stayed with the woman that he loved and he
never would have killed his best friend.
```

Fuck. Where did that come from?

I look over my shoulder slowly, hoping that Mike isn't there reading this.

So now Bud kills his best friend? That doesn't sound right. But perhaps it is more compelling.

'Fuck.'

'What are you swearing about?' Mike asks.

Shit. I said it out loud.

'Nothing. Just ... wrestling with the blank page. You know how it is.' I try to smile. It's a flimsy possibility because I don't ever have any trouble starting something.

'Look, if it'll help, I can go. I'll leave you in peace.'

I don't have to answer. Mike isn't really there, I know that. But I'm still scared.

I shut my eyes and take two deep breaths before turning around. Mike is gone.

'Fuck.' I say it out loud again. I don't know what just happened but I need to talk about it with somebody. I need to voice what I am feeling. Get the poison out. I need to speak with somebody real.

Mike is in a morgue somewhere with his lips sewn shut, wearing a suit his father bought him to be buried in. Jackie fucked me and left. One Ted has a hole in his heart and the other was shot in the chest. I don't know what is real, right now, but I do know that I still have my therapist.

I close the laptop, folding away my new opening chapter, and I move over to the sofa that Mike was just sitting on. All that's left to do is lie down and bleed.

FAKE **THERAPIST**

INT. ELI'S OFFICE/FAKE THERAPIST'S OFFICE

    FAKE THERAPIST
So, Eli, how have you been?
    ELI
My best friend killed himself. One of the Teds got shot. Jackie and I are still engaged and she's more sexual than ever. Oh, and I'm still working at DoTrue. My first day back in the office is tomorrow. That just about sums it up. Can I go now?
    FAKE THERAPIST
You called this meeting. I know all of that about you, already. So what is this really about?
    ELI
Damn, Doc, you're good. It's like you're in my head. You know?
(He laughs.)
    FAKE THERAPIST
What do you want to talk about? Be real for a moment.
    ELI
Damn it, I'm trying to be real. I've written Mike's eulogy. I've got this idea for the book but, for some reason, I'm struggling with the opening, which has never happened to me before. And now … now … I don't know … maybe … maybe I did kill him.
    FAKE THERAPIST
What? You killed somebody?
    ELI
That's what I'm saying. I don't know if I did or not.

FAKE THERAPIST
You would know if you had ended somebody else's life, Eli.

ELI
Sure. But killing somebody doesn't have to mean making the cut. I could've neglected him. I ignored one too many calls. I could've pushed him. Like, I don't know, encouraged him to do it without realising.

FAKE THERAPIST
These are the types of things a police officer might suggest to you in order to gain a false confession. That's the last thing you need.

ELI
I'm not going to the police.
(BEAT)

FAKE THERAPIST
Did Mike's mental health issues annoy you in some way?

ELI
What do you mean?

FAKE THERAPIST
Were you irritated by his previous suicide attempts? Did you see them as cries for attention? Were you bored with his lack of conviction?

ELI
That makes me sound awful.

FAKE THERAPIST
This is coming out of your head, Eli.

ELI
I wasn't as understanding as I could have been. I know that.

FAKE THERAPIST
Do you understand what it takes to commit suicide?

There is a strength to it. Missing a phone call or
telling somebody to 'Just get on and do it, then'
is not enough. You cannot be weak to pull a trigger
or cut an artery or jump from a great height. Do
you understand that?

(Eli doesn't answer. He stares at the ceiling and
breathes slowly.)

Of course I understand that. Mike had been weak before. He
thought he wanted to die but he didn't have the balls to go through
with it. I'm not stupid. He idolised me. He was obviously in love
with Jackie. Who wouldn't be?

I think about DoTrue. How every day it chips away at me. A small
piece of me dies and will never return. I know that the constant
dripping effect takes its toll on me. I know that it brings me down a
little bit further than the day before.

Each day, I get worse. Less empathetic. Less compassionate. More
cynical. Less real. And, if you can do that to a person, then there is
no reason that you cannot do the opposite. You can bring a person
up. You can prod them day by day to become better, happier, braver.

I may not know what is true, right now, but I know that much.

So I type.

THE **TEDS**
(THREE DAYS BEFORE FUNERAL FRIDAY)

Ted was alone for the first time in decades.

The other Ted had not worshipped him, he hadn't been a sidekick – they were equal. Their respect for one another was equal. Their love for one another was equal. And their history together was unequalled.

Their friendship had endured war and death and marriage and separation. The two men had spent every day working together in Gaucho's. They had a bond so strong, moments of silence were never awkward. There was a comfort in that. And understanding.

Now *that* Ted was gone.

And this Ted already missed him.

He lights a cigar. Something he used to do in secret because he knew Ted didn't like it. He can't escape it now, Ted will always be watching him, he tells himself.

Ted rests the cigar on an ashtray on the coffee table in front of him. He's at home. He's not allowed to go back to Gaucho's just yet. And part of him wants never to set foot in the place again. It's no longer their coffee shoppe, it's a crime scene. He imagines selling the place and some local trendy upstart turning it into some open-mic club called Krime Seen. Or another sex shop called Can't Buy a Thrill.

'Well, buddy ... looks like that "brave little boy" turned out to be some little fucking coward, eh? Salut.' And he knocks back another cheap whisky. He can't remember how many he's had but the part of the word that follows 'Glen' on the bottle is blurring.

It burns.

That's the point. Even the expensive stuff burns if you throw it down your neck like that.

Ted wants to feel that pain, so that he can forget for a moment how his soul aches. That he is thinking about the writer who comes into Gaucho's all the time to procrastinate and seek wisdom from his elders, and how that writer had a best friend who stopped his pain.

He doesn't want to think this way and he knows he could never go through with such a thing, but Ted has skipped the denial and anger phase and has slumped straight into depression. It's intense but it's not negative – he's too old for that, he's seen too much. Ted is not in despair, wondering what meaning life has now that he is alone, instead he is trying to discover how to go on in this new guise.

He is searching for life's meaning.

Because he wants it. He wants to go on living.

He fills another glass then sucks in a mouthful of smoke, moves it around his tongue and teeth – he likes the way it makes his fillings taste – and he blows it out across the table. A purple cloud that will eventually dissipate like his grief.

A car horn. A woman swearing in the street. Life going on. The life without his best friend. His companion. Local people knew him and were shocked at the way he was despatched, but it's so fleeting. People can't hold on to an emotion like they used to, Ted thinks. The idea of anybody having fifteen minutes of fame seems too long, now. These kids can't even listen to the entirety of a three-minute song.

He swigs.

The smoke has hit the yellowing ceiling.

Ted looks across to the other sofa.

'Fucking coward. Am I right?' He raises his glass again and stares at the other Ted.

Cue denial.

'Ilario. I tell you … when they catch him … am I right?'

This continues. He drinks. He smokes. He talks to the other Ted. His dead best friend. And, as long as that other Ted is across the room and listening, this Ted is more alone than ever.

RALPH

He does the same thing. He sits and he drinks.

So predictable.

But Ralph is not in denial. He doesn't see Mike across the room. He doesn't hear his voice. He can picture him in his mind. He's young. A kid. They're at school. They're racing on the field. They're copying each other's homework. They're kicking a ball all the way from the school gate to Mike's garden.

Then they're fighting. Then it's forgotten about. And they lose touch. And they get back in touch. They've been through it. Ralph hits the *anger* phase but it's nothing to do with Mike killing himself, it's that Eli gets to do a reading at the funeral when Ralph considers himself to be the best friend that Mike had.

He was there for him, even when he wasn't. To lend an ear. For advice. Support. Encouragement.

Ralph scrolls through his phone, finds his voicemails and clicks on the last one from Mike. He places the phone on the table, hits the button to play through the speaker and lifts his drink.

'Hey, Ralph. It's Mike. Feeling shitty. Done some things that maybe I shouldn't have. Just wondered what you were up to and if you fancied a chat. Maybe we could grab a pint. Anyway, drop me a message. If not, I'll text you soon, I guess. Cheers.'

Another missed call for Mike.

Another nail in the coffin.

People hold on to these things. A message from a deceased loved one that they cling to because it means they can still hear their voice. Or a grandparent who struggled with technology and would send nonsensical messages because they couldn't use their phone properly. They keep it. A memento. A reminder.

But Ralph doesn't feel that way. He doesn't want to hear Mike droning on. In the same way that he doesn't want to scroll through all those text messages where Mike was saying that he wanted to kill himself. How awful he felt. That everybody would be better off without him in their lives.

God, Mike, just fucking do it, then.

Ralph didn't want to be reminded of his friend in that way. It wasn't anything to do with denial; he just wanted to think of the kid on the first day of secondary school with the huge blazer that his mother said he would 'grow into'. He wanted to take a gulp of beer and laugh to himself about the time they tried to camp out in Mike's garden but the dog was so stressed out by the tent that it attacked and bit through the material and drew blood from Mike's head. Mike's father had rescued the situation and they ended up sleeping inside.

But Eli would get to say something at the funeral.

He sighs. Finishes his beer and places it next to the seven empty bottles on the floor next to his sofa.

I want to do it, but I worry about my family.

I'm overthinking it.

I can't keep feeling like this every day.

Ralph scrolls through the text conversations he had with Mike. How was he supposed to respond to these kinds of messages? They would wear anybody down eventually, wouldn't they?

Maybe not Eli. Maybe his conversations looked different. Maybe he never gave up on Mike, and that's why he gets to speak in front of everyone while Mike lies next to him in a wooden box.

Ralph doesn't want this. He doesn't want to look back and realise that his childhood friend was a drain on his life. He doesn't want to look back, reread messages and realise that he, himself, was a shitty friend.

Both of their mistakes are there to be seen. And that's the problem with the ultra-connected world. Everything we think or eat or take a photo of is out there. And it stays there. A comment on a political cartoon or a review of some film or book. You can't take it back.

You may have voted for something and since it happened, your stance has altered. But you've already been so vocal about your original view. Maybe you rewatched a film you hated, that you told everyone about. Maybe it worked better on your television than it did on the big screen. But you wrote a fucking blog about how awful it was.

Too late.

It's done.

And, maybe your friend was going through something difficult and you thought you understood it because you think that all this mental-health awareness is over-egged. Maybe you thought he should just 'man up'. Maybe you got sick of the whining. Maybe you said some things on a message that you wish you could delete but you can't. Because you puked out your thoughts and they're out there with your TripAdvisor review for the family-run B&B you slaughtered for having 'cheap sausages'.

Ralph skims through and deletes everything. Sure, it'll still be on Mike's phone, but who is going to want to trawl through that? The guy killed himself. He polished his floor and he sliced through his own thighs.

Mike deleted himself.

Now Ralph is deleting him, too.

He doesn't look across the room to the other sofa and see Mike. Because he doesn't want to see him.

He drinks a beer. Still no Mike.

Then another.

Nothing.

Ralph rattles through the rest of the pack. His vision is blurred and his head spins. He thinks back to that time when he and Mike were on the swings in the park with their friend Billy. They were swinging while Billy climbed one of the A-frame poles. They were standing on the seats, swinging, then, at the right time, dropping to the floor while kicking the seat over the bar to see if they could get it to go over and over until it was wrapped around the top. Then Billy would be there to untangle it and they would go again.

Ralph and Mike managed it. Billy untangled the swings and slid back down to the ground. As his feet hit the floor, he let out a scream that turned Ralph cold. As Billy slid down the pole, there was a nail or screw sticking out that caught him between the legs and ripped his balls apart.

Mike looked and threw up.

Ralph laughed, uncomfortably, at first, before running for help while Billy rolled on the floor crying and holding his dick.

He doesn't know why, but as the room spins and the saliva in his mouth starts to thin, Ralph decides to lie down on the sofa with that memory in his mind and he sends a text to his best friend Mike.

JACKIE

It's late when Jackie hears a message come through.

Descartes sits on the bottom of her bed. Because he knows he's not allowed to.

Jackie checks her phone but there is no text message. She read something recently about people feeling phantom vibrations of mobile phones in their pockets. Some people have suggested it is to do with anticipation or anxiety, and others say it's because you're crazy, like it's some kind of sensory hallucination.

She looks at the cat, taunting her with its quiet malevolence.

The phone makes another noise.

Not her phone. It's coming from the wardrobe.

Jackie swings her legs around and gets out of bed. She stands up and whips the bedcovers quickly to startle her cat, who jumps three feet in the air before landing on its feet on the carpet. Jackie smiles to herself. She's on to him.

Then she's opening her wardrobe door, finding the trousers she was wearing the night she found Mike dead in his apartment and she's taking a phone out of the pocket.

Three messages from Ralph.

She has no idea who that is.

Another text notification flashes onto the screen.

That scream. I can still hear that scream.

There are message notifications before this one but Jackie is yet to crack the code that will let her have full access to Mike's phone, so the longer messages are cut short. Still, she scrolls up to see whether she can get any context for the most recent comment.

Remember when Billy Embers ripped his balls open?

I don't even know why I was thinking of that. I guess I was going over some old times in my head. Trying to work thro...

She doesn't know what comes next but she gets the gist. Some kid called Billy ruined his testicles somehow. A dog, she thinks, then looks over at Descartes.

Several messages follow about the same subject, then there's a break. Jackie gets back into bed. She takes Mike's phone with her. Just in case. On her own phone, she texts Eli with a sweet goodnight message and a 'good luck' for his first day back in the office tomorrow – even though she wants him to quit. She ends with four kisses.

She uses her phone to set the alarm for the morning, turns off the light and shuts her eyes, knowing that she can't sleep.

Mike's phone:

You said that you thought nobody would care if you died.

Jackie remembers Mike saying this to her. He was obviously putting it around everywhere. Maybe hoping somebody would give him the answer that he wanted. You send the same message to enough people, eventually you'll hear the thing you want to hear.

I don't know if that's true. We'll see who comes on Friday.

But I am sure of one thing.

You made the right decision.

I'm glad you're not here anymore.

Jackie says 'What the fuck?' under her breath, her face is lit white by Mike's phone screen. If she knew Mike's code, she could text this Ralph guy back, she tells herself: *I'm not.*

That would freak him out.

She smiles. Descartes sees that ghostly image from across the room. Maniacal, he tells himself as he backs out of the door. He doesn't want to stay there tonight, no matter how comfortable the bed is or how insubordinate it is to lie on it.

The rebellion could wait.

And so too, thinks Jackie, can Ralph.

WEDNESDAY
(TWO DAYS BEFORE FUNERAL FRIDAY)

09:41

Sam's been at work for over three hours already, of course. I can only assume that he woke up to both his children defecating on his wife, or something. It's about time they upped the ante.

'Aaaaafternoon, Eli.' He drags out the first part to accentuate his point.

Thank God for Sam. This pithy, degenerate dig at my blatant disregard for punctuality drops me back into my work consciousness and reminds me just why I hate this job and Sam's misplaced sense of self-importance. I suppose I should respect his normality in this situation, especially with everyone else *handling with care.*

'Danny said it would be fine.' I knew this would goad him.

'He never said anything to me,' he mumbles, clearly irritated.

'That's because he doesn't have to. You're not my boss, Sam, he is.' I see him physically withdraw into himself as I say this and immediately I feel guilty. Sam could be me in twenty years and, if that's the case, he probably feels exactly the same as I do except he's been doing this for ten times as long and he has to deal with two miscreant offspring and a loveless marriage. So now I am the person who has taken away the one thing he has in life that makes him feel worthwhile – his power over me.

I kick the button to ignite the power in my DoTrue branded PC, then sit back in my chair, swivelling from side to side, feeling agitated.

'Look, Sam, sorry I snapped, okay? I'm just dealing with a lot at the moment, and Danny has already grilled me about being late.' It's a small lie and I'm just playing the game a little here, but I do see the tension release from Sam's shoulders and some of the colour from his cheeks is draining. I know he's pleased I said it, even though he does not respond verbally himself.

His power is returning.

For what seems like the next couple of hours I trawl through a few days' worth of emails, the obvious chronological updates from Sam, more Viagra offers, a monthly greeting from a local recruiter hoping to help with any vacancies and, surprisingly, three emails from colleagues expressing condolences for my recent loss. One from someone I don't think I know. Katie Miller. Her email signature says she works in the finance department. Payroll, in fact. No wonder she sends her sympathy, she knows how much I earn each month.

I work my way through Sam's laborious anthology of the events of the days I have missed and compose an email to him stating my gratitude for the consistent high level of shared communication on the events surrounding the campaign that were missed in my absence. I think I even used one of those business expressions that I hate, like 'thanks for keeping me in the loop'.

God, I hate being me.

I manage to resist a typical Eli response that would remark on the chronology or the fact that there are fewer updates on a twenty-four-hour news channel. I have decided not to give any clues regarding my resignation. No. Shock factor and big impact is the new strategy.

I personally respond to the recruiter, who has undoubtedly been ignored by everyone apart from Sam, who has dutifully delivered the company line that there is currently a head freeze and she should try again in six months. It's not my job to reply, and I personally think that recruiters are a special breed of scum, but I decide to give her some hope with an exclusive scoop:

Dear Angela,
Thank you for your email regarding possible vacancies within DoTrue. Unfortunately, I only occupy an entry-level position within the UK marketing team and couldn't possibly comment on any positions elsewhere within our organisation or, in fact, whether we are hiring at all right now. What

```
I can tell you is that I am going to resign today.
My bosses don't even know yet, but I'm almost
positive they will not adhere to making me work my
full month's notice.
     Please try again on Monday offering some suitable
candidates.
     Regards,
     Eli Hagin
```

I hit send and smile to myself. Sam looks at me as if to say, 'Well obviously he's not as cut up as he's making out.' And, in a way, he's right.

I wait a few minutes but Angela doesn't respond. It takes the buzz out of it for me. I start to worry that perhaps she has forwarded this on to Sam or Danny and I've blown the element of surprise for a short-term high. But surely, that would not be in her best interest.

I delete my spam and send a response to the three people in the office with a heart. I send each person an individual message thanking them for their concern and support. It feels like seconds before a blue rectangle appears in the bottom-right corner of my display, informing me that I have received a new email. Unfortunately it's not from Angela; she clearly hasn't seen the funny side of my correspondence. It's from Katie. The girl I have never spoken to.

'Wow. I can't believe you are back in the office already. That's incredible. You must really love this place.' She uses some punctuation to make a smiley face and I find it less irritating than when Jackie does it. 'Let me know if you need anything. I know it must be difficult coming back so soon.'

I'm blown away by her benevolence and her apparent disdain for DoTrue and, even though I still have no idea who she is or what she looks like or how she knows me, I think, *fuck it,* and reply to her saying that I need to get away from my desk already and will be going to grab a coffee from the canteen if she wants to join me.

10:16

I don't know why I did it. Maybe because I know I'm leaving or because I know I am breaking up with Jackie on Friday or just morbid curiosity. Either way, I did it.

'Coffee, Sam?' I stand up as if to leave.

'You've only been here thirty minutes, Eli.' I only asked him out of courtesy.

'I always have a coffee at this time of day. Besides, I need the kick-start today, you know?' I say this in a way that implies that I'm still a little fragile. It's better than coming right out and saying, *Come on, Sam, you heartless bastard, my best friend just killed himself. Cut me some slack.* That would make me sound desperate.

'Yeah, well, okay. I'll have a tea if that's all right.'

'No worries,' I say in as cheerful a tone as I can muster. It's always so annoying when he does want a drink because it means that I can't waste as much time. I know he does it on purpose.

I push my chair underneath my desk and walk off. After two steps I'm overcome with a sense of paranoia and step back to my desk to lock my computer screen. Sam peers over his own monitor quizzically.

As I enter this unknown realm of actually finishing something, I'm increasingly aware of everything and everyone, so I can't have anything go wrong, otherwise it will make it too easy for me to make an excuse and back out.

At least I'm taking something from my therapy sessions.

If I can just get through this one, simple task, I know that I will be able to push through Funeral Friday and end things with Jackie too.

Then I'm free.

I pretend I don't see the gossiping and staring that goes on as I ebb past co-workers towards the canteen. I'm the car crash they can't help but slow down for.

I opt for a coffee from the machine rather than the percolated tar sat behind the counter that went stale over an hour ago.

I enjoy my coffee. I like it black and I like it fresh, but I also love the watered-down sheep dip that you get from vending machines. I don't know why but I find it quite comforting. It has to be top-notch coffee for me or, if that's not available, weak-as-hell coffee-flavoured hot water. Nothing in between. Nothing granulated or percolated. Either high-quality sweet espresso roast from Arabica beans or dangerously addictive, flavoured chemical mixed with brown water.

The canteen lady shows me her usual look of disgust from behind the counter as I spurn her efforts once again.

Then I get a tap on the shoulder, which startles me and I spill some of my not-really-coffee coffee. I half expect it to burn a whole straight through the linoleum with a wisp of smoke.

'Eli, Hey.' She kisses the air beside both my ears alternately – quite unconventional for a co-worker to have that level of familiarity, that degree of comfort and informality. As she pushes back, I immediately realise exactly who Katie is.

I'd been cornered at the last office Christmas party. One of those Christmas parties that is actually held inside the office after work hours on a Thursday so that the following day you can all relive the terribly inappropriate events of the previous evening. Clichés such as photocopied genitalia or one-night drunken affairs behind reception are rehashed the next day to extend the alleged merriment and give most of the workers a little bit of substance to their otherwise monotonous lives.

Danny regales everyone with his conquest of whatever junior staff members he got his hands on while the girls unfortunate enough to have experienced this misery wince behind their coffee cups hoping that nobody has found out.

But we all know.

One office junior he didn't get to was the young Katie Miller. Or Kate, as she told me after we conformed with festive tradition under the mistletoe that was strategically placed over the doorway to the accounts room, where only women work and where, that night, the finger buffet was located. Nice one, Danny.

We spoke for a while, bonding over our mutual mistrust for Mr Elwes and clear distaste for the company as a whole while the rest of the office idiots leched around to the music that was kindly provided by one of the cocky, high-flying, spiky-haired, gel-soaked sales guys who likes to DJ in his spare time.

It was a drunken one-night thing that was completely innocent, apart from the peck she gave me on the cheek, but I never even really thought about her again or pursued a friendship. But I'm glad. It would be harder for me to leave today if I knew I had an ally here that I was leaving in the trenches. I wouldn't be able to neglect her and let her deal with this place on her own. So I've kept my head down and blocked everyone out.

'Katie, hi,' I say in what sounds like a normal tone to me, but I'm aware of how wide my eyes are and the fact that my pitch is also a little higher, suggesting excitement.

'Kate,' she corrects me.

'Yes. Kate. Sorry. How are you?' I'm a little flustered for some reason and feel anxious about my less-than-original salutation.

'Me? How are you? I'm fine. I can't believe you are back at work.'

This is what I remember about Kate. She's nice. It's an unimaginative description of a person but it's the word that best describes her. She's nice. Genuinely nice. You don't meet too many people like Kate in your life, I would guess, and I'm beginning to wonder whether we could become better friends.

Although, the last person I knew that was like this possibly slept with my girlfriend and killed himself six days ago. I don't think Kate would sleep with Jackie.

'So you heard about Mike. News does travel fast in this place.'

'Yeah. It's terrible. Honestly, I meant what I said in my email. If there's anything I can do—'

I cut her off. 'Thanks. That's kind but I'm not sure I'm going to be here much longer,' I confess.

'What? What do you mean?' She sounds shocked. As if I'm so depressed that I might follow Mike's example.

'I'm going to quit.' You can sense her relief.

'Wow. My hero. When?'

'Today.'

'Today? Fuck, Eli.' She puts her hand over her mouth on the curse to signify her shock and grabs my arm, pulling me to one side as if on a covert mission. She whispers, 'Today? God, that's amazing. I wish I could be so brave. When exactly? How?' She seems so excited at the prospect. Again, in a genuine way.

'I have a meeting at twelve with Danny—'

'Oh, I hate that guy,' she interrupts.

'Er, and Sam Jordane and a few of the sales managers.' I trail off thinking of ways to kill them all.

'So you want to do it before then, right?' she asks. 'Skip that boring hour?'

'No. I want to go out with an explosion,' I say.

'So you're going to the meeting?' she continues, clearly perplexed.

'I'm quitting in the meeting,' I say, with a cartoon grin and a bad-guy eyebrow-raise.

Her face lights up with a luminescent smile as she finally grasps what I am planning to do and she says. 'Well, I can definitely help you go out with a bang.'

11:24

You can smell Danny before he even walks onto the sales floor. He occupies a space at the end, with glass walls so that we can all see him on the phone or in his meetings or with his fucking feet up on the desk. And he can peer out at us, his loyal subjects, to remind us that he is watching, that he is the boss.

He's such an arrogant dick.

He comes through the door, following a cloud of cologne. He usually has his top button undone and his tie hangs low, even in the morning. I'm sure he thinks he's the forgotten member of the Rat

Pack or something but, to me, he looks like the kid at school who gets extra time in exams due to learning difficulties.

But not today. That button is fastened and the tie is in a full Windsor knot. Someone is coming in today and they are either important or attractive.

'Can I have everyone's attention?'

No 'please'. He's Danny Elwes; he doesn't need manners.

Some of the sales guys are on the telephone – if they don't show enough minutes of outgoing calls, they're in trouble. Some hang up. Some tell the person on the other end they are going to hang up, one guy tells his customer to hold and places the receiver on his desk.

'I know we were supposed to have the big meeting today, but something has come up. We'll move it to the same time tomorrow. Gives you an extra day to get your figures right or sell a few more laptops, eh?'

Sam laughs. He's the only one. But Danny still counts it as a funny comment. He's not short on confidence, that's for sure. And that can often make up for what you are lacking in other areas.

'So,' Danny continues, 'get on as you normally would today. The quarter has been strong so far, for this time of year. Keep it up. And don't disturb me once my meeting starts – unless somebody dies.'

Again, Sam laughs. One of the sales guys joins in. The customer-care team knows that it's not funny. They're further up the office and the scent has only just reached them. They don't need to say anything to each other. It's just a look, an eye-roll and a giggle.

I know what's coming and I hate it.

'Now, let's do some good.'

I look at the stapler on my desk. It's heavy. I imagine throwing it at Danny, who gets knocked out and crashes through the glass walls of his office. I picture stapling his tie to his forehead.

Danny claps his hands together loudly as he exits, as though punctuating his motto, and the sound jolts me out of my reverie and into the joys of reality.

I won't be able to quit today. I need that meeting. I need a scene.

It sounds like another excuse, but it's not. I want to do it right. Maximum impact. If I'm going to finish this job I hate so much, I want to leave a legacy.

Danny goes back into his office and sprays himself with more of his fragrance. He's like a rat in a cage, and he's forgotten that the cameras are filming him 24/7.

There's a rustling on Sam's desk. He unclips a plastic container and takes out a sandwich. The smell of tuna and mayonnaise mixing with Danny's desperation.

'Another brown-bag lunch, eh, Sam?'

'Well, you know...' He trails off as though I do know. But I don't. He'll explain, I'm sure. Just as soon as he has a mouthful of bread and fish. 'Gotta use this extra time for my forecast.'

'But ... the meeting was supposed to be today, so surely you've already done your forecast?' This is somewhere between a question and a statement.

He swallows his food and I think he's about to come back at me, but he takes another bite and then starts talking. What is wrong with him?

'Danny has given us a gift of extra time, I'm not going to repay him by not utilising it, Eli.'

'Sam, you're a fucking idiot.'

He stops chewing. His mouth drops open. I can see his chewed-up lunch.

'It's like you've got Stockholm Syndrome or something. You need to get out of this building once in a while. Breathe some air. Get a pint at lunchtime instead of an email. Fuck.' I'm exasperated. 'Don't die here, man, okay.' I mean this. It shocks me to feel any empathy for the guy. 'And finish your food before you start talking. It's disgusting. I'm going to lunch.'

I log off.

And walk out.

I hear Sam mutter under his breath, 'He's only just got here'. Still with that fucking food in his mouth.

I hope the idiot does drop dead in this place.

11:27

A minute later, I can see why Danny has dipped his torso in Old Spice. I didn't make eye contact with him as I walked past his fish-tank office. He was probably looking at his own reflection, anyway.

As I exit the DoTrue premises, a woman pulls up in a brand-new Mini. She's attractive, to me, at least. Dark hair. Professional-looking. Smart. Clearly has money to spend on quality clothing, unlike my suit, which cost so little it had to have been made by slave kids somewhere. I stand by the door and hold it open, otherwise she has to buzz in and, if it's the person that Danny has tarted himself up for, I like the idea that she will catch him unprepared. He's probably minting his breath right now.

She shuts the car door and locks it with her key fob. I watch her face as she eyes up the building and sighs. She wants to be here as much as I do.

'Are you here to see Danny Elwes?' I ask as she nears me.

'For my sins.' She sighs again and I can't help but smile.

'Ah, so you must have met him before.' I laugh. She doesn't.

'Just over the phone. What's he like?'

'He's my boss.'

'And what's he like? What am I walking into?'

I pause. It's like she is inviting me in to tell her the truth. Weirdly, she seems trustworthy. I figure as I'm about to quit, anyway, it can't hurt. Can it?

'He's a real slimy piece of shit. But that's only my opinion. Well … mine and every woman or minority that has ever met him. But you can make your own mind up.' I push the door open for her. 'Top of the stairs, turn left, keep going until the aftershave makes your eyes water.'

She walks past me and says, 'Well, fuck me.'

'I'm sure he'll think he can.'

I let go of the door and walk off.

12:02

Coffee on my own is absolute bliss. Life is better without people around.

I think about Kate.

She's wonderful. Understated. I like that about her. She doesn't stand up to Jackie, I know that Jackie is amazing. She's thoughtful and benevolent and funny. But how much does she love me? Is it as passionate as movie love?

I think about Kate.

She's resourceful. Going through all her old emails and files and secret cloud drives with compromising images of Danny. She's doing it for me. Or to see the look on that lecherous creep's face when I forward the images to everyone in the company address book.

But she's not Jackie.

Jackie is so intelligent. The idea of these pictures and stories that will dethrone our leader is child's play to Jackie. She would have a million other ways I could embarrass Danny and take him down. I bet that she could ruin him.

I think about Kate. And what she is doing for me. I know she doesn't compare to Jackie, nobody does. But she does look good and she has a brain – enough to realise that a career at DoTrue is not an option for anybody with an ounce of common sense or self-worth. She has confided in me. She likes me, I can tell. Perhaps she had intended to use all the information she has gathered to extort Danny but, instead, she is using what she has to help me.

I go through a list of all of Kate's qualities. And I compare them to Jackie. Kate doesn't really come out on top for any of the categories.

Apart from one.

She's not Jackie.

And that means she can be a complication. My complication. The obstacle in the story of my life that will help me lose Jackie, so that I can win her back.

12:50

Walking back to the office after lunch, I play 'Rocket Man' by Elton John through my earphones and walk in time. I imagine myself at the bottom of a swimming pool, looking up as the few people who have meant anything to me swim around, laughing and drinking wine from the bottle. There are pages from my first-chapter library strewn across the surface.

I don't understand the reason this image has popped into my mind, and I have no idea what it says about my current mental state, but it stays with me as I walk the next few minutes in silence.

The woman who I let into the building before I left still has her car parked outside, so I assume Danny is attempting to woo her in some way. He's either circling her chair, spouting his business speak, thinking of himself as a tiger, narrowing in on its prey. Or he has his feet on his desk, playing it so cool that she knows he is in no way cool.

It's an exciting game to play with myself. These are the things that get me through the working day.

I take the stairs, turn left, keep going until the smell of Cool Water cologne burns my nostril hairs, then I reach the glass box where Danny is sitting at his desk, his hands behind his head and his fucking feet on the desk, like some cocky private investigator, waiting for a wad of cash for the photos of some philandering husband caught in a compromised position.

I tap on the door, and I don't know why.

Maybe I want to save her.

Danny doesn't tell me to come in, but I think I see him nod his head backwards slightly to beckon me into his lair. I don't know what I'm going to say when I get in there.

'Ah, Eli.' He takes his feet off the desk and sits forwards in his chair. 'I'm glad you called in. This is Maeve. I was just telling her about the great work you did on the last campaign.'

'Good to meet you properly, Eli.' Her mouth turns up at one side. Is she going to drop me in it? Did I read things wrong? Have I just screwed up my opportunity for a grand exit?

'You know each other?' Danny asks.

'Oh, God, no. Eli was ever so polite and let me in the front door earlier.' She gives me a look. She's playing with me. Fucking with me.

'Well, Eli, Maeve and the company she works for are going to take on some of the marketing projects. The bigger campaigns across Europe. That kind of thing. Don't worry, she's not taking your job away.' He laughs and looks around the room for validation, but none of his cronies are present.

'Okay. That sounds good to me.' I don't know what else to say. It doesn't even matter if they're trying to push me out, I'm getting there before they have the opportunity.

'You were right, you know?' Maeve speaks up again.

'I'm sorry.'

'What you said to me when you let me in. You were absolutely right.'

Fuck. I feel my face start to burn.

'This *is* a really great company.' She smiles a smile that is more like a wink, and I sense my entire body sigh. This Maeve woman has got Danny down within an hour of meeting him. And if this first exchange is anything to go by, she's going to prove more than a handful for our illustrious manager.

She does not need to be saved.

'You big suck-up, Eli.' Again, nobody laughs at Danny. 'What was it you knocked for, anyway?'

I look at Maeve, wondering whether she will bail me out, but I think she likes watching me squirm.

'You know what, Danny? It has completely slipped my mind. It'll come back to me. I'll drop you an email.' I think that worked. 'Great to meet you, too, Maeve.' I start to back out of the door.

'I'm sure we will be talking more in the future.' She rolls her eyes so that only I can see.

Danny adjusts himself into his dominant-male super-pose and takes his eye off us for a moment. I screw my face up and shake my head.

We exchange another couple of looks.

Hers says, *Good on you.*

Mine says, *Good luck.*

She won't need it.

I head back to my desk, where Sam Jordane is still sitting, tapping at his keyboard, and I already want to stab him through the throat with my pen.

17:29

Ctrl. Alt.

   3 ... 2 ... 1...

   Delete.

I'm logged out, standing up, jacket on, bag in hand, walking, no goodbye, walking, past my arsehole boss, walking, out the door and onto the bus. The number eighteen bus, which takes me sixteen minutes and drops me right outside The Scam – my local pub – which is sixty-four steps from where I live.

I want a drink.

The last time I was here was with Mike and Jackie. The last supper. He sent the same text to both of us. I wonder how often he did that. I order a pint of lager to quench my thirst, and a whisky to nurse while I think.

I think about Mike. And that text. The text that got us all together that night. And all the other texts. All those messages where he was telling me that he wasn't happy, that he wanted to end it all. Was he sending those same messages to Jackie? Were there other people he was in contact with? Cousins? School friends?

I don't think he would have put that on her and, if he had, she would have told me.

The beer doesn't last long. I decide to text Jackie myself: *I'm at The Scam. How's your thirst?*

She responds almost instantly: *Give me 20 minutes then order a large Chardonnay. xx*

And I know I have twenty minutes. At this pace, that's another pint and a half.

18:17

I've had two pints when Jackie finally walks into The Scam, her hair tousled and sexy, her face bright with enthusiasm. I know she likes to go to church on Wednesday, so I assume that's where she went straight from work.

'Hey.' She kisses me. 'Sorry I'm a bit late. Buses were a nightmare. How long has this been sitting here.' Jackie picks up her drink, takes a gulp and makes a face like she just bit into a lemon.

'About six minutes.'

'Tastes about right.'

'You've been at church?' I ask, looking as though I'm interested.

'God, no. Didn't I tell you? Father Farrelly has moved on. There's a new guy, Father Salis. Comes from some backwater village where everyone is in everyone else's business. Hinton Hollow, or something quaint like that.'

'Sounds delightful.'

We clink glasses.

The mood is high. We drink and laugh, and talk about everything. Almost everything. She tells me something about her snobby cat, and I end up with tears streaming down my cheeks. I talk about Sam's kids and how Danny was made up today, trying to impress some marketing guru from Hampstead. There's a stupid moment where we are both laughing at the same story detail and we look towards the empty chair at our table, and I feel the atmosphere drop.

'I know. You felt that, too, huh?'

Jackie nods.

'It's like he's still here. He'd always kill the vibe somehow. One of his boring do-it-yourself projects...'

'Ha. Yeah. That's true.' Jackie agrees.

'A job he was applying for...'

'His latest blurb.'

It turns into a game.

'How he wants to kill himself.'

There's a hush. One of the moments where you feel as though you have said something inappropriate and everyone around you has just finished what they are talking about as the music stops.

Jackie spits her mouthful of wine into my lap.

'Fucking hell, Eli. I was not expecting that.' She knows she shouldn't find it funny but she can't help it.

'You'll have to get the next round because I can't go to the bar with wet trousers.'

'We could always take you home and get you out of those things.'

It's very tempting but I want to wallow some more.

'His dad is going to burn him to ash in a couple of days. The least we could do is have one drink too many in his honour. Then we'll go.'

'Makes sense.' She stands up. 'Same again, or a gin?'

'Yes,' I say, raising an eyebrow.

'Maybe you can work on your speech while I'm at the bar. I can't lie, I'm worried about what you consider to be appropriate.'

Damn, I love this woman.

Tonight we can be close. Tomorrow, I can fuck it up.

23:52

It's still Wednesday. Just. Jackie is asleep in my bed. My head is pounding. I look at the clock on the bedside table. It takes a moment to click into reality, where I am, how I got here. I panic for a moment. Forget how to breathe. Then I calm. Jackie is naked. We almost had sex but ended up falling asleep. I remember that.

I don't know how we got home. We must have walked. It's sixty-four steps. A hundred if you are weaving and winding down the pavements. Maybe Mike's death has brought us closer together. Jackie and I had fun. We didn't finish it off with a bang, so to speak, but that wasn't detrimental.

I'm dazed. Blinking. Something woke me up. Jackie is face down on the mattress. The pillow is above her head, her hands beneath it. I squint to make sure she's breathing. I think it would be a great idea to open a book with this situation but the woman is dead, and her partner can't remember what happened or whether he killed her.

I write it down in the notes app on my phone.

Then I hear it again.

A notification. On a mobile phone.

Then another.

Somebody messaging late at night. The sound is coming from Jackie's bag. But I know that she always keeps her phone on silent. We've had discussions about it. It's annoying when I'm trying to get hold of her.

This is beep after beep. It's coming from her bag. I can't see her phone on her side table, so perhaps she knocked a switch or pressed a button that unmuted it in her bag.

But who the fuck is messaging her this late? Over and over. It's the kind of thing Mike would do. If you didn't answer him straight away, he'd keep poking and poking until he got what he wanted.

All the signs were there.

But what are these signs? Jackie is talking to somebody else late at night? Could be a friend. Could be another man. Surely she'd be more careful if that was the case, she would keep her phone silenced.

Fuck. I'm not the kind of person to snoop. I wouldn't go through her bag. I wouldn't read her texts. I wouldn't hack her emails. The alcohol still swills around my brain and I can't even remember the code to get in to Jackie's phone.

Not that I would.

I want to. But I won't. There has to be some privacy in this world where everything is so out in the open. There's dirty laundry everywhere you look. You can know where everyone is, what they're eating, who they are with, what they think of the boutique hotel they stayed in. Anything. Everything.

I can't go into Jackie's bag and look at her phone. There has to be boundaries.

But I want to.

It beeps again.

And again.

I can't remember the code. I know my own. I even know Mike's.

He loved a good conspiracy. He read everything about the assassination of John F. Kennedy. But he hates the way that Americans write their dates. 11/22/63. That's when they think JFK was shot. To everyone else in the world, it happened on 22/11/63. And that was Mike's code.

Another notification from Jackie's bag.

It's infuriating.

I pick up my phone, open the notes app again and type: *what happened to Mike's phone when he died?*

I'm definitely still drunk, so the note actually says: *what happened miles ohone when he irie.*

I'll have to decipher that in the morning. Right now, I need to lie back down. I throw a pillow over Jackie's bag in an attempt to muffle the sound of her admirer and I shut my eyes. Tomorrow is my last day at DoTrue.

I'm finishing things, Mike.

THURSDAY
(THE DAY BEFORE FUNERAL FRIDAY)

I get up early. 4:38. Jackie's bag is no longer ringing, but my ears are. My brain is so dry that my thoughts woke me up, banging against the inside of my skull, begging to be released. I have to write.

A note on my phone says, *what happened miles ohone when he irie*. It shouldn't make any sense but it somehow sparks me in to action. I take a look at Jackie as she sleeps and shake my head in disbelief. What is it they say about the guilty sleeping well?

She is out of it. I don't want to wake her but I also don't want her to think that I've left her here, so I decide to text her phone. It's the first thing she looks at when she wakes up.

> Hey. I couldn't sleep. Got an idea for something to
> write, so I'm just downstairs in the office. Didn't
> want you to worry.

I hit send and get out of bed.

Halfway through pulling a T-shirt over my head, I realise that the message sent but there was no sound from Jackie's bag.

So I send another text. Just a couple of kisses. Nothing suspicious. To test.

It sends.

There's no sound.

Maybe the phone died in the night.

Downstairs, I take one of the black capsules – strength twelve – and place it in the coffee machine, boot up the laptop and sit down at the desk. No checking emails. No social media. No flicking through news stories about the old man who was shot in the coffee place next door.

I write.

And it flows.

~~THE PRINCIPLE~~
~~KING LIAR~~
~~UNTITLED PROJECT~~
QUEEN LIAR
(WORKING TITLE)
BY ELI HAGIN

F I R S T   **C H A P T E R**

'He was sat there. His hands in his legs.' That's
what Bud Ellis told the police as they grilled him
for hours, desperate for some kind of confession.

Bud's best friend had taken his own life. He'd
threatened it on many occasions, never felt awkward
about discussing the prospect, but Bud never thought
it would actually happen.

Jenny had called Bud, crying.

'He's dead, Bud. He's fucking dead.'

'What? Jenny. What are you talking about? Where
are you?'

'Oh, don't play dumb with me, you know exactly
where I am. Get over here. We need to call the
police.'

Four hours of questioning. Bud wanted to sleep.
But they wouldn't let him. They had dispensed with
the good cop/bad cop routine and were opting for bad
cop/worse cop.

Why did she say that it was your fault, Ellis?

You made him do it, didn't you?

Let's face it, you wanted him dead. You wanted him
out of the way.

You're telling us that there isn't even the

possibility that you could be responsible for your friend taking his own life.

This is how they entrap you. They scare you. They trick you into saying that something is possible because anything is possible. They record you out of context. And they get a false confession.

Case closed.

But not Bud Ellis. He was tired, he was upset, he was confused, but he wasn't stupid. There was no way he was going down for a goddamned suicide.

The cops left him in the room alone to stew. Bud thought about Jenny. How she was probably just upset. That's why she had told the police it was his fault. That was all it was. Grief.

The detectives re-entered the room with smiles on their faces.

'Looks like we've got you bang to rights. New evidence. The victim's phone. We can see what you said to him. You wanted him to die. You told him to do it.'

Bud had to control himself. There was no context. Surely they didn't believe that telling somebody to end their life is not murder? It's not easy to commit suicide. Nobody could be blamed but the person who shot the gun or hung the rope or jumped in front of a moving train. Bud knew this.

But they looked so smug.

And they started to read him his rights.

If Bud Ellis was looking for a complication in his life, something he could fight to overcome, to make his life feel more like a movie, he'd found one.

Look, I know that 'Jenny' is a thinly veiled version of Jackie but I had to get the words down quickly. I know it's not good. Worse than a first draft. And, yes, it's not necessarily about Bud Ellis's Hollywood dream of losing his ideal woman on purpose just so that he can prove how strong his love is and win her back. Sometimes, when you are deeply entrenched in a story, you can't see it fully. You have to take a step back to see what is working and, more importantly, what is not.

This isn't a story about dysfunctional love. It's about friendship and betrayal.

I don't think I have ever written anything this real before.

And that scares me.

Where has this new string of thought come from?

There's a tap at the door and Jackie steps in.

'Hey, I got your text.'

'Your phone's not dead?'

'No. Why? That's a weird question to ask.'

'Oh, it's just … just that we collapsed when we got in, so didn't put our phones on charge through the night. Mine is so old it runs out if I don't plug it in six times a day.' I attempt to laugh it off.

'It's fine. My phone is newer than yours. I need to get going. Drop me a message later to see what's going on tonight.'

She comes over to my desk and kisses me on the head as though everything is okay.

I can't focus on Jackie now. I have to quit my job today.

RALPH
(THE DAY BEFORE FUNERAL FRIDAY)

There's a new routine to Ralph's days since Mike passed. It involves time alone, drinking and howling at the moon. It's unhealthy. And he knows it.

Yesterday was the worst.

He wakes up to see the devastation that is the image of his grief counselling. A tableau of his despair. Two bottles of Canadian whisky. It's cheap and easy to drink. He's a week or so away from bottles with labels that contain no origin, no age, just a barcode. A real betrayal to his tastebuds.

There are eight cans of lager, too. A pizza box. Two movie-sized bags of Doritos. An empty pot of hummus. He's disgusting and he feels it. And he knows it. But he opens the pizza box, takes a bite out of one of the leftover slices and washes it down with a mouthful of warm, flat beer. Then he calls in sick to work.

He's taken tomorrow off as part of his annual leave. Funeral Friday. Ralph figures it will be the closure he needs to move on.

But not today.

He plans to pick up exactly where he left off on Wednesday. There's a crate of beer in the garage and some wine in the kitchen that most people wouldn't even cook with.

Ralph checks his phone. No messages. Nobody asking how he is feeling, even though he hasn't been at work. Nobody checking in on him about the death of his childhood friend. Nothing incoming. But he sees Mike at the top of the list. Ralph sent forty-three messages last night to his dead pal.

Spite. Vitriol. Name-calling.

Puff. Wheeze. Spit.

Ralph sees it as cathartic. Calling Mike a selfish cunt. Telling him that this will kill his father, too. Expressing glee at his death. The joy that will come with watching Mike burn. It's mean, it's hateful but it helps Ralph.

It's screaming into a vacuum.

It doesn't matter what he is saying, because nobody is listening.

JACKIE

Jackie is listening.

She leaves Eli to write and heads back home for a shower. On the Tube, she opens her bag and takes out Mike's phone. She counts. Forty-three separate text messages.

This guy is fucking crazy, she tells herself.

Some are perfunctory and she can read them in their entirety as she scrolls. Others ramble and she can't tell where they are going without unlocking Mike's phone.

And she remembers talking to Eli about it last night.

He knows the code to get in. But she can't recall if he mentioned it or not. He told a story to remember it by. But he's always telling stories.

Fuck. That would be so useful. A window into the mind of her friend who took his own life. Plus the bonus of reading all these messages from Ralph. And anything that Eli had ever said to Mike. Maybe even about Jackie.

In a world where everyone's business is online, where insecurities are dressed up and camouflaged to mask reality, where you find out that your cousin is openly racist or that an ex has put on three stone, you may find that you crave some privacy.

Jackie does not.

She wants to get into Mike's mobile phone and she wants to read everything.

KATE

Kate hasn't had a drink since that night. That stupid, drunken night.

He'd seemed so nice. He paid her a lot of attention, made her feel important to him. And she had taken it in the wrong way, apparently. That's what he told her. 'I can't help if you took it the wrong way.'

He said that.

After he fucked her.

Or tried, at least.

Kate had let Danny Elwes in because he had hired her, given her a job straight out of university. But it wasn't enough.

He very rarely hired women based on their aptitude for the job or experience. Kate was young and fresh and optimistic. She wanted to earn her own money, be self-sufficient and independent. And she wanted somebody to share her time with. She chose badly. And, since that office party, she has felt dirty.

To this day she has denied it. 'Ha! He wishes something had happened.' And that was enough to throw anyone off the scent, because nice-person Danny doesn't show his face too often in the office. It's bravado Danny, look-at-my-new-car Danny and punch-them-between-the-legs-so-it-feels-tighter Danny. He's an animal.

How could she have been so stupid?

It had started out okay. There's nothing romantic about being pressed up against a vending machine, but it wasn't like that – it just felt raw and naughty and they'd been drinking and it was a festive time of year, and pretty soon he was inside her. And pretty soon after that, he went soft. He had tried to keep it going but he couldn't.

He was embarrassed, and that's when the nice Danny evaporated.

It had never happened before. Maybe it was her fault. That kinda bullshit.

Then, it would be her word against his. He said/she said. Don't even try it.

Not once had she said anything to make him feel bad. Danny's best defence was to immediately go on the offence.

So, Kate was stuck. She figured her best bet was to deny anything had ever happened. People in the office would assume it was more of Danny's bombast, anyway. She could go on the offensive herself and say that he couldn't get it up, but he could make life hard for her even if he couldn't do the same to his dick.

And she didn't want to leave because he could then say anything he wanted about her. Besides, she needed the job.

She was stuck.

But she wouldn't be if, for some reason, it was Danny who left. And even better if he could leave in disgrace. And God or fate or the Universe has listened to her and sent Eli to help.

When this is over, maybe she can have a drink.

THURSDAY

I'm excited about work today.

With Mike now deceased and my apparent break-up with Jackie in two days, it's really just my current employment that's holding me back, surely – that and a deeply psychological torment that my therapist is yet to uncover. Besides, I need to focus solely on the funeral tomorrow and the kind of message that I am to deliver to the congregation that ultimately honours the memory of my back-stabbing best friend but also puts across the point that we should all be happy that he is dead.

I feel like I've hated my job since before the position I so vacantly inhabit even existed. I don't just want to leave because I feel low or because my soul has been systematically ripped from me piece by piece on a daily basis for over three years via an emotional technique more invasive than an anal probe.

I feel raped.

I can't even pretend that my reasons for wanting to quit have any kind of therapeutic value whereby I actually manage to finish something. It's not that at all.

It's far simpler than that.

It makes me hate myself.

I hate being diplomatic in situations where I would rather tell the truth no matter how brutal. I detest spending the majority of my waking life not caring. I loathe myself for agreeing with theories or ideas that I know are useless, self-indulgent, commercially inept, or all of the above, just because it's easier to ignore than voice an original thought; this just stems from not caring.

I feel revulsion for Sam Jordane for being such an all-round pathetic human being, yet at the same time I should thank him for being a constant reminder that he personifies an unwritten fate that my life will mirror his in twenty years if I am not firm in my convictions on this historic day.

I abhor Danny Elwes for seeing something in me that suggests I may be good at my job or may even want to progress within marketing and admit that this job that I find so odious is actually the career path I have chosen.

But most of all, more than corporate life or promotions or 'let's do some good', or wasting two hours each day drinking coffee or breaking down in the disabled toilet once a week for a short cry, even more than Sam or Danny or the rude woman on the register in the canteen, I hate myself. And I hate the fact that I hate myself.

So today I have decided to resign. I'm going to start the day by giving them every clue that this is coming, and they are all so self-involved that they won't even notice.

I haven't shaved for days, and I've been drinking fairly heavily and consistently since Mike died. I went back to bed and I'm waiting for the snooze tune, so I'm definitely going to be late again today.

I care less than I normally do right now. All I have on my mind is how to make this the coolest resignation in history. It needs to be memorable. I want people to be talking about this day for years to come. I want to leave my DoTrue legacy and I don't want it to have anything to do with the fucking back-to-school campaign of 2020.

Then I hear the waves.

And Otis starts to sing.

There are three things I know about 'Sitting on the Dock of the Bay':

1. It's the only song with whistling in that doesn't remind you of Roger Whittaker. I'd rather listen to an album entitled *All Your Favourite Gay Anthems on the Panpipes* than hear him churn out another rendition of 'The White Cliffs of Dover' merely by blowing his own breath through a gap in his lips. Otis makes it sound cool.

2. I know people from San Francisco hate it when people call their beloved city San Fran, but it grates on them even more when it's

referred to as Frisco. But again, Otis Redding just makes it sound so fucking cool.

3. This song is definitely going to make me stay in bed past 9:00. The time I am supposed to be logged in and raring to update the website or send out an e-shot or wish a horrendous and mysterious incurable wasting disease on Sam.

I don't catch my bus until 9:30. Half an hour after that, I'm strolling through the lobby, bumping straight into Danny Elwes.

'Morning, Eli. How are you feeling?' Fuck. Either he doesn't realise that I am late or he doesn't care for some reason. 'Look, Sam has explained to me what's been going on.' He's going to ask me to pay him back in some way for letting me skip work for the last few days. 'I know how hard these things can be and that some mornings it is just tough to even get out of bed. You probably feel that you have to force yourself into work.' I've actually been like that since my second day. 'I just want you to know that I have an open-door policy and you can talk to me whenever you feel the need.'

I'm gob-smacked.

I can't believe he is being so reasonable. I can't trust this apparent sincerity. But, with everything that is wrong with Danny Elwes, the motivational speeches, the jokes that aren't funny but are always met with rapturous hysteria – Mike called them 'career laughs' – the dodgy marketing invoices, the questionable expenses claims and the elaborately over-embellished yarns detailing his string of imaginary conquests, when it comes to family he is actually consistently accommodating.

I wonder whether quitting today is my best option.

How long can I ride out this goodwill?

What is my period of grace?

Then he speaks again.

'So, you have a couple of hours to catch up on emails etcetera and I've called a catch-up meeting for 12:00. Brown-bag lunch today and we'll debrief you on the BTS.' He's speaking a little louder now as more people are around and he enjoys showing his seniority over me. 'Good to see you back, Eli.' And he pats me on my back quite roughly as if to say, 'Now be on your way, cretin.'

It's possible I could have utilised this opportunity to exercise my contempt and instigate my plan for the day but I diplomatically thank him and stomp slowly up the stairs as the weight of my own self-loathing pushes down on my shoulders, reminding me that I allow people like Danny to strip me of dignity on an almost hourly basis.

That's when I trip and fall up the stairs.

Normally the crowd who turned abruptly to witness the event would laugh or cheer as you do when a waiter drops a tray of glasses, but not today. They just feel sorry for me. And I feel very sorry for myself.

KATE

There's a function on the photocopier that allows a document to be scanned and a digital copy to be saved to the shared drive. Kate has created a sub-folder within another folder from years ago that contains sales figures against targets for each quarter. Nobody would ever look there. And the folder will only exist for a few minutes until she drags it onto the DoTrue-branded flash drive she has in her pocket.

Expenses forms are not stored on the shared drive. There are only hard copies. They are printed off, receipts are stapled, and they have to be signed off by Danny. But who signs off Danny's expenses? Danny does.

He has an inflatable hot tub in his garden that he expensed.

There's the man cave next to the hot tub. Also expensed.

When he said he had claimed off the company healthcare for an operation that was 'desperately needed', that was the time he took four days off to travel to Las Vegas for a major boxing event.

Thousands claimed, and claimed in months when commissions had to be capped, apparently.

There are pages of these, but Kate doesn't want to raise suspicions, so she's grabbed five of the worst examples.

Danny even made Sam organise a whip-round in the office so they could send a card and gift when he went in for the imaginary operation. He was so committed to the lie and his own ego that he organised his own get-well-soon card. The guy is such a braggart that he eventually forgot he'd lied about being unwell and regaled the office with a story of the time he saw a boxing match in Vegas. The piece of shit even won a tonne of money with his bet.

Kate has always liked Eli. He's not like the other people who work at DoTrue. He doesn't laugh at the awful jokes. He never goes on the team nights out. Sam once asked him why, and Eli told him, 'You're not my friends, you're just people that I work with. I don't want to go bowling.' She has been sniggering at that for years.

It's nervy. Kate is paranoid. But nobody is looking at her. People don't really notice her. They only want her when they haven't been paid on time or the expenses claim hasn't gone through or a customer's account is on hold. She's the perfect person to do this. But she's also the perfect person for Danny to take advantage of.

She has to scan the papers, send them to the sub-folder, move that to the flash drive, delete it from the shared drive, and return the hard copies to the filing cabinet. Then add all the other evidence of corruption and depravity to the drive and deliver it to Eli. Who she doesn't really know but feels she can trust.

It's a huge risk on her part but, like Eli, like so many people who hate their job, she can't quit. If she were ever fired or made redundant, it would be a blessing, but it takes a certain courage to resign. It's the same kind of courage you need to resign from life.

It has to come from you.

As Kate is placing the paperwork back into the filing cabinet, Danny comes up behind her.

'Kate,' he says softly, but it frightens her, and some of the people in the customer-care team notice.

'Jesus Christ, Danny.'

'Sorry,' he laughs, 'I didn't mean to startle you.'

Kate still has the expenses from the Vegas trip in her hand. She flicks through the files, trying to appear as relaxed as possible.

'Is there something you need?' She locates the correct slot and drops the hard copy inside then shuts the drawer. She's sweating.

'Everything okay, Kate? Are you feeling well?' Danny appears to be showing signs of sympathy, which is unlike him.

'Yes, yes, fine. Women's issues.' That's always enough to get a Neanderthal off your back. 'Now, what can I help you with.' Kate walks a few steps towards her desk, to pull Danny away from the files. Then realises that she has a flash drive hanging out of her computer and stops.

'I need you to take some money from petty cash and pay for a taxi when it arrives.'

That's not what it should be used for, but she doesn't argue because she just wants him to go away. She never argues. And he knows that.

'Sure thing. Just drop me a message when they arrive and I'll go out.'

She doesn't even ask who will be arriving. She wasn't listening to the announcement because she was too busy retrieving the CCTV footage of the party when Danny pinned a customer-care girl to the wall and kissed her.

She knew about the incident. Just as she knew about Vegas. And the client trip to the factory in Germany that ended in a strip club and brothel bonanza, funded by DoTrue via Danny's credit card and expenses form.

Reason for Claim: Marketing/Client Entertainment.

Kate knows all of this, and more. And now she is ready to see that information released.

Maybe losing her job will be her punishment for being complicit.

THURSDAY

Sam must be able to tell that something is up. I never look this excited at work. I don't have that long to put this thing together before the meeting, and I am dying to see what Kate comes up with.

Sitting at my desk tapping a pen repeatedly on the surface is just drawing attention to the fact that I am fretting and waiting for something.

'Everything okay, Eli?' Sam asks with his usual brilliance.

'Yeah, fine, just thinking, you know?'

'About the BTS campaign, I hope. A lot has developed in the last week that you need to be aware of.' It looks as though my earlier outburst at Sam has left him unscarred and as condescending as he ever was.

'Yes, Sam, of course I am thinking about the campaign. I'm sure all will become clear in the meeting.' My lie seems to have quelled his interest in me for at least another twenty minutes.

Come on Kate, where is it? I lift myself up higher, like a meerkat trying to see into the finance office to make sure that she is even there. She is stood by the photocopier with some documents. I stare intently at her, waiting for reciprocation. Eventually she must feel me stalking her and turns in my direction. She smiles cheekily and slyly gives me a wink before putting another document onto the machine.

What does she have for me?

I didn't even get a chance to ask her earlier before she ran off to get started. She seemed more excited than me.

Danny comes over to my desk while I am still looking over at the finance department. In my state of wonder I do not notice the rancid stench of cigarette breath that follows Danny wherever he goes.

He puts his face next to mine, mimicking me to detect what I am gazing at. That's when I taste the nicotine.

'Oh, yes, she is a pretty one.' I fall back into my chair, startled. He brings his face closer to mine and whispers, 'Lovely little body too, if I remember the Christmas party correctly.' He nudges me and winks, and Sam joins the conversation with a career laugh. I just can't force myself to play the game, so look at him blankly. He doesn't remember the Christmas party at all. He's lying about another conquest. Kate would never touch him. I wish one of these girls would just make an issue out of his behaviour. I'm sure many more would follow suit.

'Anyway, Eli, I just wanted to let you know personally that the meeting has been pushed back thirty minutes because one of the board will be attending and his flight has been delayed a little. So it may drag on a tad later.' I move my view to Sam, who has a knowing look in his eyes, like he is privy to information that I am not and knows exactly what is going on.

I'm just glad that I have extra time to prepare myself for my extravagant exodus.

I manage to type out a sentence to Kate on the intra-office messenger while Danny and Sam blather nonsense to each other: *Come on, this breath is killing me.* Danny turns to me as I hit send and it disappears from my screen. I smile with accomplishment, like a child who has successfully executed a practical joke on a parent.

'See you shortly then, men.' And he walks off to harass another team.

'Sam, what is going on? Why do we have someone from the board flying over for a meeting about this campaign? I know you know something.'

'Eli, I am not at liberty to say. It's not that far away now, just get on with your work until then and you will be debriefed in due course.' He's so frustrating. He likes to hold any bit of power he can over me. He knows nothing. He's bluffing.

'Fine. I just thought we were a team...' He knows I am baiting him into telling me something and even though we don't really get on, he would love it if we could become more of a team – with him at the helm, of course. But he just rolls his eyes and continues tapping away slowly at his keyboard.

Then I get a reply from Kate:

Sorry, Eli. I've been scanning some documents using the photocopier so they will be sent as files to my desktop.
Nearly done.
K x

What could she possibly be scanning into the photocopier? I don't want her to get into trouble but this will definitely lead a trail to her if I decide to use these documents. While I am grateful for her enthusiasm I can't possibly incriminate her with my own personal vendetta, so I start to write my resignation speech without her help.

It's the second speech I've written this week.

Almost as soon as I hit the first few keys, the blue box appears in the bottom right hand corner of my screen, signifying that I have received an internal message from Kate. And, although I don't want to read it, morbid human curiosity is a powerful emotion. Besides, I like to take the chance at any distraction to get me away from completing my writing.

Hi Eli,
Would you mind coming to my office? Won't take long.
Regards,
Kate.

It seems very formal, as if trying to disguise the contents as banal or usual so as not to alert any echelon detectors.

I lock my computer screen. I made the mistake of leaving it open once while I went to get a coffee and one of the sales guys changed the wallpaper on my monitor to a naked, obese woman stuffing her face with cake. Another time he changed it to two men kissing. Childish, but kind of a funny prank if anyone in the world but him had performed it.

Danny is watching me, I can feel it. He's just mentioned how hot he thinks Kate is, and now I am walking towards her office. If he asks me what I was doing, I'll say I went to ask her out.

'Hi, Eli. Look down at my desk.' I do as I'm told. 'Everything you need is on that drive. It was too much to mail over once I put the video footage on.' Kate stares over my shoulder at Danny's glass office, then her eyes flit down to the desk.

I reach down, trying to be as inconspicuous as possible and place the USB key into my trouser pocket. I haven't been this excited at work ever.

'If Danny asks why you came into my office, just tell him you wanted to change the account that your wages are paid into, okay?'

'I was going to tell him that I was asking you out for a drink.' I laugh. She smiles.

'Maybe you should when this is over.'

That hangs in the air as I walk out.

I hear her start typing and there's a message for me when I get back to my desk and log on:

I'm sure that if you decide to use them I will be implicated and reprimanded accordingly, but to be honest, it will get me out of here and maybe we can go for that drink or something when we are both unemployed.
Speak soon.
K x

JACKIE

Six numbers. How hard can it be?

000000. Denied.

123456. Denied.

Mike was stupid but not that stupid, it would seem.

She tries Mike's date of birth. Then her own. Then Eli's, and is locked out of the phone for a few minutes.

You always see it in TV shows and films, when they try to guess the password to somebody's laptop or email account. It takes them a few wrong guesses and then they recall something personal about that person that is so obvious, they would surely never use it for their password.

But this was real life. Not a movie.

She tries the time that the snooze choon comes onto the radio. Mike loved that thing.

Denied.

Locked.

Fuck.

It's not the date that he finally killed himself or when he finally got to make love to his best friend's girlfriend. What was it about Mike? What was it that would encapsulate his Mikeness? He loved DIY. Was it how many days it took him to polish that stupid fucking floor?

Denied.

Books. He loved books. Writing blurbs for Eli. But there aren't enough books in the first-chapter library to fill the six digits. What was the name of that book he loved? The Stephen King one about JFK. He was always going on about it.

Jackie swipes to the internet on her phone and gets a list of Stephen King books.

11/22/63.

Of course. That's it. That's the thing about Mike. That's what will break this thing wide open.

She types:

112263.

And the phone makes that vibration and click to say that you have entered the wrong password.

Denied. Denied. Denied.

She gives up.

And she was so close.

THURSDAY

I take my laptop and the flash drive into a toilet cubicle.

Looking at the files I see that she has copied a stream of outrageous expense claims from Danny Elwes that must have gone unnoticed. Many are for after-work drinks with alleged clients that go on until late in the night, where they apparently often go to a health-and-fitness centre, which I can only assume is a smokescreen for a brothel. There is a receipt on here for a dining table to be delivered to Danny's personal residence and a brand-new refrigerator, which was meant for our staff room but mysteriously never materialised. There are receipts for plane tickets to Morocco and Ibiza, both places that Danny visited on holiday in the last year. The list goes on.

There are emails in here and even a video of him with a woman in his office after hours, taken from the CCTV.

It's like she has been compiling this for a while, waiting for the right opportunity.

I shouldn't liken her to Jackie.

I compile all the information that I need over the next forty-two minutes. Danny leaves his office and waves at us to signify that it is time. Before I go, I respond to Kate's message:

Kate, this is all too good not to use. Thanks for your help on this but let's not wait until we are unemployed and have no money. I'll meet you at 18:00 for drinks and I can tell you what happened. The Royal Scam.
See you then.
Here I go...

FUNERAL **FRIDAY**

After the exhausting day today – Funeral Friday – it's no wonder that, when I return from the kitchen with a freshly opened bottle of Cabernet Sauvignon, Jackie is fast asleep on my sofa with the stereo remote control still in her hand. It makes me smile. She looks so, dare I say it, cute. I can't allow myself to have these feelings towards Jackie; it will just get in the way.

I pull her legs up from the floor and lay them gently on the sofa, taking her shoes off in the process. Using the throw to cover her in case she gets cold, I stroke her hair back from her face and kiss her on the forehead. I turn the light off in the living room and take her full glass into the kitchen.

On the walk back from The Scam, Jackie was holding on to me tightly so as not to fall over, but she kept squeezing my ribs where Ralph had only recently booted me in the toilet cubicle. I felt like screaming but I didn't want to alarm Jackie with the fact that everything wasn't actually all-bloody-right. I lift my shirt under the kitchen light to peruse my wound. My ribs have already turned a quite striking shade of purple and my back has definitely cut and bled because I could feel it sticking when I lifted my shirt.

I lean backwards against the kitchen work surface and quaff Jackie's unwanted glass of wine, then I grab the bottle and a clean glass, and head down to the library for a late-night therapy session.

Upon arrival I see that the sofa is in the correct place and the tape recorder is standing on my therapist's chair, ready to start. I don't recall having set this up, but it doesn't matter; I am late and I should just get down to it.

Never keep a woman waiting.

I switch the machine into record mode and start with the cursory, *How I have been since our last meeting*.

INT. ELI'S OFFICE/FAKE THERAPIST'S OFFICE - NIGHT

    ELI
To be honest, not good. We buried Mike today. I can
still see him on his living room floor.
    FAKE THERAPIST
And how have you been coping?
    ELI
Well, I think fairly well, if you consider pickling
myself on the inside with gin and wallowing in my
own filth as coping. You think I'd be better at this
sort of thing after Mum.

I wish I hadn't brought her up so soon. Usually we run out of time
before getting to Mum, but this is still very early on in the session
and will certainly pique my therapist's interest. They always seem to
want to talk about your parents.

I sit up, turn off the tape recorder for a moment and take a gulp
of the wine to boost me into finally confronting this issue. Shit. I'm
going to talk about Mum in therapy. It only took three years and the
suicide of my best friend to prompt it out of me.

I lie back on the sofa.

    ELI
I went to see mum today. After the funeral. I found
her grave and I sat there and spoke to her, just
like I'm speaking to you now.
    FAKE THERAPIST
How was that?
    ELI
I couldn't do it at first. You see, I don't believe
in all that anymore, as you know. I don't think she
is looking down on me, or up at me for that matter.
I don't believe that she can hear me when I speak;

I don't believe there is any higher being out there
that can hear me when I speak. What I am sure of is
that there are some bones and hair six feet under a
piece of white marble, and it doesn't resemble the
woman I once called mother. There is no brain
activity, and the little soul she had left is not
lingering in the ether with some unfinished
business. But I spoke to her anyway.

This really is just a rehash of the last time we spoke about Mum,
and she tried to convince me to visit her and see how it made me
feel. I know she thinks that I lost my faith when I prayed for Mum
and it didn't make a blind bit of difference. It's textbook.

    ELI
It helped. I didn't think I would make it here today
and I needed to talk to someone. I always used to
talk to Mum about everything and now I don't have
Mike…

(He trails off, getting upset.)

I sit up and take another mouthful of wine and realise that the
tape recorder is not on. I forgot to switch it back to record. My most
important breakthrough and I'm not even getting it down.

I stand up and pace the room for a few minutes, flicking through
some of the first chapters I have not looked at in a while, and I think
about the first chapter I wrote last week – *King Liar*. I feel like there
is something in that story, that something is holding me back from
progressing with it. I straighten my life's work and lay back down on
the sofa, not forgetting to press record this time.

    ELI
I just wanted to fill her in on some of the things

she has missed, but for some reason I ended up lying
to her.

>   FAKE THERAPIST
Why do you think you did that?

>   ELI
I don't know why I did it. I'm ashamed, I suppose.
Of who I have become since she died. I can't let
myself get close to anyone; that's not a secret, I
know that. It's not a revelation.

>   FAKE THERAPIST
Because you think they might die?

>   ELI
They are dying. I only had Mike and Jackie, and now
I only have Jackie.
I think that maybe being on my own is the best thing
for everyone. I couldn't save Mum from her illness.
I couldn't make her see that it was worthwhile for
her to want to save herself. I couldn't save Mike,
either. I couldn't even tell what was going on with
him and I was supposed to be his closest friend.
The only good thing I can think to do is to save
Jackie. I can do that, I know I can. The best thing
is for her not to be around me.

Saying Jackie's name wakes her from the sofa in a daze. With her
vision blurred and her mouth dry, she sits up slowly, waiting for the
strength to return to her limbs so that she is able to get herself a glass
of water.

She slowly sips at the glass so as not to fill herself up too quickly
and end up vomiting on my coffee table or something. She can hear
a mumbling downstairs so tip-toes her way down in the dark.

>   FAKE THERAPIST
Do you really believe that?

> ELI
> Of course. I won't be as dramatic to say that
> everybody around me dies, but I do not bring out
> the best in people. Far from it. I held Mike back,
> so now I am letting Jackie go.
>   FAKE THERAPIST
> Do you feel responsible?
>   ELI
> For Jackie?
>   FAKE THERAPIST
> For Mike. For his death.
>   ELI
> You mean, did I kill Mike?

Oh my God. Is that it? I have tried to dissipate the blame in front of an entire congregation of Mike's friends and family; I have taken some of the blame, but really is it entirely my fault?

Jackie pushes through the door.

'Eli...' She scares me and I jump up out of the seat, spilling half of my wine onto the tape recorder. 'Who are you talking to?'

'Jackie, what are you doing? I thought you were asleep.' My heart is racing. How long has she been down here, what has she heard, what does she know?

'I was asleep but then I could hear talking, and I thought I heard my name, but you weren't upstairs so I came to find you. What are you doing?'

'I'm writing. That's what I do, you know that. I get all my best ideas at night and I was just recording them because I feel a little too tipsy to write anything down. I can't focus.' This seems pretty believable and I've managed to shift some guilt onto her for interrupting me.

'Oh, right. I'm sorry. I'm going to bed, you carry on.' She goes to walk out, but I grab her by the arm.

'No, no, it's okay. I'm finished now.'

'You want to go to bed?'

'My mind is whirring now. We've opened up some wine, let's have a nightcap, make sure we get a good night's sleep.'

Jackie kisses me. She agrees. Which is great because I need to make sure she's knocked out.

THURSDAY
(THE DAY BEFORE FUNERAL FRIDAY)

This is it. My big moment. I've been building up to this for three years now, sat at the same desk, looking at the same screen and the same face of Sam Jordane, listening to the same motivational talks from the ever-sickening Danny Elwes, tasting the same stale nicotine breath and coffee-coloured water, feeling the restriction of wearing a shirt and tie for five days a week, except for the last Friday of the month on which we are allowed to wear a polo-shirt with trousers. I have always rebelled against this as I think it looks ridiculous and typifies everything I hate about our sales-driven culture. So I punish myself by sticking to the shirt and tie, even on these semi-casual days.

'Well, here it is, the moment of truth,' Sam says to me without moving his lips, as if nobody would know it was him. What does he mean – the moment of truth? How could he possibly know what I am about to do unless he has been monitoring my emails again?

We all fall in line as we are shepherded into the boardroom, where Danny is sitting at the end of the table, laughing with Mr Kohler, one of the board members. It's the first time I've seen Sam on time for a meeting; he is always the last one in, pretending his work is important, but today he is almost first in the room. He doesn't sit down beside Danny or Mr Kohler; he sits at the other end of the table directly opposite them, as if of equal importance, as if they will be talking directly to him.

The mumble as everyone enters fades into a hush, and we all stare at the end of the table, waiting to hear what is to be said. Danny looks particularly nervous and fidgety but also has something of a smile/grimace on his face. Mr Kohler clears his throat and begins to address us.

'Good afternoon, everyone, and thank you for your time today. Sorry I am a little late but I had trouble with my plane, as I am sure some of you are aware. Now, I have some news today and I know that rumours have been circulating for a short while now, but Danny will no longer be the managing director of the DoTrue UK office.'

What? Danny is leaving? Oh, this is just great; we are not here to discuss the back-to-school campaign at all. I don't understand why it all had to be so cloak-and-dagger; we could have just called an impromptu meeting. Why have I even been called in here? I am not part of the management team.

'I know you will all be sad to see him go' – Danny smiles smugly – 'but he will still be around. I don't want to lose him, especially after all the success he has brought to the UK. His new position will be to manage the Benelux region along with UK and Ireland. It's more responsibility but he's up to the task.'

I feel annoyed that we have been messed around like this; that they have made me produce a presentation for this campaign and we are not even here to discuss it. But I find that I have to keep bringing my hands up to my face to hide the smile. It is almost hurting my cheeks.

Danny chips in with his usual dose of insincerity.

'I'd just like to reiterate what Herr Kohler has said. I have really enjoyed my time here at DoTrue UK, and it will always hold a place that is dear in my heart, which is why I could never leave entirely.'

Kohler nods and smiles like a good little puppy. I can't help it but I snigger at how trite that sounds. What heart? He may have ruined my dramatic exit, but I am going to leave a scar on his apparently impeccable reputation within this organisation.

'Is there something you wish to say, Eli?' Danny says, as if I am a school kid passing a note round in class.

'I was just wondering when your last day would be.' A good enough question that also implies that I am looking forward to him leaving.

Kohler interjects, 'That has not been confirmed yet, but Danny is likely to still be around as usual for the next month to hand over responsibilities while we work on the restructure. Are there any other questions?' This is always a bad idea when Sam is in a meeting, because he always has questions, most of them irrelevant, and he can make a fifteen-minute meeting drag on for hours.

And then he speaks.

'Well, Mr Kohler, it's not so much a question, but I would just like to say that, on behalf of everyone here, we really appreciate everything that Danny has done, and it has been a real privilege working with him and we wish him the very best in his new role.' A few people join in with a 'yes, definitely' or murmur some feeling of agreement, but I give Danny a look that lets him know that Sam certainly is not speaking for me.

'Thanks, Sam, that means a lot, and I really am going to miss seeing all of you guys every day, but we can still go for a beer sometime when I'm back in the UK.'

To Sam this is a firm booking, but Danny doesn't mean it; he wouldn't want to harm his imaginary reputation on the streets of London by being seen with a bedraggled middle-aged gimp like Sam. It's just another lie coming out of his poisonous mouth.

'In the meantime, we need to shuffle things around here.' Everyone comes to an immediate quiet as Kohler utters the words that could spell promotion or redundancy for someone in this room. 'As Danny has been acting as sales and marketing director, we have decided to split this into two roles to give it more focus and make it more manageable for the handover.' I can see Sam's eyes light up. He's been here so long, and there is a distinct possibility that he will soon have the power that he craves so dearly. Extra official responsibility would also give him more of an excuse to stay away from home.

'The plan is to add an office manager, who will support sales and marketing.' Kohler looks around the room not making eye contact with anyone; but it is obvious that Giles will look after sales because he has always been Danny's little pet, and Sam will finally manage the marketing team. I don't know what all the fuss is about.

'Giles' – shocker – 'you will take over as the sales manager for the UK and have come highly recommended by Danny.' Everyone in the room applauds the decision, trying to hide their envy like the losing nominees at the Oscar ceremonies. 'And marketing will be controlled by...' He looks down at his notes, keeping Sam waiting, perspiring, holding his breath, preparing his gracious face as if he didn't know. This must be what he meant by *the moment of truth*. 'Eli Hagin. Congratulations, Eli.'

The room is stunned into silence as we all literally hear Sam's heart break. But then Sam, as English as ever, starts the clapping to suggest that he is okay with this decision to have a junior member of staff hurdle him in a career he has pledged so much to.

I laugh because I can't quite believe what has transpired. It's a mystery to me. My idea has backfired. Showing that I don't care about my job has backfired. It has lent an air of enigma and coolness that has been misconstrued. For some reason, they think I have something to offer.

I want to stand up and say, 'Thanks for the opportunity but you can stick your job and your failing company up your arse.' But that is so base compared to the elaborate exit I had planned. So I bite my tongue.

Sam looks at me like he wants to die. I want to say sorry to him, but that is too condescending. I know that's how he is with me all the time but this really is his life. This is his reality.

I don't know what to do to make him feel better. I can't trust him, I know that, but he looks like the biggest loser, so I mouth the words 'I'm leaving', but he doesn't understand.

Everyone exits the room, but Giles and I are asked to stay behind. Our hands are shaken firmly as we are welcomed into the management circle. I still have it in my head that I am going to leave, but I am going to waste their time just as they have wasted mine.

Outside, Kate is waiting for me. I see her through the glass talking to Sam. He clearly explains what has transpired, and she looks at me through the window in disgust, shakes her head and goes back to her office.

I feel disappointed that I have made her feel like that and the air of Sam's misery plagues me throughout our discussion of how the business will be run going forward.

I've been caught off-guard.

When the meeting finishes I rush over to the finance department, but Kate isn't there. Returning to my desk I am greeted with the sullen face of Sam, who sarcastically says, 'So, what do you want me to do, boss?'

Great, this is just what I need.

'Don't be like that, Sam. I didn't want this position.'

'Then why don't you say that?'

That's how desperate he is. If I rejected the position and they offered it to him as second best, he would take it and his pride wouldn't even dent. You leave your pride at the door when you take a job at DoTrue.

I tell him, 'Don't worry about it, Sam. I'm sure they'll soon see the error of their ways.'

If he'd have been able to read my lips earlier, he'd know what I mean.

I can't let this derail me.

The plan goes ahead.

KATE

The toilets at DoTrue are immaculate. Whoever's job it is to keep them clean clearly takes pride in the work. And that's a real perk of the job because it's where people go to cry.

Eli has done it. Sometimes it's through frustration, sometimes fruproyance, sometimes just to get some sadness out.

Sam has done it, too. He picks the cubicle furthest from the door and calls his wife. She is less than sympathetic to his woes when she has spent the morning chasing their demon offspring around the house or supermarket. He wants to call to tell her about being passed up for a promotion but he knows that she won't give him what he needs. That makes him want to go in there without his phone. And just cry.

But it's Kate's turn today. For her, it's a release. The pressure of sneaking around all morning, and then the waiting around for the clandestine meeting between sales and marketing. The emotions have built up and they have to come out. She's paranoid, too, that she backed the wrong horse in Eli Hagin.

When she returns to her desk there's a message from him saying that Danny is trying to slip away and take over the Belgium office, or something, and they had the audacity to promote Eli.

Her heart sinks.

She messages to see if he is going to stay now. She's paranoid that he has that information, even though she'd like to get out of there, Eli is right, she can't get sacked.

Then, a message at the bottom of her screen:

It's thrown a spanner in the works, for sure. I need to rethink things. But I am not staying at this company for one more fucking day. See you at the pub.

THURSDAY

So I sit at my desk and I start to type up my resignation to send to Danny, but I want to copy in Mr Kohler and Sam. Then blind copy Kate in so that she can see I am a man of my word.

I type:

```
Danny,
I resign.
Eli.
```

A little abrupt and doesn't necessarily convey my every feeling. I'm not sure brevity is the angle I want to take. I delete it.

```
Hi Danny,
When I heard you were leaving, it upset me somewhat
because I will now have to focus all of my loathing
towards Sam and he isn't really that bad, to be
honest. I only hate Sam as much as I hate terrorism,
but you rank about one notch below a child-molester.
```

Too hostile. I don't want to come across as hostile. I want to achieve a certain level of indignant wit.

I think. A hard copy. Something poetic about that. More personal.

```
Hi Danny,
Please be advised that I will be unable to take the
position of UK marketing manager as this goes against
everything I have worked so hard to avoid. Please
reconsider this role for someone who is actually
stupid enough to care about what we do, I think this
will better serve the company's interests.
```

I also do not feel that I can adequately perform my job as a marketing executive any longer as a result of a three-year soul-battering that leaves me feeling raped each day.

Speaking of rape, you will find a disk enclosed in this envelope that clearly shows you having sex in your office with what looks like Tina, who was here on work experience. I cannot say for certain because I do not have her birth certificate, but I would be surprised to find that she was over sixteen. Luckily the video is time-stamped so I will leave that up to you to work out.

You will also find a file containing a selection of your more colourful expense claims. I have circled the items where you have paid for sex with prostitutes and charged personal goods to the company expense account.

I really think that you may have a problem with sexual predation and may in fact have a disease, judging by the frequency that you are visiting the Regency Health and Fitness Centre at 3:00 a.m. Perhaps this is something that you could get on the company health package, as I can see from the enclosed record, they did pay for your pec implants.

I would suggest that you increase the security on this level as I found it remarkably easy to obtain and copy these records. They have also been backed up in a digital format for ease of distribution, but I wouldn't worry too much about that as they will have been emailed to the entire company address book by the time you have finished reading this.

This is my resignation, by the way. I assume you will not want me to work my month's notice.

However, as you may have heard, I like to write,

and I really need some time to do that. So, in order for me to hold on to this information, I will need you to continue paying my wage for the next year while I get this story finished. I'm sure you will find a way to get it through accounts. Perhaps you could cut down on the number of clients you take to that midnight 'health spa' each month.

Yours contentedly,

Eli Hagin

I print the page out and place it into the envelope with all of my other files and seal it with a loathing kiss.

'I'm just popping out, Sam.' And that's the last thing I ever say to him. I get up, grab my belongings, put the large manila envelope under my arm and check to see if Kate is back in her office. She looks over at me, and I make a sign with my hand that looks like a phone. I mouth the words 'thank you' to her but she still seems perplexed. I hope I have done enough in my resignation letter to keep her out of the loop.

I can see Danny and Kohler through the glass, talking jovially in the office about something.

I don't knock. I just open the door and say, 'I've got something for you.'

'Eli, you should really knock before entering a private meeting,' Danny exclaims with his usual air of arrogance.

'I don't have to do anything you say, Danny. Here you go.' And I fling the envelope across the table. It whizzes over the surface and falls off the edge. They both bend down to pick it up but by the time Kohler appears with the envelope in hand, I have already walked out and am heading out of the building.

I quit my job and, even though that may seem a little self-destructive, I've finished something.

I'm nearly there.

KATE

'You're my fucking hero.' That's how she greets him. 'What are we drinking?'

Eli is sitting at his favourite table, half a lager left in his glass.

'Ah, you came. I am finishing this lager and then I will be having whatever it is that you are having.'

'We'll be sharing a bottle of wine, then.'

Kate goes to the bar and Eli watches her. She is the complication he has been waiting for. He's her 'fucking hero', apparently. It feels like a green light to Eli. A few drinks. More talk of heroics. A flirtatious comment. Drinks at his. Maybe hers, to be safe. Explain what he did to Jackie. Get dumped. Show how much he loves her. Sell the idea to Nancy Meyers.

She returns with a bottle of Chardonnay and two glasses. Eli feels guilty about Jackie. That's what she would have ordered. But he persists.

Kate tells him that the office was in uproar after he left. Everyone wondered where he'd gone. Danny brushed it aside until Kohler left with more money from the petty cash. He did an announcement. Said that Eli had decided to leave. That he was taking time out to pursue his passion for writing. That there were no hard feelings. That we should all wish him well.

'He looked shaken.' She seems buoyant. Revelling in Danny's misery.

'All thanks to you.' Eli raises a glass.

Flattery.

'You are the one who had the balls to follow through.'

'Sometimes it's important to just put an end to things.'

They drink the entire bottle of wine, all the while laughing at Danny's arrogance and Sam's desperation. Kate reminds him of the time he said he didn't want to go to the work bowling event.

'God, I sound like such a dick.'

And they laugh at that, too.

'To be honest, I half expected to get the sack for getting you that information.'

'I didn't tell Danny where it came from.'

'Oh, right.' She seems disappointed.

'You don't want to get sacked, Kate. It'll look bad when you go for your next job.'

'I guess. Besides, it'll be better there when Danny Elwes is gone, right?'

It dawns on Eli that he didn't do what he was initially going to do. He was supposed to take down the king. He was supposed to ruin Danny's already sketchy reputation.

Instead...

'You really are a fucking dick. You set yourself up nicely, didn't you? A year off. Paid. While we endure that slimy fuck. I wondered why he didn't want me to fill out your leaver's paperwork. I thought you were one of the good guys.' She stands up. If there was any drink left, she would throw it over him. He knows that.

'Look, Kate, it's not like that.'

'It's exactly like that, and you know it.'

'I saw an opportunity and I took it. It was in the moment. I don't really care about the money.'

He just wanted to beat Danny. Make him suffer rather than wreck him.

'You don't have to stay there.' He's making it worse with this. He's finished one thing and now he's an expert.

'Go fuck yourself, Eli. Keep your blackmail money and good luck with your shitty little book.'

Kate walks out. And Eli is glad. He can't feel guilty now that she has insulted his writing. If there is such a thing as karma, then he is ready to take what is coming to him. He thinks, maybe Kate's punishment is to stay at DoTrue. Nothing could be worse.

Eli is pleased that he didn't complicate things.

Why would he ever end things with Jackie?
He texts:

I'm at The Scam.

Again?

Judging?

It's the funeral tomorrow.
If you want me to come over, I'll have to drag all my stuff with me.

We can celebrate.

That's not the right word for it.

I mean tonight.
I have news.

Oh, God. What have you done now?

Come. I'll tell you when you get here.

Tell me now or I'm not moving off this sofa.

Come on.

Tell me.

Spoil sport.
I quit my job.

Well, it's about fucking time.

JACKIE

Tomorrow is all about Mike. It's going to be sad, of course. Traumatic, maybe. Goodbyes are almost always a wrench to the heart. And the circumstances are tragic; he was young, he killed himself. But Jackie has the ability to compartmentalise. She pushes Descartes off the arm of the sofa. He lands on his feet and stares at her. She stares back until he gives up. It's a small win that she knows she'll pay for at some point.

They are saying goodbye to Mike tomorrow and Jackie feels happy.

Because he's done it.

Eli has done it.

He quit that evil job. That weight around his neck.

He will have time to write. That's all she has ever wanted for him. To do the thing that he loves most. And to be with the person he loves the most. She knows he has what it takes. And not just because she loves him, she can be objective about his prose. There is something there, she is sure of it.

And she should know because she has read everything he has ever written.

Everything but those text messages to Mike.

That'll come. Tonight is about Eli. Eli and the future.

Jackie packs some beauty products into a bag with her hairdryer and straighteners, and calls a cab. The dress she plans to wear for the funeral is hanging on the doorframe of the bedroom, she's surprised Descartes hasn't scratched it to pieces. He's too classy for that. His revenge will be far more nefarious. She leaves a bowl of dry food out for him as a peace offering and exits her apartment, a bag slung over her shoulder, dress in one hand, heels in the other.

She tells the driver to take her to Eli's address.

'Sorry, love, I'm not sure I can get down that road. They've shut it off because of the shooting in that coffee shop, but I'll get you as close as I can, alright?'

'That's fine, thanks. I think they've taken the police tape down now, though.'

They have. He drops her outside Eli's flat. She has a key. Just as she had a key for Mike's flat that she won't ever get to use again. Jackie drops her things upstairs in Eli's flat, goes into his office to read his latest first chapter then walks sixty-four steps to The Royal Scam.

FUNERAL **FRIDAY**

Three nights in a row at The Scam with Jackie, both of them drinking heavily. With the funeral over, it's time to cut back on the alcohol. But I needed it tonight. More importantly, I needed Jackie to have it.

Wednesday night was crazy. That midweek slump. The height of fatigue plus a thousand beers, we didn't even get our underwear off before we fell asleep on each other in my bed. Thursday was different. There was a buoyancy. A sense that sex can be fun as well as sensual. And she let me know how pleased she was that I was no longer a part of the corporate machine.

Tonight, it was that sad sex. That at-least-we-have-each-other sex. That let's-feel-good sex. For me, though, it was that let's-get-going-as-soon-as-we-walk-in-the-door-so-you-have-to-leave-your-bag-downstairs sex.

It's niche.

But I needed to get a look at that phone.

Jackie is passed out again. Face down on one pillow with another draped over the back of her head. I slip on a pair of joggers that have been left on the floor but can't find a T-shirt. It doesn't matter. I need that bag.

There's underwear on the stairs and a tie on the bannister. In the hallway, next to the wall that I pinned Jackie against is a skirt and my shirt. I shake my head free of the flashback. I need to focus. Leaning against the skirting board is Jackie's handbag. It's half unzipped. I can see inside. Her phone and purse and lipstick and tissues. There's a host of paraphernalia I'm sure she never uses, but not the phone I'm looking for. The one with all the text messages.

'Fuck,' I whisper under my breath. 'Waste of fucking time.'

My mouth is as dry as my brain. I go into the kitchen and down a pint of water and immediately need the toilet.

In the bathroom, on the drawers that Jackie made me buy to store things in 'so they're not all over the side', is another bag. Make-up, straighteners, clean underwear, tampons and another phone.

Immediately, I feel the need to look over my shoulder at the door. I shut it and lock it and go back to the bag.

I want it to be what I think it is.

And I don't want it to be that, too.

But I know.

That's why I type 221163 and watch as the screen springs to life.

I could check everything. His emails, all his social-media apps, how badly his bitcoin investment is going, his Uber trips, what food he has had delivered. I could cancel his subscriptions or make outrageous bids on eBay. I can see the songs he played the most and go through his internet browser history to see the kind of pornography that worked for him. Maybe I could get into his bank account with a bit of effort.

All of this information, carried around in a pocket on a device made largely of glass. It seems wrong that something so important is protected by something so fragile.

I don't want any of that information, though. And I don't think anyone else should have access to it. I just want to see who he was talking to near the end. I could find Mike's final words.

Top of the text list is Ralph. My heart sinks. No wonder he was so irate with me – Ralph was the last person Mike spoke to before he died.

On closer investigation, there are maybe fifty unanswered messages. The texts have been sent after Mike died. My instincts were right, Ralph is the psychopath I always knew him to be. And, God, some of the words are harsh. Evil, even. I scroll to see whether he spoke to Mike like this while he was alive but there's nothing, really. He was a good friend. It's clear. Supportive and tolerant, like the rest of us.

And I see that Mike was sending Ralph exactly the same messages that he was sending me.

Ralph only lost his patience a couple of times. Towards the end.

Then a noise.

Feet dragging.

Water running.

Feet dragging.

A light knock.

'Eli, are you okay in there?'

Breathe.

'Yes. Yes. I'm fine. That tonic water goes right through me, you know? I'll be up in a second.'

'Tonic water. Ha.'

Feet dragging.

Stairs creaking.

She doesn't suspect anything. She's still half asleep. Maybe half drunk.

I don't have much time now. I have a quick scan through my messages to him, to make sure I wasn't always a dick and then I read through Jackie's.

When I'm finished, I lock the phone, put it back in the bag, flush the toilet and spray air freshener, even though I never went. To maintain the pretence and to stop her from wanting to come in here.

I lie back down in my bed. Jackie rolls over and drapes her arm across me.

She tells me that she loves me.

I reciprocate the sentiment and stare at the ceiling.

My mind will not stop buzzing.

There is no way that I am going to get any sleep tonight.

A story is forming.

SATURDAY
(ANOTHER BEGINNING)

I haven't slept.

I know that people say it when they've had a bad night's sleep. 'Oh, I didn't sleep at all, last night,' and what they mean is that they kept waking up or they had a period of unrest that has made them feel more tired than usual.

That's not what I mean.

I have not slept.

I've been running through what I saw on Mike's phone, what Ralph did to me at the wake, and I have a new chapter in me. It's bursting to get onto the page. It wants to live. To be real.

Like I do.

Like Mike was.

He was real.

Jackie had her head on my chest for an hour. My heart was racing, I don't know how it didn't wake her up. Eventually, our breathing levelled and became in sync with one another. She calmed me without even realising.

But I still couldn't sleep. There were too many ideas. Too many thoughts.

I'm sorry, Mike.

I needed a plan. That was my focus. A plan.

Jackie rolled over eventually. She likes to sleep on her stomach. She likes to have sex that way, too. That was my opportunity to get up. Not to check the phone again. I don't need to see it. I just need to be up. If I'm lying in bed awake, it's an inconvenience. At least, if I'm up, then I'm up; I'm supposed to be awake.

It's Saturday, so Jackie will want to hang around. There's no work today, she might want to get up late, have a lazy day. I need her out, so that I can write in peace. So that I can hone my ideas and get my thoughts together.

First I get my fiction right. Then I'll worry about my reality.

She's stirring.

I cough on purpose to jolt her from slumber.

She turns over to see me sitting on a chair, reading.

'Morning, sunshine. How are you feeling now?'

I wonder what she's talking about at first, then remember what I said in the middle of the night.

'Not to be too disgusting first thing in the morning but I got it all out.'

'Delightful. What are you doing?'

'Relaxing. Reading a bit.' I've read 184 pages waiting for her to wake up naturally. It's a great book. Something else I need to finish.

Jackie sits up.

'You want to go out and get some breakfast?' she asks, like we are some kind of professional couple with mountains of disposable income to fritter away on whatever sourdough and avocado concoction is the most trendy today.

I don't want to go to breakfast. I want her to go home so that I can write. And I want her to notice the book.

'You know, I still feel a bit ... tender. Think I'll stick to the water and a slice of dry toast, this morning, while I relax with my book.' I raise the book. Come on. Look at the book.

'What are you reading?'

Finally.

'Stupid, really. That book Mike was always going on about. Should've read it while he was still ... you know. It's really good. He was right. He had great taste.'

'Well, he loved your writing, Eli.' She smiles at me with nothing but love in her eyes and gets out of bed. She looks incredible. She pokes the cover to read it. 'Ah, yes. *112263*. He was always talking about that. His favourite, I thought.' It's not quite a question.

'It was. Of course, that's not what he called it.'

'Eh?'

'He hates the way the Americans write their dates, with the month first. So he called it—'

'*221163.*' I see the lightbulb. She has the code to get into Mike's phone.

'Exactly. Silly really, but that was Mike, sometimes.' I pretend to look down at my book for a moment and allow this new information to percolate. I can see that she is looking around the bedroom for her bag. 'So, what do you want to do today?'

I know the answer.

'Well, I don't have anything clean here to wear, apart from underwear. I didn't really plan this far ahead. So I'll probably go back to mine, get clean, get changed. If you're not feeling great, anyway, maybe you should rest. We could talk later?'

'Sure. I mean. That's probably best. I'm not a hundred per cent. But you know how I get thirsty at lunchtime on the weekend.'

She pretends to laugh but she's almost out the door, into her clothes, with both bags slung over her shoulder before I have an opportunity to suggest anything else.

Jackie kisses me and goes. Then I move just as quickly into my office, open the laptop, pour a coffee, sit down.

Mike is behind me on the sofa.

'Ready, Mike? You're going to want to see this.'

JACKIE

She can't wait. She thought about getting home, locking the door and devouring the contents of Mike's phone. She will do that, but she needs to check that her hunch is right, that she has the code to get in to the phone she took from her friend's flat after he made a gouge in both of his thighs with a piece of glass.

Twenty-four steps at a decent pace and she is around the corner of Eli's road. She leans against the doorway of a small gallery selling paintings adorned with neon words called Countdown To Ecstasy, and takes the phone from her bag.

112263.

It vibrates.

Denied.

'Fuck.'

She tries again.

221163.

A click, then Mike's home screen. It's almost bare. No apps that don't come with the phone. No social media. No games. No internet banking. Nothing but music and contacts. Photos. A calculator.

She clicks open the photos.

Nothing.

Even the trash is empty.

She looks around. Nobody watching. Across the street is a Vietnamese restaurant called Aja. A man in his twenties drops two black bags of rubbish onto the street outside.

She opens the emails.

Empty.

'What is going on?'

All she wants are the texts but now she is scared. She looks around again. Then taps the green icon. She sees Ralph's name at the top and that's enough. The messages are there. That's all she needs.

Jackie turns the phone off, stuffs it back into her bag and runs towards the next bus stop. She can wait until she gets home to read.

SATURDAY

'As close to the end as possible,' I tell myself.
I write.
And I write fast.

QUEEN LIAR
BY ELI HAGIN

F I R S T **C H A P T E R**

You can't blame her.

She wanted him to die because he wanted to die.

It was love.

Support.

Read all of her messages: *Are you going to do it today? Just drink bleach. Stop overthinking it or you'll never do it. If you want this as badly as you say, tonight could be the night. Why would you want to keep living this way every day?*

It looks like she pushed him. Like she forced him towards his end.

A few messages taken out of context and suddenly, she's a murderer. Somehow, her words were a weapon.

Her words made a grown man smash a mirror, take a piece of the glass and jab it into his thighs so that he would bleed to death as quickly as possible.

He was so fragile that her words could make him do that.

No gun or knife or baseball bat or brick.

Words.

It seems unlikely.

But the court of public opinion will not see it that way. It's better to have a monster. It's a better story. Real life is more interesting than fiction because fiction has to make sense. But nothing here makes sense.

It doesn't help her case that the texts went on for days and weeks. It starts to look more like taunting and goading. And nobody needs the full story any more. Nobody requires the complete truth. Instead, they pick samples that fit their own opinions.

She kept pushing and pushing until he snapped.

All of this talk and now you're backing out? You're not making any sense. I'm messaging a dead man. Just drink the fucking bleach.

Taking the conversations in their entirety, keeping things in context, it's clear to see that she was on the wrong end of an abusive relationship. Gaslighting. Belittling. Insults dressed up as playfulness. Co-dependency.

Go fuck yourself, he would say. For a laugh. *Don't you dare tell anyone I'm going to do this*, he would instruct. Trapping her.

You read this side of the story and you still end up on his side. Because, maybe she didn't do it for love, for support, to help him end his daily suffering.

She did it to get out.

She did it to get away from the heartache of being leaned on every day, from being chipped away at, from being walked on.

But he can't be the monster because he is the one who died. He is the one whose parents need somebody else to blame for their inadequacies, for their lack of attention. Another young man with mental-health issues, committing suicide, is not a front-page story.

A woman who can kill a man with her words is a headline.

This will get people talking. Discussing the dangers of technology and social media. This will divide a population.

If anyone ever sees those text messages.

Jenny had been texting Matt about killing himself for weeks. He was determined not to just attempt it this time. He was hurting more every day. The pills weren't helping. The therapy wasn't working. He felt so shit he wasn't even sure death would solve all of his problems.

But he was going to do it. And Jenny was going to make sure he did.

He'd told her to come over and use her key to get in. That she would find him. She could call the police.

Jenny had her own key. All the friends did. She let herself in and he was sitting on the floor, a gash across each leg, puddles of blood.

But he wasn't dead.

Matt saw her and wanted to take it back. To make it stop. He dug his fingers into the wounds to try to restrict the bleeding. He called for her to help.

Jenny was still.

She watched him die.

Then she took his phone.

JACKIE

Her texts have been deleted.

When Jackie gets home, Descartes is waiting smugly in the hallway like he has just pulled off the greatest prank in the war between pet and owner. But Jackie ignores him in the way that he always ignores her.

She kicks off her shoes, takes the phone out of the bag and throws the bag onto a different chair.

221163.

She's in. Straight to the texts. Pages of unanswered messages from Ralph, including two new ones where he apologises to Mike and says that he now understands what it must feel like to want to die.

Ralph knows that Jackie will see it. He wrote it for her.

Jackie doesn't care.

Beneath Ralph's texts is her conversation, her thread of thought, her dialogue with a dead friend, and it is empty. There's nothing there. No record of their relationship at all.

She sits back on the sofa, looks up and smiles. As if Mike would be looking down at her. She stole his phone after she found him at his flat. After she had fucked him and called it off the next day. And he had the foresight to delete any evidence of their conversations.

That's what she thinks. That Mike deleted his apps and messages to erase himself from everything. Maybe even to protect her.

She doesn't need to know that it was Eli who did that. That he is the one protecting her. Keeping her safe. Keeping her around. Because Mike didn't care. And Jackie doesn't need to know.

Fiction is more comforting.

SATURDAY

EXT. GRAVEYARD. MIKE'S TOMBSTONE - NIGHT
(The stone says 'Beloved son, dear friend and man of words.'
Eli, holding a bottle of red wine, laughs as he reads.)

ELI
A man of words, eh, Mike? Bloody hell, I think Ralph
was right, your dad has lost the plot.

(He swigs the bottle and pours a little on the ground
for Mike.)

Look, you can't blame her. It's not her fault, you
know? You wanted to do it. She couldn't make you.
It wasn't fair to leave that out there for people
to get the wrong idea. That's not cool, man.

(He drinks again but doesn't share.)

So, Ralph's a real piece of shit. And not your
biggest fan, it would seem. I have to say, I'm
starting to see where he's coming from.
I'm annoyed with you. I think you could still be
around. I think it could have worked. Life is shit
for everyone, and it's over so quickly. We shouldn't
be wasting it.
 Oh, I quit my job. Finally. I know, I know. Look
at me finishing stuff. Sorry, I'm all over the
place. I should have written something down. Like I
did at your funeral. That went down well.

(He laughs loudly, and two mourners, crying at another grave, turn around in disgust. Eli puts a finger over his mouth.)

Shhhh. Anyway, I don't have anything poignant planned. I just wanted to come and get it out. My therapist is always telling me to stop bottling up my emotions. And I don't want you sitting in my office anymore, okay?

I'm getting on with things now. I've got direction. I thought that maybe I had you to thank for that. That if you couldn't face living in this world, you'd at least leave me with some metaphorical toe up my arse.

I just came here to say goodbye. To tell you to leave me alone, now. That I understand you only killed yourself for you. And that's okay. Because I have Jackie. And I know that what she did, she did it all for me.

(He finishes the dregs of wine and drops the bottle on the ground in front of the epitaph.)

I guess I should go and see Mum while I'm here.

SUNDAY

It was obvious what he was doing. Mike wanted permission to kill himself. He was pushing everyone. His dad was too loving and weak to be anything but supportive. That wouldn't help Mike.

Ralph was the first to go.

Relentless prodding and poking. Never asking Ralph about himself. Pushing the self-pity until he snapped with 'Just do it, then, and stop talking about it.' It was off-the-cuff. Ralph regretted it instantly and has been regretting it ever since. That led to fear and anger, hatred and violence in a men's toilet. All that's left is self-destruction.

Mike didn't care. He wasn't close to Ralph by choice. He only needed three signatures for his petition and he already had one.

The second would be tougher. Jackie was a good friend. He did love her. In all the ways he knew. Maybe he did trap her. Maybe he did use her. Maybe he was abusive and it forced her to push back against him. Maybe Jackie was supporting his wishes. Maybe the only way to push him over the edge was to break his heart.

Those messages are gone. And if I believe that she did it all for me, for us, then I can forgive her indiscretion. She can't be blamed. Jackie and our relationship was never the complication to my story, it was Mike. He was holding me back. He was holding *us* back. And Jackie resolved that. She cleared the chaos. Order could be regained.

Mike had two signatures, now. Ralph and Jackie had been beaten down.

I was the last one to give up.

But I couldn't.

I never did. Mike was my best friend. My partner. We were going to get there together. So I never told him to do it. I never got mad and said he should fuck off and die. I never betrayed him while he was alive.

Perhaps it was this that pushed him over. The guilt of sleeping with my girlfriend and still having my undivided support.

Maybe I am glad that he's gone.

I'm not even sure what is true anymore.

And who is worse off? The person who trusts what is real or the one who believes something that has been made up?

Jackie brings me a coffee in my office. She's decided to move in. She's bringing her evil cat. I'm not keen but I've said yes. I've only got a year of money coming from DoTrue and that could stop if Danny finds somewhere else to abuse. Jackie can keep us going for a while if anything crops up.

It doesn't make sense to break up with her now. I don't want to finish with her.

Endings are overrated.

It's time to start something new.

'Working hard, I see.' She kisses my cheek and checks the screen.

I type:

S E C O N D **C H A P T E R**

```
You have to stop putting it off.
There's never a right time.
Do it now.
Just drink the fucking bleach.
```

ACKNOWLEDGEMENTS

Thanks to the people that I usually mention in the back of my books. Most of you have been great.